# THE
# TOWER

# part one

# MURDERS UNDER THE SUN
## SEASON FOUR; INTRO

**MOLLY:** Welcome to *Murders Under the Sun*, a podcast that explores a series of unusual crimes that have occurred in sunny Southern California.

I'm Molly Shure, your host. For the past five years I've worked as a journalist at a local news outlet. Stories of murder and mayhem come across my desk weekly, if not daily. However, one day last March, I noticed something startling.

There seemed to be a connection between several crimes that transpired over a five-year period—seven crimes to be precise. What connected them? Location for one. They all took place within a twenty-mile radius of each other, but that alone wasn't significant.

The thing that pinged in my brain was that many of the people at the center of these crimes knew each other. Not the criminals, which would be an obvious thread, but the victims. I know, I know, six degrees of separation. Didn't I already say the crimes took place in a twenty-mile radius? But we're not talking six degrees here. It's more like one degree.

You'll see if you stick with me for all seven seasons of the show, the crimes circle back around. The people you meet in the first season play a role in Season Seven's story.

Am I imagining things? Is the connection real? Is there one mastermind behind the crimes? Or are they linked by some kind of social, psychological or even spiritual force? I'm afraid that's something you'll have to decide for yourself.

Each season, I'll do a deep dive into just one of these stories. You'll hear from the people who were victimized, and listen to transcripts of journal entries, memoirs, and letters from others who were involved—sometimes the criminals themselves—and behind the scenes information you can't get anywhere else.

So, get out your sunglasses. We're pulling back the curtains and letting the light shine on some of Orange County's darkest mysteries.

# part two

# MURDERS UNDER THE SUN
## SEASON FOUR; EPISODE ONE

**MOLLY:** Welcome to Season Four of *Murders Under the Sun*. I'm Molly Shure, your host.

As I mentioned at the end of last season, the story we are about to delve into is the one that tipped me off to the connection between the seven crimes we are exploring in the podcast.

I've titled this season after the house where the drama unfolds. The Tower is what the locals nicknamed an imposing stone structure on the cliffs in Laguna Beach. Oddly, it's on Cliff Drive, only a block and a half away from the Cliff House where the Real Estate Killer committed his crimes a few years earlier.

Coincidence? I don't think so, but you can decide for yourself as the episodes progress.

The woman I interviewed for this season is Rosie Ring, an interior designer who was hired to remodel the tower by Jacob Rinehart. If that name sounds familiar, it's because Mr. Rinehart is a fabulously popular horror fiction writer. He purchased the house on the cliffs to hide from the media after a woman was killed in the same manner of the victims in his latest book.

Rosie Ring, if you remember, was the designer Mimi hired in last season's story to renovate the garden house of Season Two. You can see that these crimes become more and more entangled as the stories go on.

I made an analogy last season to the ripple effect of a pebble thrown into a pond. Each widening circle encompasses whatever is within its trajectory.

Was the pebble thrown by REK at the Cliff House? Or did it happen before his time in the events of *The Dark Room*, a story about a cottage in Capistrano Beach where a series of very strange events occurred?

This is what we are exploring in the seven seasons of the podcast. Will we have a definitive answer at the end? Or will each of you have to arrive at your own conclusions?

This season, I'll be telling Rosie Ring's story to the best of my ability. In addition, I was able to procure the transcripts of psychiatric patient interviews. Since these transcripts were presented as evidence in a trial, they are part of the public record.

As usual, you won't know the identity of the patient until Rosie learns it. I believe experiencing the events as she did brings the story to life, so I'll just refer to them as Patient Zero.

I'm beginning the season with the testimony of a woman known as Kate. We only hear from her once, but her story is both disturbing and compelling.

Let's get started.

# 4.1.1

THE BUSH SHOOK and emitted strange snuffling noises. "Hurry up," Kate said and pulled her coat more closely around herself. She wished she was better prepared for the weather, but Jake had acted like it was an emergency. The dog was five months and not as housebroken as he ought to be, so if Jake wanted out, she took him out. The dog sniffed more than he peed this morning, however.

Kate tugged the leash, and Jake trotted out from under the foliage and onto the gravel path. "Are you going to go, or what?" Jake didn't answer, only dragged her to the next stand of bushes and resumed his olfactory research.

It was early, five-thirty. The sun had just begun its climb from beneath the horizon. Morning fog muted the little light and warmth it offered. Kate shivered.

Jake had jumped onto her bed and awakened her with a volley of slobbery kisses. Once she was up, he ran in circles from the front door, to her, and back, emitting the frantic yips that she'd learned the hard way meant he had to go. She slid her feet into flip flops, pulled a jacket over her thin cotton pajamas, and took him out. Her clothes were scant protection against the wet chill.

She had made a left onto her street and walked two blocks to a path leading into the park adjacent to her Seattle neighborhood. She'd trudged along Jake's favorite route, patiently waiting for him to do his business, but now all she could think about was warmth and coffee.

"Okay, that's it. We're going home," she said to the dog and started to turn, but paused. The silhouette of a man moved toward her. She didn't want to see anyone. Not this early. Not in her pajamas. She made her way to a small cutoff ahead on the right. She'd take that, circle to the main path and get behind the man.

The cutoff was narrow and not well groomed. Soggy branches reached across it. Weeds poked up through the dirt. She avoided the dew-drenched leaves as best as she could with Jake pulling her this way and that, but her feet were completely soaked after a few yards. She cursed herself for procrastinating about obedience classes. Jake wasn't easy to manage.

A snap behind her echoed in the quiet morning. She glanced over her shoulder. The man she'd seen had followed her onto the cutoff. *Followed her.* She was overreacting. The dim light and lack of people in the park made her feel vulnerable. He'd probably been intending to come this way all along. She picked up her pace anyway.

Soon the crunch of boots grew louder, closer. A thin prick of anxiety traveled up her spine. She began to jog, her shoes flipping mud onto her calves. Was it her imagination or were the heavy steps matching hers?

Jake frisked beside her, jumping and biting at the leash in her hand, happy with the new game. Kate stumbled over a tree root, righted herself, and looked behind her again. The man was so close now, she could see his beard, brown and curling. The rest of his face was invisible, covered by a black hoodie.

The cutoff opened onto the main path. She bolted forward, branches slapping wet stripes across her pajamas. She burst into the open area and looked left then right for an early morning jogger. For someone else walking a dog. For safety.

There was a bench a few yards up the path. On it lay a reclining figure. Probably someone who'd holed up in the park for the night to sleep something off. Normally she'd avoid the kind of person who slept on park benches, but this morning anybody was better than nobody.

She ran to the figure. "Hey, wake up. Please." Her words were quiet pants.

Kate eyed the place where the cutoff had joined the gravel road, but the man hadn't appeared. Maybe he was hanging back because he'd seen the person on the bench too. "Can I sit with you? I don't want to be alone. I think someone is following me."

The sleeping person was dressed in dark slacks and a print top and appeared to be female. Kate felt a surge of relief. A shaft of early morning sun shone in her eyes but she could still make out the outlines of the woman, and the open book that covered her face as if she'd fallen asleep reading. Jake sniffed at the figure and whined.

Kate put out a hand and touched the woman's legs, pushing them to the side ever so slightly so she could perch on the edge of the bench. The woman didn't acknowledge the shove. She must have had one heck of a night out. "I'm sorry. But I need to sit here for a while, until I'm sure he's gone," Kate said.

She settled on the bench and scanned the bushes. Jake sat at her feet and scratched himself. Long minutes passed, and Kate's heart rate began to slow. Jake curled into a ball and fell asleep. The man had to be gone by now, but she'd wait a bit longer to be sure.

When the sun began to warm the gravel path with watery rays, she decided it was safe. "Well, thanks, not that you even know the good deed you did," she said to the still form. Kate put a hand on the bench readying herself to rise, glanced at the woman and sucked in a breath.

The hands resting on the sleeping figure's stomach weren't hands at all. The cuffs of the floral blouse lay empty. A jolt of adrenaline shot through her. Kate's heart thudded. Probably an accident. Probably why the woman was sleeping in parks.

There was nothing to be afraid of, but she was. Kate jerked away, an awkward movement, and jarred the woman's legs. The figure's arms fell open. The book slid to the ground.

Kate screamed. Not because the woman's face was horrible. Because it wasn't there.

**MOLLY:** I warned you. This was disturbing, but also strangely compelling. Why would someone pose a headless, handless body on a bench with a book? That's the question I'll do my best to answer this season.

Now, let's jump ahead six months and pick up the story from Rosie's point of view.

# 4.1.2

The tower was being invaded. Rosie slowed as she made the sharp turn onto Cliff Drive. The large stone house reminded her of a fortified medieval castle, hence the nickname. Well-muscled men carried an expensive replica of a French settee, circa 1890, from the moving van in front through an open door.

Rosie craned her neck to get a peek inside. She'd never been in the tower and had always wondered what the interior looked like. The house had stood sentry on that cliff overlooking the small cove beneath for forty years. All its inhabitants had been rich, reclusive, and mysterious—her dream clients.

A horn tooted behind her. A woman in a Mercedes SUV threw up her hands in exasperation. Rosie stepped on the gas. She'd seen all she was going to anyway. Based on her glimpse of the furniture in the van, the new owners were like those of the past.

She'd have to get a hold of Gwen Bishop to find out more. Gwen was a realtor and knew the neighborhood. She'd listed a house on this same street two years ago, and although it had been a terrible experience it had opened doors for her.

That home, although only a block and a half south of the tower, couldn't have been more different. Rosie drove past it slowly, noticing the changes that had been made since the days of its notoriety. Money had been spent; it was obvious. But despite the improvements, the place made her shudder.

The owners couldn't pay her enough to take that project on. Not that they'd asked. On the flip side, she'd redecorate the tower for a song just for a chance to see the interior and brag about the job.

Rosie navigated her way through the tight streets and onto the Coast Highway, next stop, the Nightshade Gallery. One of her clients had seen a painting in the window and wanted her to look at it, see what she thought.

Rarely did anything from Nightshade work in the homes she decorated. The art Peter carried was dark and disturbing, the opposite of Rosie's style. She prided herself on creating open, fresh, and comfortable spaces. She would look, however, so she could tell her client why they didn't want the piece.

Despite their dissimilar taste, she and Peter Stiller were friends. They'd met through a marketing mastermind group he used to run. The group was too pseudo-spiritual for her to stick with, but they'd connected. He referred business to her regularly. She recommended his gallery to anyone who might like the unusual art he specialized in.

She parked behind the building and trudged through the alley toward the highway. Normally she'd enter the gallery from the rear entrance. However, today she wanted to see the window display as her clients had seen it. She made a left on Coast Highway and walked to the main entrance. She picked out the painting immediately—a magenta dahlia.

At first glance it was lovely, so real you could feel the drops of water on its petals. She understood why her clients thought it would look beautiful in their home. Rosie had chosen creamy white for the walls and pale wood for the flooring. Those formed the backdrop for the antique furniture the couple had accumulated on trips to New England. Deep, saturated jewel tones were a perfect complement.

Rosie stepped up to the glass and examined the painting. She knew the kind of surprises Peter's art held. It took a second or two for her to find what was hidden in this one, however. When she did, she grimaced.

A worm, so fat and swollen with blood it was hardly distinguishable from the magenta flower, was attached to one of the petals. She tracked a slender, green slime trail from the worm to the corner of the painting. A dead beetle, small enough to be overlooked, lay on its back, feet in the air. In its belly was a red gash from which mammalian looking entrails protruded.

Her client had missed this, Rosie was sure. She pulled her phone from her purse and snapped a picture of the worm and its victim. She'd text it to the couple with the recommendation to keep looking. As she replaced her cell in her purse, the front door of the gallery opened. Peter thrust out his head.

"Are you coming in? Or are you just going to stand there?"

She gave him a half smile. "Have any coffee made?"

"Was Leonardo Catholic?"

She followed him into the dim interior of the gallery. Peter, small, pale, and partial to black clothing, almost disappeared as he moved deeper into the shop. Black, the color of mystery and hidden things, was the perfect hue for him. "So who are you going to talk out of buying one of my paintings this time?"

"You don't know them," Rosie said. "They were in town for dinner and saw the dahlia. But for the worm and the beetle, it would be perfect."

"But for the worm and the beetle you could buy it online from a paint-by-numbers artist. I don't carry frivolous art."

Rosie sat in a purple Victorian-era chair. It wasn't comfortable. Vicky hadn't believed in creature comforts. But it was authentic. "Then you can't complain when I don't encourage my clients to hang it over their couch."

He waved a hand in the air, fanning away the subject. "Did you hear?"

"Hear what?"

"Someone bought the tower."

"I just drove by it. I saw the moving van."

Peter set two small, china cups on a low table and took a seat in a mismatched chair across from hers. "I know who the new owner is." He gave her a smug smile and raised his cup to his lips. Peter liked to be in control. Rosie guessed it was what her husband referred to as "small man's syndrome." Eric believed short men made up for their stature by puffing up what they did have.

"Are you going to tell me? Or make me beg?" Rosie said.

He set down his cup, dabbed at his mouth with a napkin and reclined in his chair. "Jacob Rinehart."

"You're kidding?" Rosie had expected a Hollywood producer or business mogul, not an author. At least, not an author who was a household name. She felt a pang of disappointment. She wouldn't have to call Gwen after all.

"How did you find that out?"

"I know his publicist. She's one of my best customers."

That Jacob Rinehart's publicist would enjoy the kind of art Peter sold didn't surprise Rosie. Rinehart wrote macabre, gritty books. She'd read his first novel, *Cage*, but never tackled another. *Cage* had given her enough nightmares. Six months ago, there had been a real-life murder tied to one of his books. Another reason to avoid his novels.

"It's the perfect house for him. He can decorate it like one of his stories, complete with a dungeon in the basement," she said.

Peter shook his head. "By all accounts he's a very nice man, a gentle soul."

"That's hard to believe."

"Thriller and suspense writers are some of the nicest people you'll ever meet. It's the romance authors you have to watch out for."

Rosie laughed.

"You think I'm joking? Jacob was so disturbed by the murder, so distraught that someone would mimic the crime he'd imagined, he couldn't write. Complete block."

"I bet it sold a lot of books."

"You are a cynic, Rosie Ring. That's a terrible thing to say. Cecily—his publicist—said he was tortured by the idea he was responsible."

"I'm not saying he was happy about the crime, but I'm sure the attention he got helped pay for that big house." Rosie took a sip of her coffee. It was excellent. Thank goodness Peter's taste in java was better than his taste in art.

Peter shrugged. "He moved here from Seattle to get away from it all."

"The murder was like the ones in his second book, right?"

"No. That was *Deep*. Everybody drowned in that book. It was like the ones in the third, *Pillory*. Gruesome. Very upsetting."

"Eric thinks it was the Mexican mafia and not related to the book at all. He thinks the publisher exploited the murder to boost sales."

"Your husband might be right, but my understanding is the mob mutilates the bodies of its victims and sends the heads to their families or their gangs as a warning. This was quite neat. Head and hands severed and never found."

Rosie replaced her cup with a shaky hand. It clattered onto its saucer. Talking about murder and dismemberment wasn't pleasant anywhere, but here in Peter's gallery it was intolerable. She glanced around at the paintings closest to her.

Most were like the dahlia—nice enough at first. But the field of poppies dripped blood. The lovely dark-haired woman in the portrait had dead eyes and blue lips. And the crystal waterfall hid a demented, demonic face. Nothing in Peter's shop was as it seemed. Including Peter.

Rosie stood. "Thanks for the coffee."

"Leaving so soon?"

"I have to get going."

Peter walked her to the door. "I'll tell Cecily about you. I'm sure Rinehart will redecorate."

"Why don't you wait on that? Let me think about it."

"What's there to think about? It would be a great job for you. Money. Prestige. What's the downside?"

"Rinehart. He's the downside."

"I told you, Cecily said he's a terrific guy."

Rosie didn't want to talk about it anymore. "Just give me a few days."

Peter shrugged. "You want to lose another job to Twila, take your time."

She tightened her mouth. "I'm going to have to talk to Eric."

"You're a very good wife, Rosie, but you're also a very good interior designer. I think it's time to step out of Eric's shadow."

Rosie flushed. She couldn't stand it when Peter psychoanalyzed her. He'd made his money as a success guru with a New Age coaching organization called Manifest. About five years ago, accusations of sexual impropriety against the founder shut it down. Peter moved to Laguna, bought the gallery, stocked it, and retired to become an art dealer. Sometimes he reverted to his roots, however.

As much as she disliked his intrusion into her psyche, she didn't argue with him. She did feel more comfortable staying in the background. A bad habit left over from her stay-at-home-mom days. She pushed against that tendency every day. No, that wasn't why she was undecided about having Peter promote her to Rinehart.

The reason was twofold. She felt cautious about working with someone whose mind traveled such twisted roads. But, more importantly, Eric would hate the idea.

There had been a death associated with his own company around the same time the killing in Seattle had taken place. Time might heal wounds, but six months wasn't long enough to mend the ravages of murder.

# 4.1.3

Rosie stopped at the market on her way home. She wanted to get something special for dinner. Things between Eric and her had been tense ever since the scandal at his office. He'd started traveling more on weekends and working late on weeknights. When he was home, he was often sullen and moody.

Last night, she'd lost it. She knew he was under a lot of pressure, but she was tired of the drama. She'd said things she now regretted. Tonight, she'd cook up an olive branch. She could feel him out about the tower job too. They could certainly use the money.

An hour later Rosie had dinner prepped. She heard a joyful yelp from Peach, their golden lab mix, followed by the sound of the front door opening and closing. She checked the pot of rice steaming on the stove, and went to join the party in the front hall.

Eric was wearing a navy-blue suit that brought out the blue in his eyes. "Hey there," she said and pushed Peach aside so she could greet him. She wrapped her arms around his neck and pressed in for a kiss. Eric gave her a peck then untangled himself from both her and the dog who'd wiggled between them. Whether he'd intended it or not, Rosie felt the sting of rejection.

"It's like having a little kid again," he said scratching Peach's head.

Peach trotted alongside him when he walked to the kitchen. She got between him and the fridge when he opened the door and pulled out a hunk of cheese. She followed him with her eyes as he uncorked a bottle of wine, found a glass, and poured. And she collapsed in a heap at his feet when he sat in an overstuffed chair in the family room. Rosie didn't plan to put on the same kind of performance to get affection.

"How was your day?" she asked, pouring herself a glass of wine.

"Not the best." Eric's voice sounded heavy and weary.

"Really?" Rosie perched on the arm of the couch.

"I don't want to talk about it." Eric shook his head. "It's Friday night. I want to forget about work for the weekend."

"Nothing too serious?" Rosie said. Eric used to share the week's issues with her on Friday nights over a glass or two of wine. That hadn't happened in months.

"I hope not," he answered, but she watched his shoulders tense.

She twirled the stem of her glass between her fingers and changed the topic. "I was in Laguna today. I drove by that house—the one that looks like a castle with the turrets—on my way to the Nightshade. There was a moving van out front." Eric slid off one shoe and rubbed Peach's stomach with his foot. Rosie went on. "Guess who bought it?" Peach rolled over. He rubbed her belly, but didn't say anything. "Jacob Rinehart."

That got his attention. His eyes locked on hers in surprise. "The Jacob Rinehart? The horror writer?"

"Yup."

"How'd you find that out?"

"Peter is friends with his publicist."

"Why doesn't that surprise me?"

"Peter is from Seattle. That's where Rinehart lived, until now. The city isn't that big."

Eric nodded. "Creepy people tend to find each other."

"That's not a nice thing to say. Peter is a friend."

"Yeah, but he's a strange one. You gotta admit." Rosie didn't admit anything. Eric sipped his wine, then said, "So, what's his background?"

"Who? Peter?"

"Yeah, does he have any family? Ever married? Kids? He's such a mystery man." He wiggled his eyebrows at "mystery man." Eric wiggled his eyebrows when he thought he was being clever. Rosie used to think it was cute. Now she found it annoying.

"Why are you asking me this? We've known Peter for years."

"You may know Peter, but I don't know Peter. I've met him, but he's. . . Evasive."

"He's not evasive."

"Then what's his background?"

Rosie paused. "I don't know much—"

"See?" Eric said, a look of triumph on his face. "I think he appeared in Laguna one night with a coffin and a hunchback guy with an Eastern European accent."

Rosie pulled a face. "You're so funny. Peter has never been married. His parents have passed, but he has a sibling in the Seattle area."

"Brother or sister?"

"Yes." Rosie brought her wine glass to her mouth to hide a smile. Truth was, she was pretty sure Peter had told her which it was, but she couldn't remember. Before Eric could do a victory dance, she said, "Peter is going to mention my name to Rinehart."

Eric stopped massaging the dog. He sat up straight. "I'm not sure that's a good idea."

"It would be a high paid gig. Things aren't going well at Pacific—"

"You don't need to worry about Pacific, Rose. We're working things out."

"If I don't need to worry about Pacific, then why do you go around looking like your dog just died?" She glanced at Peach. "Sorry," she said to her pet, then let her question for Eric soak in. He wasn't entirely logical on this issue, and she wanted him to face it.

His lips thinned. "Don't worry about Pacific, but don't throw hand grenades at it either."

"Hand grenades?"

"We lost three more accounts, big ones, this week. We're under a microscope. Any hint of impropriety, and the clients scatter like cock-roaches."

"How would my working for Jacob Rinehart be an impropriety?"

He looked at her like she was five. "Seb broke the law. He was involved in bad, illegal stuff. Rinehart might not have broken the law, but he's under suspicion for doing bad, illegal stuff. It's guilt by association."

Several months ago, it came out that one of the partners at Pacific Financial was involved in criminal activity. Nasty criminal activity. The firm had been scrambling to recover their reputation ever since.

"I don't work for Pacific," Rosie said.

"You're my wife."

They stared at each other for a long minute. She stood. "I think the rice is done."

Eric went upstairs to change out of his suit, and Rosie set the outside table. The evening wasn't going the way she'd planned. The garden was beautiful under a lavender sky, the sun almost down. She walked into the kitchen and came out with a wide candle and matches.

When Conner, their youngest, left for college, she'd thought their marriage would have a romantic revival. It hadn't. Maybe it would have, if it hadn't been for Seb's death and everything that meant. He'd died months ago, but there were still reverberations. New circles emerged daily from that rock that had been dropped into their peaceful pond, but they had to stop living on the defensive. It was time to take charge of their lives again.

She kept the conversation light during the meal. Eric did most of the talking for a change. It seemed the company was planning a move. "We've lost almost half our client base," he said. "But the good news is, we also lost Seb. We can downsize. Save money. Put a fresh face on things."

"That's great," Rosie said and meant it.

Eric pushed his chair onto its rear legs. "Have any more wine open?"

"I'll open one I've been saving for a special occasion."

"What's special? Did I forget something?"

"You. You're special." She gave him a self-conscious, sultry smile, and went into the kitchen to get the wine. Maybe the evening was salvageable after all. She pushed all thoughts of Rinehart and the tower job from her mind. She'd worry about it tomorrow. Tonight she'd celebrate Eric's victory, however small it seemed.

Through the window over the sink, she watched him get up from the table and walk across the grass to the old-fashioned love seat in the corner of the yard. It was a comfortable couch for two suspended from a metal frame by chains. Rosie'd found the swing at a garage sale in a nearby senior-living community. It was love at first sight. It reminded her of her childhood.

Eric had laughed when she dragged it home. It had been a sight, covered in rust and torn fabric, but Rosie had a vision. She spray-painted the frame shiny red and recovered the cushions in a brightly colored, retro-design fabric. The kids had fought over that swing in the summers. Three kids, two seats, always a problem. But tonight there were only two of them. Nothing to fight about.

She opened a bottle of wine they'd bought on their last wine tasting adventure in the Central Valley. It had a stupid name, Red Ravish, but it had been delicious. She poured them each a glass, brought them out to the swing, and handed one to Eric. "It's from that vineyard in Paso."

"The one with the goats?"

Rosie nodded.

Eric sipped. "It's good."

It was good. The smell of raspberries and coffee filled her head as she brought the glass to her lips. She inhaled and took a small sip savoring the explosion of flavor. They sat in silence, leaning against each other, the gentle motion of the swing lulling her.

"Tell you what," she said after a while.

"What?"

"When you get your new office, I'll do the design work. No charge."

Eric slipped an arm around her and pulled her close. "That's magnanimous of you."

Rosie rested a hand on his thigh. "I'm a magnanimous person."

She could feel his strong muscles through his jeans. He was in good shape. He ran, biked, swam, and played tennis. She began to run her thumb in a circular motion, massaging, offering comfort, and more. He lifted a hand to her hair and rolled one of her curls around his finger.

The quiet became thick. Only crickets and a few night birds broke its density. Eric leaned closer and kissed Rosie's shoulder and neck and ear. She turned her face to him and met his mouth with hers.

When he broke away, he looked into her eyes. "Want to go upstairs?" His voice was gruff. She could feel the anger in him. Not directed toward her, but there. The tenderness she'd hoped for was absent. But the warmth of the wine traveled to her belly, and she found she didn't care. "Sure."

# 4.1.4

The bell of Sweeter Than Honey Gourmet Cooking Supplies jangled as Rosie opened the door on Tuesday morning. "Honey," she called.

"In here." Honey's voice traveled through the shop.

Before Rosie could maneuver her way around the pile of boxes between her and the office, Honey appeared. Her blonde hair was pulled into a disheveled ponytail, her plump arms filled with boxes, and she had a black smudge on her nose. "Thank the Good Lord you're here. I don't know what I'm doing." Frustration peppered her Southern twang.

Honey's full name was Honeysuckle Wells. She hailed from Kentucky, where she'd left behind a bevy of sisters (Rosie still wasn't sure how many) with names like Lavender, Lilac, and Primrose. Her mother was an avid gardener. Honey said she knew she and Rosie were meant to be friends the first time she heard her name.

A smile tugged at the corners of Rosie's mouth. "I got here as quick as I could. What's going on?"

"I just told you, I don't know."

"Can you give me a hint?"

Honey dropped her load on the counter and spread her arms wide. "Look at this mess."

Rosie's gaze traveled around the showroom. The glass shelves along the walls were sparsely stocked with pots, pans, and small appliances.

One lone spatula hung from a wall hook in the corner section that had been devoted to grilling for the summer. The half-filled gadget baskets were in disarray.

"My Thanksgiving inventory came yesterday, but..." Her words trailed off.

"You don't know how to organize it." Rosie finished her sentence.

"Oh, I can organize it. Kind of. But I can't make it look pretty."

Honey could create a banquet beautiful enough to grace the cover of *Gourmet* magazine, but when it came to nonfood items, she fell apart.

"Start clearing the shelves. I'll unpack the boxes and see what've we got," Rosie said.

An hour later, the new items were grouped on the floor near the shelves they'd inhabit, summer goods were packed away, and everything had been dusted. "What now?" Honey said, hands on hips.

"Don't you have paperwork to do?"

"You want me to leave you alone?"

"That'd be good."

Honey disappeared into her office, and Rosie got to work. She liked to work alone. She had a hard time concentrating with the chatter of voices around her. It wasn't a good trait for her profession. Rosie knew she'd have more clients, make more money, if she worked for a larger interior design company instead of going solo. However, other people's thoughts and ideas cluttered her mind and stifled her creativity the way the new merchandise overwhelmed Honey.

A half hour later, Honey's voice broke her concentration. "That's beautiful."

Rosie looked at the shelf she'd just arranged. On it was a pumpkin-colored bowl, a bright green, retro looking mixer, a wooden spoon, and a seasonal cookbook with a colorful cover. "I'm not done," she said in a distracted tone.

"Alright, I'm leaving." Honey walked away, but. didn't get far. The doorbell pealed. "It's a bit of a mess, but come on in," she called out.

Rosie sat on the floor loading appliance boxes onto a bottom shelf and tuned out the conversation going on at the counter. Her mind flitted to the front window display. She'd have to make a trip to the market for pumpkins and gourds, but she could start organizing merchandise today. The new espresso makers would look great with the autumn-themed platters and dishes.

She was so focused on her plans, she only peripherally noticed the presence of a person standing near her left shoulder until she heard the voice. "So, you're doing retail now?"

Rosie spun on her bottom and glanced up the cool, elegant length of the woman who towered over her. She took in the black Louboutin pumps, the eggplant-colored Helmut Lang suit, the perfectly high-lighted hair. Maybe it was Twila's outfit—purple being the color of royalty—that made Rosie feel small and insignificant, her Nordstrom Rack jeans and Costco t-shirt like a peasant's clothing. She pushed herself to her feet with the aid of a cardboard box. "Twila," she said.

"I turned away a shop owner just last week. The project was too small. If you're interested, I could introduce you."

"I'm not," Rosie said between stiff lips. "I'm just helping out Honey."

Twila's interior design business was bigger and more successful than Rosie's one-horse operation. In the past three years she'd managed to build an exclusive base of wealthy clients. Many of whom Rosie had pitched to as well. Twila had an uncanny way of knowing exactly what people wanted before they knew it themselves. If Rosie could develop that skill, she might be able to give Twila a run for her money. Not that it was a competition or anything.

"It's wonderful you have the time. I'm swamped," Twila said.

"I make time for friends." Rosie paused, allowing the silence to grow long and pregnant. "Why are you here?" she finally asked.

Twila gave her a frigid smile. "I popped in to see Honey. One of my ladies wants to show off the dining room and kitchen remodel we just finished. I suggested a cooking class."

The shop was only part of Honey's business. She was a trained chef who'd retired from restaurant work after the birth of her first child. Ten years ago she got the idea to offer in-home cooking classes. They took off and became a popular girls' night in for Orange County's wealthy housewives.

"How nice," Rosie said. "Speaking of swamped..." She glanced at the boxes still piled on the floor.

"Right. You'd better get to work." Twila took a few steps, then turned to face Rosie again. "Funny running into you like this."

"Why is that?"

"I just saw Eric."

"Eric?"

"Yes. Pacific Financial is moving, but I'm sure you know that."

Rosie didn't answer. Something heavy settled onto her shoulders—dread maybe.

"I'm going to be designing the new office space for them."

The rush of blood in Rosie's ears almost drowned out the rest of Twila's words. She heard them as if from a distance. "Their lease on the current space is up at the end of the month. Auspicious timing for them, don't you think? Under the circumstances."

Eric was using Twila's services instead of hers—his own wife? His own wife who'd offered to work for free? The idea couldn't find a place to lodge in her brain. It didn't fit.

"Well, have fun. I miss the days I could take on a little project like this. So uncomplicated." Twila left the shop. Rosie stood unmoving, staring at her retreating, purple form. Eggplant was in the nightshade family. It contained trace amounts of solanine—a poison alkaloid. The color suited her.

"That was an unexpected boon." Honey emerged from her office. "I was wondering how I'd pay for all this stuff. Twila isn't my favorite person on the planet, but I have to say—" She stopped talking midstream. "Rosie, what is wrong with you?"

Rosie met Honey's eyes. "You didn't hear?"

"Hear what?"

"Pacific Financial is moving. Twila is doing their office design."

Honey didn't say anything for a long moment, then her face crumpled with sympathy. "Oh, Rosie."

"I can't believe it. What's even worse than Eric choosing her, of all people, is I offered to do it for free."

"Oh, Rosie," Honey said again.

"I don't get it. That woman has beaten me out of five big jobs this year alone." Rosie began ticking them off on her fingers. "The Wilson's place—

somehow she knew they were expecting their first grandchild and suggested doing one of the guest rooms as a nursery. Broadchurch—Nellie Broadchurch was all set to sign with me, but found out Twila loved cello music. Nellie's son is a music major at UCI. Guess what his instrument is?"

"Cello?"

"Of course, although I don't know what that has to do with design. Then there were the Shankers, the Conrads, and the Hadads. I have no idea how she got those jobs. All I know is they were ready to hire me, until they met her. And now my own husband has thrown me over for TW Designs."

Rosie buried her face in her hands and groaned. "Is my work that inferior to hers?"

"Of course not. It's better. I'm sure it's not that."

A wave of frustration hit Rosie and pushed her into motion. She began to pace. "Then what is it?"

"You can't let Twila get to you."

"She does. She gets to me."

"I've heard she had a bad childhood and had to learn how to fend for herself early. People like that know how to read people."

Rosie had learned some uncomfortable things about Twila's childhood during the ten minutes they were friends, but she wasn't in the mood to sympathize. "Seems like she's doing okay now."

"Maybe her business is doing okay, but her personal life is a disaster."

Rosie didn't give two figs about Twila's personal life. "Why wouldn't Pacific Financial use me?" She heard the whine in her own voice and hated it.

"It's probably a misunderstanding." Honey hugged herself, gazing at Rosie's trek back and forth across the showroom. "You remember the firehouse's family picnic last year when they put one of the new recruits in charge of the barbecue?" Honey's husband was a local firefighter. "I was hurt, really hurt. I blamed Booker, but it turned out he didn't have anything to do with it. And afterward, everyone said my events were better."

Rosie stopped moving. "We used to be a team. When things got tough, we were there for each other. Now, I don't know, everything revolves around him and that damned company."

Honey reached Rosie in two steps and wrapped her arms around her. "It's like that every fire season in my house. It'll pass. I promise. You two have always been great together."

They used to be, but since the newspapers broke the story of Seb Skandalis's human trafficking exploits, Rosie felt like she lived alone. She stepped out of Honey's embrace. "I'm okay," she said.

"You're clearly not okay."

"Maybe not, but I'm not going to cry. I'm going to call Eric. Find out what the hell is going on."

"Is that a good idea? Maybe you should calm down first. Give the dirt a chance to settle."

The dirt, an apt analogy. Rosie felt as if a dump truck had backed up to their lives. Her cheeks flamed when she thought about the intimacy of Friday night. She'd imagined it was a fresh start, a reuniting, that they'd dug themselves out of the mess.

"You've got to be the strong one right now," Honey said.

"I'm tired of being the strong one." The air in the room seemed thin, like she'd moved to a higher altitude. Rosie needed to get outside, catch her breath. "Can you load this stuff on the shelves? I'll stop by tomorrow and arrange it."

"Sure, but what are you going to do?"

She gave Honey a quick hug. "Don't worry about me."

# 4.1.5

Rosie closed her car door and stared out the windshield at nothing. A long moment later she pulled her phone from her purse and hit number one in favorites—Eric's number. It rang five times before his voicemail message came on. "You've reached Eric Ring's cell phone. I can't answer at the moment—" She clicked off, tossed her phone into her purse and drove out of the lot.

When she got home, Peach greeted her with enthusiasm. The affection raised a lump in her throat. Rosie sat on a low stool, pulled as much of the dog as would fit into her lap, and buried her face in warm fur.

Only for a moment, though. It was difficult to keep the eighty-pound dog still when she was intent on licking her cheeks. Rosie pushed her off and stood. "Let's get out of here." Peach ran to the hook that held her leash.

Fifteen minutes later, Rosie pulled into a parking space near Heisler Park in Laguna Beach. She needed to move. Emotions warred inside her making it impossible to think clearly. If the external commotion matched the internal, maybe she could find equilibrium.

Salt air pinched her nose. A sea breeze whisked her hair into her face. Waves pounded the shore below the path. Peach pulled her along the path.

After a mile she began to calm. Her heart rate was still elevated but from exertion, not anger. A thought entered her mind now, one too quiet to have been heard earlier. *Maybe I'm jumping to conclusions.*

Maybe Twila had pitched the firm and didn't have a definitive answer. Maybe she assumed she'd get the job and wanted to rub Rosie's nose in it. It was the kind of thing she'd do.

Or maybe Bob, Eric's remaining partner, had spoken to her before Eric had a chance to tell him about Rosie's offer. The whole thing could very well be one big misunderstanding. She and Eric hadn't been communicating well. She might have made a leap she shouldn't have.

She was glad now that Eric hadn't answered his phone. Honey was right. She'd needed to get some perspective.

Rosie slowed her pace and noticed the beauty of the day for the first time. The sun sparkled on a cerulean sea. Seagulls swept past her riding the air currents. A pelican dove into the water like an arrow shot from a bow. She inhaled, filling her lungs with the salty air. She'd talk to Eric tonight, clear things up.

She stopped to let Peach sniff a tree. A tired peace, the kind that comes after an upset, enveloped her. It would be okay. She and Eric would work it out. You couldn't demolish twenty-six strong years with a handful of rocky months.

She turned toward home and gave the dog a tug. Before she'd gone three steps, her fragile peace shattered. A black form darted under Peach's golden one. Peach whirled around with a yelp. A tangle of leashes, fur, snapping teeth, and snarls erupted.

"Fury, no. *Fury.*" A man's voice rose above the fray. A moment later, strong arms reached into the fight and dragged out the snapping Fury. Peach slid behind Rosie's legs.

"I'm so sorry," the man said.

Rosie pulled her gaze from the small, black dog her big golden one was hiding from. The man's eyes were a startling green. A shock of light brown hair covered his forehead. He wore an expression of vulnerable concern that gave the impression of youth. When she looked more closely, however, Rosie saw laugh lines at the edges of his mouth and eyes.

"Is your dog okay?" he said.

Rosie turned to the cowering Peach, felt her haunches and belly for blood. She didn't find any, but would do a better exam when she got home. "I think she's fine. Just shaken up."

"I stopped to watch a pelican dive, and Fury bolted. He's a rescue. Traumatic puppy-hood and all that."

"Have you thought about obedience classes?" Rosie heard the irritation in her voice.

"I'm going to hire someone, but I haven't had time. I got him two weeks ago, and I was in the middle of packing and moving and all that."

Rosie softened. "This one was a rescue too. It took a while for her to settle in."

"I hope he does. He's very affectionate at home, but he's got a protective streak a mile long. He's decided I need supervision."

He looked at Fury, who'd plopped onto the pavement to chew a leg as if nothing had happened and smiled. His face transformed. Rosie had thought him pleasant looking, but when he smiled, he was almost beautiful. Beautiful, and familiar.

"I'm sure he will," she said. She wasn't sure, but wanted to make him feel better. He seemed so genuinely sorry. "You're new in town?" She changed the subject.

"Yes. Moved in last week."

"That's very new."

He nodded, paused for a moment then put out a hand. "Jacob Rinehart."

Recognition and surprise hit her in equal measures. Of course, she'd seen his picture on his book jackets and occasionally in the papers. He looked older than those photos, his hair longer, but it was him. She took his hand and shook. "Rosie. Rosie Ring."

Jacob patted his pockets. "I don't have a card on me. Can you take down my number?"

"Your number?"

"Yes. If you get home and find anything wrong with your dog, I want to pay the vet bill. In fact, maybe you should take her in and get her looked at. On me."

Rosie dismissed his words. "I'm sure she's fine. It wasn't a serious fight. Just a lot of noise."

"I'd feel better—"

"I can get in touch with you if I need to." He raised an eyebrow. "Peter Stiller, a local gallery owner, knows your publicist. He and I are friends."

"Small world."

"Laguna may seem cosmopolitan, but it's an illusion. The tourists are the only thing cosmopolitan about it. The locals are small town, believe me."

He smiled again, and Rosie was charmed, again. "Thanks for the warning."

They said goodbye, said it was nice to meet one another, despite the dog fight. Rosie promised to call if she took Peach to the vet. He promised he'd keep a better grip on Fury's leash. And they parted ways. He went north. Rosie headed south. Jacob Rinehart was nothing like she'd thought he'd be. She should have given him her business card, but she'd been taken off guard.

Before she reached the car, she made a decision. She'd have Peter get in touch with Rinehart's publicist. She'd ask for his contact information, call, and make an appointment. Eric was wrong about this situation. If Jacob Rinehart was truly a suspect in what was now being called the *Pillory* murder, the police wouldn't have let him leave Seattle.

He was an innocent victim, like Eric. It would be the highest form of hypocrisy for her to hold him accountable for someone else's crime. Besides, her husband didn't want her involved in his business, why should he get a say in hers?

# 4.1.6

The grandfather clock in the living room gonged once as Rosie walked through the door. It was four-thirty. Eric wouldn't be home for at least two hours. Plenty of time to satisfy her curiosity.

Questions about Jacob Rinehart clamored in her head. What had inspired such a seemingly nice man to write such disturbing literature? Was there a deep, dark secret lurking in his past that he needed to purge? Was he more twisted than he seemed? Many famous writers were substance abusers, depressives, haunted individuals. She'd assumed he fell into that category when she'd read *Cage*. Of course, he might be emotionally healthy. She'd only had one conversation with the man. She didn't know him.

After filling Peach's water dish, she poured some water for herself and settled in her sun porch on a rattan chair. Fifteen years ago, the glassed-in room had sold Rosie on this house. It was still her favorite spot to sit and think. It was on the southeast corner, warmed by early morning rays and bejeweled by stars at night. Diffused gold light from the late afternoon sun reflecting off the stonework in her backyard filled it now.

She put her glass on a side table, tucked her legs under herself and opened her laptop. The first story that appeared after she typed Jacob Rinehart's name was about the murder named for his third novel.

### *The Pillory Killer Strikes Fear in Seattle*

She already knew more about that than she wanted to. She started to scroll down the page, saw Jacob's name in the opening paragraph, and clicked on the link.

The beginning of the article was a rehash of old news. The previous March, a flight attendant, Marianne Kennedy, had been laid out on a bench, feet crossed at the ankles, handless arms resting on her belly, and an open copy of *Pillory* covering the area of the bench where her head would have been if she'd had one.

The article went on to summarize the plot of Jacob's book. Rosie read this with more interest. The stories he invented must be a key to the man himself.

In *Pillory*, a husband discovers his wife is a member of a special club. She frequents a house on the outskirts of town where married people go to swing. Men deposit business cards into a basket. Women draw them at random. The couples hook up for the evening.

The husband in the story manages to get the business cards of every man his wife has slept with and dispatches those men over the course of 353 pages. Each is decapitated, dismembered, and posed in a public place. Cold crept over Rosie's limbs. Thank God she'd stopped reading Rinehart's books.

The article went on to say the police discovered the real crime mirrored the fictitious in more than just method. The flight attendant was a member of an online dating service that targeted married individuals looking for extracurricular fun. The profile picture of the victim smiled up at Rosie from her computer screen. She was an attractive, thirty-something, brunette with wide-set eyes. It was tragic. What she'd done—cheating on her husband—was wrong, but not deserving of a death sentence.

Jacob Rinehart was questioned, but he was never a person of interest in the case. He claimed to be at home when the crime took place, and it seemed the police believed him. There were no other murders that followed the pattern of any of Jacob's books. That didn't stop the media frenzy, however.

His publicist, Cecily Cranston, made a statement on his behalf and on behalf of the publisher.

*All of us at Trammel Publishing are shocked and horrified by the crime. However, murder mysteries and thrillers are a beloved institution. The genre sells more books than almost any other and gives rise to countless movies and television dramas. Neither Jacob Rinehart, nor Trammel Publishing can be held accountable for the act of a deranged individual.*

The article ended with questions: How closely would real life reflect fiction? Would the body count rise to match that of the books? Was the murderer done? Or could Seattle expect more corpses?

Rosie closed her laptop, and the room plunged into the deep, colorless gray of evening. She shivered and reached for the throw on a nearby chair. As she did, she saw movement from the corner of her eye. Her heart skipped a beat. Her eyes cut to the wall of darkened windows.

A head of short curls and a frightened face stared back at her. She exhaled. The windows had become mirrors, the way they did every evening after sunset.

Instead of pulling the throw over herself, she stood and began flicking on lights. The colors of her home revived in the lamp light, deep blues, ruby reds, emerald greens. The pure hues soothed her jangled nerves. She wished she hadn't read the article, hadn't looked at the face of the victim. She hadn't learned anything new about Rinehart; all she'd accomplished was to scare herself.

She entered the kitchen and looked at the clock. It was after six. Eric wasn't home yet, and the house felt hollow. Only the echoes of family life remained. Five comfortable seats in front of the TV. A basket next to the stairs for school books, socks, sweaters—anything that needed to go up the next time someone made a trip. Too many dishes in the cupboard. Too many forks in the drawer.

She rummaged through the fridge and pulled out things to make a salad. Based on Eric's recent schedule, there was no point in cooking. When she was done assembling her food, she took it to the living room and turned on the television. She scrolled through the channels until she found a comedy, something light that had nothing to do with murder.

Twenty minutes later, she heard the front door open and close. Peach exploded from her spot by the couch, but Rosie didn't get up. Eric entered the living room through the kitchen. He looked tired and disheveled. His tie was askew, his shirt untucked, and his hair stood on end as if he'd been tugging at it.

Rosie turned off the television. "Hi."

His lips curved into a brief smile. He poured himself a glass of wine from a bottle on the counter left over from the weekend.

"How was your day?" she said.

He collapsed into an easy chair. "Long."

"Problems?"

"The usual. It's like we're on trial with the accounts that haven't bailed. We're guilty until proved innocent."

"You didn't lose any more today, did you?"

"No. But I'm working twice as hard for half as much."

Neither spoke for a long moment. Rosie wanted to bring up what Twila had told her, but didn't trust her voice. Anger still simmered under her calm surface. Finally, she said, "How's the move going? Have you set a date?"

"Yes." Eric took a slug of wine, dropped the glass to his lap, and stared at it. "We're moving at the end of the month."

"So soon?" Twila was right about that anyway.

"Not soon enough. The rent is much lower on the new place. We need to cut expenses." He glanced up at her. "Anything to eat?"

"There's turkey. You could make a sandwich."

Eric didn't rush into the kitchen, so Rosie forged ahead. "I saw Twila today." A frown creased his forehead, but Eric didn't speak. "She said something interesting, especially in light of the financial issues you guys are dealing with." He raised his eyebrows. He wasn't going to help her. She'd have to spell it out. "She said Pacific had hired her to design the new offices."

Silence dropped like a stone. Eric fiddled with the stem on his wine glass for a full minute. Then he cleared his throat. "Bob felt it was best not to hire someone in the family. Easier to spell out what you want. Correct the things you don't like."

"You weren't going to hire me. I'd offered to do the work for nothing."

"Right. I told him that."

"You told him I offered?"

Eric wouldn't meet her gaze. "I did. He said he didn't want to work with someone related to the business."

"Don't you have a say in things?"

"Division of labor. Bob handles the office stuff. I handle marketing. We defer to the guy in charge when we don't agree."

"So you don't agree?"

Eric stood with a suddenness that made Rosie jump. "Of course I don't, Rose. I know how you feel about Twila." He strode into the kitchen and threw open the refrigerator door. "By the time I found out about it, it was a done deal. There wasn't anything I could do."

Rosie followed him into the kitchen. "Couldn't you explain that you wanted to use me? That she is difficult to work with?"

He slammed a package of cold cuts and a loaf of bread onto the counter. "How would I know if she's difficult to work with?"

"Because I know her, and I told you."

"I'm sorry, Rose, but you're not exactly unbiased."

"I'm telling you, she's aggressive and controlling. You'll find out."

"She's a business woman. Aggression is another word for assertiveness. Control for good management skills."

Rosie filled a wine glass. She didn't really want it, but she needed something to do with her hands. Twila's personality was more suited to the business world than her own, that's what he was saying. Maybe he was right.

Rosie had been in the Fine Art department at the University of Colorado-Boulder before she switched to the more practical interior design major. She approached design as an artist, not always as a businessperson. Artists starved. Businesswomen didn't. She'd changed a lot over the years, but it didn't come as naturally to her as it seemed to for Twila.

"Look." Eric took the glass from her hand, set it on the counter and held both her hands in his. "This isn't personal. Bob is gun-shy after what happened with Seb. He's trying to do everything by the book. Nobody would know you weren't charging us, and nepotism is frowned on."

Rosie looked into the blue depths of his eyes, blue like the ocean, like the sky, true-blue. His eyes had won her twenty-six years ago. They won her over now. "You're right. I just wish he'd hired someone else."

Eric released her hands. "Let it go, Rose. Don't let it get under your skin." He took two pieces of bread from the bag and began making a sandwich. "Besides we need to think about us. We can't afford for you to be spending your time doing volunteer work. Conner and Becca are still in college, and we haven't even finished paying off Ryan's loan. We need your income."

Rosie opened her mouth to tell him about her meeting with Rinehart that afternoon but shut it again. She didn't want to argue, not before there was something to argue about anyway. She'd fight that battle when, *if*, she got the tower job.

# 4.1.7

On Thursday morning, Rosie drove to Laguna to talk to Peter. She wanted a chance to work with Rinehart, whatever Eric thought. The rear door of Nightshade was locked, which was unusual but not unheard of. Sometimes Peter went in through the front and forgot to open the back. She walked around the building to the main entrance.

The showroom lights were out, and a red sign was propped in the window—closed. She stared at it for a long minute. It wasn't like Peter to close the gallery on a Thursday. If he closed at all, it was on Mondays and Tuesdays.

She thought about asking one of the other shop owners who shared the courtyard if they knew where he was or when he was returning, but decided against it. Peter wasn't particularly close with his neighbors. Besides, he had a right to his privacy.

She felt deflated as she trudged to her car. There had been a constant argument playing in her brain since she'd met Rinehart: Should she make a bid for the job, or shouldn't she? She was tired of the noise. Talking to Peter would have shut it down.

She could call, but if he hadn't come in there had to be something big going on. She didn't want to bother him. She'd wait. Call tomorrow. Meanwhile she could finish up at Honey's place.

Forty-five minutes later, Rosie backed through the door of Sweeter, her arms full of bags of pumpkins and gourds. She'd intended to get there on Wednesday, but Wednesday had disappeared in a flurry of activity. She'd had to take tile samples to a client in San Juan Capistrano who was considering a kitchen remodel, drape another client's windows with fabric options, and meet with Gwen about staging a house she'd listed. Then she'd gotten a phone call from Becca who was in her third year at San Francisco State, and that was that. Life stopped when one of the kids called.

The bell chimed, and Honey popped up from behind the counter like a prairie dog. "What'd you bring me?"

"Stuff for the window." Rosie dropped her bundles on the floor. "Sorry I couldn't get here yesterday. It was crazy."

Honey crossed the room and peered into the shopping bags. She wore a sky-blue sweatshirt today, that contrasted with her taupe-colored eyes. "Don't apologize. I appreciate your doing this. I wish you'd let me pay you."

"As my New England grandmother used to say: Spit in one hand, wish in another, see which gets full first."

"Nice." Honey wrinkled her nose. "What do you need me to do?"

Rosie opened the plywood door leading into the window space and began to unload her purchases. "Get me five items you want to move before Halloween."

Rosie didn't like doing windows. Correction, she enjoyed the creative process. What she didn't enjoy was being on display herself.

She'd never been one of those here-I-am, look-at-me kind of kids. Give her a box of paints, brushes, and a quiet space, and she'd disappear for hours. Her sister had been the gregarious one. No surprise. She was also the pretty one.

Liz, older than Rosie by three years, had the celebrity status older sisters often have with their younger siblings. She also had straight, shining hair that hung to her narrow waist like a lace sheer, eyes almost as deep blue as Eric's, and a laugh that made everyone within earshot smile. And, she didn't have severe asthma. As a teenager, she'd lived a whirlwind life of boyfriends, parties, and sports, while Rosie sat home and sucked on an inhaler.

An hour later, Rosie crawled out of the window. She and Honey exited the shop and walked around to the front to view it. It looked good. Rosie had arranged a set of autumn leaf coffee mugs and matching plates around one of the new coffee-brown espresso makers. White, orange, and green winter vegetables spilled from one corner of the display. Fall colored bowls and platters were perched in another.

"I don't care what you say, you are so much better than Twila," Honey said.

"Thanks, but when have you seen Twila's work recently?"

"At that cooking class she booked for her client."

"That happened already?"

"Yeah, last night. Twila was so sure I'd say yes, she told Marybeth two weeks ago to go ahead and send out invites. Kind of presumptuous, don't you think? How'd she know I wouldn't be busy?"

Rosie didn't answer. How did Twila know anything? If Rosie could figure that out, she wouldn't have lost those five jobs to the woman.

"Anyway, I wasn't impressed with the kitchen. Everything was cold and blue and silver. All the wrong colors." She gestured to the flame-red tablecloth Rosie had covered the floor of the window display with. "You know color."

Rosie had studied the effects of different hues on people's moods. It was part of every design school's curricula, but for her, the class had only scratched the surface of something she'd already known on a much deeper level. Rosie had a gift. She wasn't beautiful like her sister. She couldn't turn food into art like Honey. She didn't have commercial insight like Twila. But she intuitively understood color. She felt its effects on her soul.

Rosie knew red, particularly a shade edging toward joy-filled yellow on the color wheel, was good for a cooking shop. She knew it objectively. It caught the eye and inflamed the appetites. Many restaurants included red in their color scheme for those reasons. But she also felt its vibrations, knew which shades would sing in harmony with those that soothed and brought comfort. She could combine colors in a way that beckoned people to sit and eat and enjoy each other's company.

"And it wasn't functional." Honey wasn't done criticizing Twila's work. Rosie smiled to herself. Twila was good at her job. She hated to admit it, but it was true. Honey would never admit it, however. She was too loyal to Rosie. "Everything was in the wrong place. I must have walked across that kitchen a hundred times if I walked across it once."

"At least you got some exercise," Rosie said. Honey was on a perpetual quest for the perfect exercise routine, one that required no time or sweat but burned as many calories as a ten-mile run.

"Funny." Honey turned on her heel and walked into the shop.

Rosie trailed after her. "Did you get any new gigs from the event?"

"No, but Twila did. I'm telling you Rosie, you need to get your clients to have showing-off parties like she does. Friends come. They get envious. They got to keep up with Joneses. At least two of the ladies made appointments for her to come check out their kitchens."

"I don't know. I hate the idea of taking advantage of my clients. I'm finishing up a Laguna Niguel home now. We re-did all the living spaces except the kitchen. The only thing left to do is find the right painting for over the mantel. It's their home. Their sanctuary."

"You're not taking advantage. People love bragging parties. Besides, you can ask for me. I need more business."

It was easier to ask a favor for a friend than for herself. Rosie pondered the idea for a long moment. "Okay." Reluctance oozed from the word.

Honey grinned. "Tonight is the Art Walk in Laguna. Get down there, find that painting, and let's get that party started."

Eric's words of Tuesday echoed in Rosie's head: *We need your income right now.* Which meant she needed to think more like Twila. Maybe not Twila. More like Honey—assertive, but with a heart. "I'll do it."

*If I get the tower, I might not need to have a party.* Rosie shut down that thought as quickly as it flashed through her mind. She had no idea what Jacob Rinehart was planning to do with his place. The job could be as simple as helping him chose paint colors and hiring a crew to do the work. And, there were no guarantees she'd be the one to do even that. She couldn't count the money before the deal was hatched.

Rosie focused on the walls of shelves around her. Honey had put everything where it ought to go, but nothing about the arrangement said "buy me." She began reorganizing. Honey headed behind the counter. "Twila wasn't pulling your leg about getting Eric's company's business." It wasn't a question. It was a statement.

"No. She wasn't, but how do you know?"

"Estelle, Bob's wife, was at the party last night."

Rosie stopped working and turned to face Honey. "Estelle was at the party?"

"She's friends with Twila's client, Marybeth. The one who threw the shindig."

"Five degrees of separation."

"Six."

"Whatever. You know what I mean."

"I think that's how Twila got Marybeth's remodel and the Pacific Financial job. She did some work for Bob and Estelle a few years ago. She works those connections, I'm telling you."

Rosie sighed and returned to the shelves. "Eric said it's a good thing I'm not volunteering for them. I need to spend my time wisely right now."

"Oh, Rosie, I am—"

Rosie put up a hand and cut her off. "Not you. Not this. This takes no time at all. Besides, you've referred more work to me than anybody. It's the least I can do."

Neither woman spoke for the next half hour. Rosie made her way around the shop, moving a bowl here and a cookbook there, creating small pops of color with each mini display. When she reached the kitchen gadget baskets near the front counter, Honey looked up from her work.

"Twila didn't get the Pacific job because she's better than you," she said. Rosie raised an eyebrow. "There's something going on with her and Estelle. Some kind of tension."

Rosie laughed. "Those two are a couple of pit bulls. Put them in the same ring, and there's bound to be a fight."

"There was a fight all right."

Rosie hesitated. Did she really want to know? She hated the idea of gossip, didn't want to fall into that all too stereotypical female trope. But wasn't it all fair in love and business? "What happened?"

Honey lowered her voice even though there wasn't anyone in the shop to overhear. "I'd brought a tray of cauliflower au gratin into the dining room, and as I was walking back into the kitchen, I heard two people arguing.

"I didn't want to embarrass anyone, so I ducked into the butler's pantry—that's the only thing Twila did right, by the way. You should see it. It's got all those hanging metal baskets for crackers and things and those big pull out bins for flour and—"

"The argument," Rosie interrupted.

"Oh, yeah, right. So I ducked into the butler's pantry." She paused on the last two words, savoring them for a moment before continuing. "I was going to cough or something, let them know I was there. But I heard Estelle say, 'You got what you wanted.' Then Twila laughed that Cruella de Vil laugh of hers and said, 'Really?' all sarcastic like."

Honey widened her eyes as if Rosie should say something, so she did. "Then what?"

"Well, then Estelle said, 'Don't push your luck.' I wondered what she meant, so I stayed quiet for a tiny bit longer." She paused again.

Impatience skittered over Rosie's skin. She wished Honey would get to the punchline. "And?"

"And then Marybeth came into the kitchen and everybody acted all happy snappy like they were the best friends in the world."

The story was anticlimactic. Rosie had been expecting more. Her face must have shown it. Honey said, "Don't you see? It doesn't make sense. Why would Bob give the Pacific Financial job to Twila if Estelle couldn't stand her?"

Why would he? Honey was right. It didn't make sense, and that rankled. Rosie shrugged. "Bob must like her for some reason."

"Exactly," Honey said, a look of triumph on her face.

"Exactly, what?"

"She has a reputation, that's all I'm saying."

Rosie groaned inwardly. She didn't want to go there, no matter how much she disliked Twila. It smacked of high school mean girls. "A reputation?"

"Don't play dumb with me, Rosie Ring. You know what I'm talking about."

"You mean, she sleeps around." Rosie had heard the rumors.

"With other people's husbands." Honey tightened her mouth into a thin, disapproving line.

"I think that's an exaggeration. She might have had an affair with a married man years ago—one of those he-was-planning-to-leave-his-wife kind of things." Rosie couldn't believe she was defending Twila.

"That's not what I heard."

"Have you seen Bob lately?" Rosie liked Eric's partner, but he wasn't exactly an Adonis. He spent half his life in restaurants, and the other half in a chair.

Honey turned her palms skyward. "I'm just telling you what happened. I don't know what it meant, but I thought you might be happy to know Twila isn't as popular as you thought."

"I am. Thanks." Rosie knew Honey meant well, but the conversation left her feeling unsettled.

As she cleaned up the odds and ends she'd left around the shop, she gnawed on the situation the way Peach gnawed a rawhide bone. She would love to believe Twila got the Pacific Financial job because she was a devious flirt and not because she was a good designer. She didn't.

On the other hand, if Twila was a shark, Rosie wasn't happy about Eric swimming in the same waters. Not now. Not when things were so strained between them. It was a lose-lose scenario.

Later, when Honey clicked the lock on the front door of the shop, she asked, "Do you want me to go with you to the Art Walk tonight?"

"No," Rosie said. "You wouldn't have a good time, and I work better alone." Truthfully, her brain was too burdened to absorb Honey's rapid fire dialogue.

They each got into their respective cars. Honey pulled out first, and Rosie followed her up Town Center Drive. They both made a right onto Alicia Parkway, crossed over Crown Valley, and drove up the hill to an older Laguna Niguel neighborhood. A right, then a left, and they each pulled into their driveways, got out of their cars and waved goodnight. Honey walked up the walkway to 29241 Via Las Mares, while Rosie unlocked the front door of 29243.

**MOLLY:** We learned a lot about Rosie in this first episode. She and Eric are still reeling from the crimes committed last season in *The Hiding Place*. And she's struggling in her career thanks in no small part to Twila Wilkes, an unlikeable competitor.

Before we wrap up, however, let's hear the first of the patient transcripts.

# patient zero

Excerpt of recorded patient interview
from the files of Dr. Lewis Carver:

Some people have no ambition. They let others walk all over them. Live in everyone else's shadow. They cover their lack of drive with feel good drivel about doing unto to others, and karma, and all that crap. But they don't really believe it.

You know how I know? I know because they get bitter when someone takes them up on their sacrificial offer. If they were really into the Mother Teresa stuff, they'd suffer in silence. Or, better yet, they'd thank you for giving them another notch on their sainthood belt, for helping them earn another martyr credit.

But they don't. They don't like being taken advantage of. They don't like it when other people show a little backbone and get ahead either. I think it's because it highlights their laziness, laziness and cowardice. They don't take risks, and they don't like it when other people do.

Once when I was a kid, my parents took us to a lake for the summer. It was one of those out of the way places you could only get to by boat. You had to park your car on one side and take a ferry across the water to get to the cabins and hotels on the other.

I saw an opportunity right away. When people got off the ferry on the far side of the lake, they had to drag their luggage to their lodging. So I took my wagon to the dock every day, met the ferry and, for a fee, I carted suitcases, bags, and boxes, and whatever else people needed carting.

Pretty soon there was a group of kids doing the same thing. It didn't bother me. It was good for business. There were always more people looking for a wagon than I could service, and it built credibility and confidence in the program. Credibility and confidence are important.

Then one day this geeky kid shows up. I think he was slow. Don't get me wrong, I don't have anything against people who aren't intelligent. They're fine. No threat. But this kid, he started offering to take people's suitcases to their cabins for nothing. No pay.

Of course, the people paid him anyway. But they paid whatever they felt like paying. They'd throw a couple of quarters at him, and he'd be happy.

I bet you can guess what that did to business. The rest of the kids started to feel bad about asking for two dollars when this kid was doing the same job for nothing. Before you knew it, we had a charity organization going on at the docks.

It didn't sit well with me. I stuck to my two buck guns. People gave me disapproving looks, like they thought I was ripping them off, or I was less noble than the other kids. But, hey, I ask you who was doing the ripping off? They had more money than I did. Why should I work for slave wages?

Needless to say, most of the kids stopped bringing their wagons to the docks. I mean, if you're only getting a quarter what's the point? The geek was there every single morning regardless. My father said it gave him purpose. But I had purposes too, and he was screwing them up.

One morning, as I headed out to meet the 10:30 ferry I made a decision. This was it. If business didn't pick up, I was going to find another line of work. I was industrious, always have been. I'd come up with something.

When I got to the dock, I saw four or five kids all standing around in a tight circle. I pushed my way through to see what had happened. A wagon hung onto the dock by one wheel, halfway submerged in the water. It belonged to the geeky kid.

He was standing there crying, asking the other kids to help him get it back on dry land. Nobody moved. It was like they were playing a game of "Mother May I" and nobody said they could, so they didn't.

I knew then and there they all felt the same way I did. They wanted the kid to go away, but they weren't going to do anything about it. So I did what I always do, I took charge.

I walked over to the wagon. The kid started thanking me because he thought I'd help him. I felt bad about that, but you can't let those kinds of things stop you from getting the job done. I put my foot on the Radio Flyer and gave it a shove. I still remember watching the wagon disappear in slow motion, bubbles popping to the surface long after it was gone.

The kid ran off crying, which I expected. What I hadn't expected was the way the other kids reacted. They stared at me like I was an ax murderer—ironic now, I know. But, hell, I did what I did for the common good. And I'll tell you, word got around. The next day the whole gang was at the dock to meet the ferry with their "Wagoning-$2.00" signs.

But, not only weren't they grateful, they wouldn't even talk to me. They treated me like I was some kind of pariah for the rest of the summer. A bunch of hypocrites, that's what they were. Based on my experience, most people are.

**MOLLY:** Interesting perspective. We're obviously dealing with a hard-nosed character.

Now, for the question of the week: Would you pursue the tower gig if you were Rosie? Or would working with someone like Jacob Rinehart be a no-go for you? Let me know your thoughts in the Facebook Group. The link is in the show notes.

**(cue music)**

**VO:** If you enjoyed this episode, please leave us a five-star review on your favorite podcast service—it really helps. *Murders Under the Sun* is edited by Jim Wilbourne, theme music is by Eclectic Blends, and I'm your host, Molly Shure.

# part three

# MURDERS UNDER THE SUN
## SEASON FOUR; EPISODE TWO

**MOLLY:** Welcome back to Episode Two of *The Tower*. I'm Molly Shure, your host.

Before we get into today's story, I have to say I loved hearing from all you long time listeners on the Facebook page. The community is so supportive, and it's growing. Many podcasters feel like they're speaking into the void. I'm so thankful I have you.

And speaking of long time listeners, many of you wanted to hear what I learned about the missing CSU-Fullerton students over the break. I'll fill you in, but first here's a recap for the people tuning in for the first time.

Way back in Season One, a listener asked how I got into crime reporting. After all, these stories aren't exactly light, fluffy butterfly and puppy-dog tales. My answer was that my college roommate, Melissa Shilling, disappeared during the 2005-2006 school year and is still missing to this day.

That was a life-changing event for me. After it happened, I pivoted from pursuing an English Lit degree to a journalism path. My goal became to tell the world the hard stories in the hopes that others might avoid the same fate as the victims. I also strive to understand why these things happen. I believe if we know the why behind these tragedies, we're better able to prevent future tragedies.

When I shared all this with the listening audience, relatives of two other students who went missing that school year contacted me. My initial reaction was that they should take their information to the police. But when Camilla Jimenez wrote telling me about her son Raphael, I was really touched. He sounded like such a great kid, and she was naturally heartbroken. Consequently, I relented and promised I'd see what we could find out.

This is what we learned over the break. Three students, Melissa Shilling, Ariana Blackstone, and Raphael Jimenez all went missing the same week. I hadn't realized their disappearances had happened so close together.

But while that was odd, we couldn't find any other connection between them. At first, anyway. Melissa was in the Psychology department. Ariana was a Drama major. And Raphael was in Cinema and Television Arts. It didn't appear their paths had crossed.

According to news stories at the time, everyone who knew them agreed they were serious students, close with their families, and all-around good kids. Not the kind to get into trouble, or to run away. Two weeks ago, we finally discovered this wasn't the only thing they had in common.

In the first season I told you The Raven's Perch, a local bar, was the last place Melissa was ever seen. Well, it turns out it was one of Raphael's favorite haunts, and Ariana actually worked there. She was a waitress.

I realize that isn't much to go on, but it's the only tangible link between them we've found thus far. Abby, my assistant, and I plan to pull that thread and see what unravels. We'll keep you in the loop.

But, meanwhile, let's get back into today's episode of *The Tower*. Last week we learned that Rosie was leaning toward pursuing the tower gig.

Jacob Rinehart didn't fit the horror writer image she'd created in her mind and actually seemed like a nice guy. Whether that job was actually a possibility was still up in the air, however. We'll find out about that today.

Here's Rosie.

## 4.2.2

The parking spot seemed an auspicious start to the evening. Rosie had a cousin who prayed for good parking spaces and considered it a miracle when she got them. Rosie didn't believe parking spaces had any cosmic importance, but on the night of a Laguna Art Walk it was fortuitous to get one so close to the gallery she wanted to visit.

She crossed Coast Highway when the light turned green and headed toward Myrtle Street. There were lots of people out and about. Couples holding hands and groups of friends bundled against the cold moved from gallery to gallery chatting and laughing.

The first Thursday of every month, galleries stayed open late and offered snacks. Restaurants featured local musicians. A trolley was scheduled to transport people to and from the parking lots out in the canyon.

Rosie was headed to a gallery in North Laguna that featured still lifes from local artists. Last time she'd been there, she'd seen several that had the modern-meets-traditional look she was after.

She passed by a gallery showing city skylines, one filled with portraits, an antique shop, then entered Canyon Art. The front of the store held the Laguna Beach scenes so popular with tourists—ocean vistas with bougainvilleas, or roses, or bird of paradise blooming in the foreground. She navigated around a bank of movable partitions covered with them to the rear of the store. The two side rooms held the paintings she was interested in.

On the far wall of the first were five pictures, all by the same artist. They depicted local homes. One caught her eye. It was the tower.

Gray clouds hovered over the stone building. Whitecaps slashed across a churning sea in the background. In the foreground, star-shaped mock orange blossoms glowed like constellations in a deep-green leafy night. It was beautiful, and it was disturbing. She could feel the coming storm through the artist's strokes.

A familiar voice broke into her musings. "Let me show you. It's perfect for you." Rosie tore her eyes from the piece and glanced over her shoulder. Twila, elegant in a black flowing jumpsuit, was speaking to someone hidden behind a large art display.

"Okay," that someone said, then stepped into Rosie's line of vision. She realized with a start it was Jacob Rinehart. Twila had cast her spell, and his eyes were fixed on hers. They walked toward Rosie, but neither had seen her.

"I know the artist. If you don't like the painting, you could commission her to do another. Maybe something a little sunnier," Twila said.

Rosie's head pivoted right, then left. She didn't want to run into them right now. She needed a moment to think. On her left was the entryway to the second back room of the gallery.

She darted into the hushed space, slowed her pace, and swallowed something that felt an awful lot like rage. Twila had bagged the tower. She'd done it again, taken Rosie's job. Well, not her job in fact. She'd never spoken to Rinehart about it, but it should have been hers.

How many nights had she and Eric sat in the park that bordered the stone house, sipping wine and nibbling cheese and dreaming? How many stories had she imagined about bumping into the inhabitants as they sat picnicking?

"Lovely sunset," she'd say.

"We're so lucky to be able to watch that show from our windows every night," they'd say.

"Oh, do you live here?" she'd say, knowing full well they did.

"We do," they'd say, and then they'd tell her how they'd purchased the house but hadn't gotten around to remodeling. Eric would mention Rosie was an interior designer. They'd exclaim about the coincidence and schedule an appointment.

The next day, two days, week, Rosie would enter the tower, the building that had held her captive since the first time she'd seen it. The imposing stone walls, the soft foliage surrounding it, the miles of shoreline that could be seen from its windows made her itch to create something beautiful. If someone was to ask her to choose one home in Orange County to redecorate, one home to build a career on, she'd have said the tower. Twila had stolen more than a job this time, she'd stolen a dream.

A headache erupted behind Rosie's eyes. She massaged her forehead. Why hadn't she given Jacob Rinehart her card that day in Heisler Park? Why had she let Eric's paranoia influence her?

Rosie closed her eyes and willed the bitterness that coursed through her to settle, to dissipate. It wasn't like this was a new experience. Twila had taken many jobs she'd wanted. This may be the worst, but it wasn't the only and probably wouldn't be the last time it happened.

She had other clients. She'd come here tonight to shop for them. *Pull yourself together, Rose.* She inhaled and exhaled, then surveyed the room she was in.

The walls had been painted a deep umber. The lights were low. Each piece of art glowed like a jewel under its own lamp.

She strolled to the wall on her left and considered a painting of a brass vase of pink peonies on dark background. It was well done but the blooms were too pale for the setting she had in mind. She viewed bowls of fruit, roses in a vase, apples on a wooden sideboard. Too ordinary. She could hear Peter's critique, *paint-by-numbers art.* She turned right and a work on the entry wall caught her eye. This was it.

An azure jug of black-eyed Susans sat on a windowsill in a shadowed room. Slanted rays of light played like music over the blues, yellows, and blacks. A green sun-drenched field, visible through the open window, beckoned. Rosie walked closer and checked the price. It was within her budget. She pulled out her phone, snapped a photo, and sent it to her clients, John and Carol, along with the artist's name.

While she waited for their response, she peeked into the room she'd escaped from. Twila and Rinehart were gone she noted with a stab of her earlier emotion. *Forget it. Forget them.* Rosie wandered around the gallery, looking without seeing. After making a full circle, she found herself in front of the painting of the tower again. The piece had power.

She stared at it, losing herself in its turbulence. She thought about buying it. Not for a client. For herself. But it wouldn't go with the decor in her home, and she wasn't sure she'd want to live with it even if it did.

When Rosie was ten, someone had given her a book of Poe's short stories. They'd captivated and repelled her at the same time. "The Tell-Tale Heart" had ruined her sleep the night she'd read it. Every shadow in her bedroom was a demon, or murderer until the early morning light dispelled the illusion. The next night, she opened the book again and scared herself silly with "The Pit and the Pendulum". This painting had the same effect on her as Poe's stories. The fact that it depicted the house she longed to feature in her portfolio only increased the tension she felt when she viewed it.

"That's the one piece in the place worth the canvas it's painted on," said a voice behind her.

She turned to face Peter. "Why doesn't it surprise me you'd feel that way?"

"Because you know I have discerning taste."

Rosie suppressed a *humph*. "It's unsettling, I'll give you that."

"Good art should evoke emotion."

"The emotion doesn't have to be horror." Rosie's phone dinged, and she checked her texts. "In fact, I'm about to buy a painting that evokes a completely different emotion."

She walked to the room with the jug of flowers to get the information from its placard. Peter followed. "It's not horrifying, but it is melancholy," he said.

"It's not melancholy. It's wistful."

Peter shrugged. "Melancholy. Wistful. We're nattering over nothing. My point is, it's not all sunshine and butterflies." He waved a hand at the wall of roses, fruit, and peonies.

Rosie didn't answer. She didn't feel like massaging his ego by agreeing with him. She may not enjoy the art in his gallery, but she got its point. Art should have an element of mystery to captivate the viewer.

They walked to the desk together. A middle-aged woman with asymmetrical hair sat behind it leafing through a glossy magazine. She set the book down and smiled brightly as Rosie and Peter approached. "Can I help you?"

Rosie gave her the information on the piece she wanted to buy and opened her wallet. She flipped through the cards inside, but didn't see her business bank card. She pulled out the stack of plastic and leafed through it again. The card wasn't there. Then she remembered she'd used it for an online purchase recently. She must have left it next to the computer in her office.

She didn't like to use her personal credit card for client purchases. It made bookkeeping a nightmare, but she'd have to make an exception this time. She handed it over. The asymmetrical hair lady slid it through a swiper and handed it to her. While the payment processed, Rosie wrote her clients' address on the delivery paperwork.

"Hmmm. Can I see that card again?" the woman said.

"Was there a problem?" Rosie said.

"Probably the swiper. You know how temperamental these things are." She took the card, rubbed it on the hem of her long shirt, and ran it again. "Nope."

"That's strange." Rosie felt a niggle of worry. Identity theft was such a problem these days. She'd heard the stories, although she'd never experienced it herself.

Asymmetrical hair lady returned the card. "It says it's unauthorized." She sounded apologetic, as if she'd committed a social blunder by reporting the news.

Rosie took it, the niggle turning into a brick in her stomach. Eric monitored their family accounts. He was meticulous. If someone had figured out how to hack their credit card, what else had they gotten into?

"Can you hold the painting for me?" Rosie said.

The woman frowned.

"I'll be by in the morning."

She looked at her watch.

"Oh, come on," Peter said. "I own a gallery on the other side of town. I can assure you, you're not going to sell that piece to someone else tonight."

It was true. The Art Walk was winding down. The crowd on the street had thinned out, and there were only three other patrons in the shop.

"Okay." The woman's mouth tightened. "I'll hold it for twenty-four hours."

Rosie and Peter walked outside. The night air cooled her flushed cheeks. "I'm going to have to call the bank, put a stop on the card."

Peter pulled his jacket collar up. "Hate to leave you, but I'm going to head home."

"Me too." She'd found the painting she'd been hunting for, and now all she could think about was telling Eric what had happened with the card.

"Where are you parked?"

Rosie pointed toward the ocean. "Heisler Park."

"I'm there too." He threaded her arm through his.

"I stopped by Nightshade this morning," she said.

"I wasn't there."

"I know."

Rosie waited for him to tell her where he'd been, but he didn't. She broke the silence. "Everything okay?"

He waved his free hand in the air. "Fine. I had business in Seattle. And it was a good thing for you that I did. I spoke with Cecily, Jacob Rinehart's publicist."

"You did?"

"Yes, and I put in a good word for you. She didn't know Jacob's plans for the house, but knew he was planning to make changes."

"That was sweet of you, but I think we missed the boat."

"What do you mean?"

"I saw him with Twila tonight."

Peter turned his gaze to the sky. "God help us."

"She's assertive," Rosie said.

"She's a witch. I mean that in the literal sense," Peter said. Twila was the one person Rosie knew who had gotten the better of him on an art deal. He'd avoided doing business with her since. "But are you sure it was him? I'm told he doesn't look all that much like the picture on his book jackets."

"I'm sure. I met him last week."

Peter stopped in the middle of the Coast Highway. "What? Where?"

Rosie took his arm again and pulled him forward. "His dog attacked Peach."

Peter laughed. "Nice introduction. Reinforces your belief that horror writers are dangerous."

"You know what they say about dogs and their owners," Rosie said.

"Cecily insists he's a kind and thoughtful man."

"Actually, he does seem nice. He wanted me to take Peach to the vet, said he'd pay for it."

Peter's steps slowed. "Was she hurt? I didn't mean to be callous."

"No. She's fine." Rosie said in a reassuring tone.

"Good." He didn't speak for several steps, then said, "You did give him your card, didn't you? You told him what you do for a living."

"No. I didn't."

"Well, there you go." Disapproval seemed to float above his head like a gray cloud.

"It was a mistake, but I had other things on my mind."

Peter sniffed. "Obviously."

"I'm not as aggressive as I should be, okay? I'm working on it."

"I merely suggest you apply a little networking savvy." He sighed to make his disappointment clear as if it wasn't already.

One of the reasons Rosie had left the marketing mastermind group was because of its Manifest mindset—everyone in every situation was a potential sales victim. She didn't want to be one of *those* people. But perhaps Peter was right, perhaps she'd fallen into the ditch on the other side of the road.

They reached her car before she had to comment. "Goodnight. See you next Saturday?" she asked. She and Peter had a meeting that morning to plan the annual Nightshade Halloween party.

"Right. Breakfast on me." He walked on, his footsteps echoing in the quiet night. She opened her car door, and the click of his heels halted.

Peter, a silhouette now, stood outside a streetlamp's circle of light.

"I'll tell Cecily about the dog fight. Maybe Rinehart can be guilted into using you."

Rosie opened her mouth to tell him not to bother—Twila always got her man—but closed it again. What was the point? Peter would do what Peter wanted.

## 4.2.3

*The bank card.* Rosie stopped with her hand on the doorknob. She'd almost walked out of the house without it again. She ran to her office, grabbed it from her desk and hurried to the car. She wanted to arrive at Canyon Art when they opened at 10:00.

It was inconvenient, to say the least, not to have a back-up credit card. Eric had asked her not to use any of their personal ones until he got the problem sorted out. Rosie was upset and not only because of the inconvenience, but because he didn't seem to be. When she told him what happened at the gallery, he didn't even glance up from his book. He mumbled something about looking into it and kept reading. That was it. He'd look into it.

When she asked him what she should do about household expenses, he'd offered to put more money into her checking account. Cash wasn't her problem, however. It was the unexpected things. The things you couldn't prepare for. Eric was better at thinking ahead than she was. He was the financial guy. She struggled to balance her books every month.

She fished her phone from her bag. He told her he'd call the fraud line as soon as he got to the office. She wanted to know what he'd found out, but it rang before she could dial. It was Liz. "Hey there, sis."

"What's going on?" Rosie couldn't keep the worry from her voice.

Their father had a heart attack four months ago. He'd been doing well, but she was afraid a call from home meant bad news.

"Nothing. Don't worry. Dad's fine," Liz said.

Relief washed over her. "So, what's up then? You don't usually call on weekdays." Liz was a probate attorney who billed by the minute. She didn't spend precious time on frivolous chats during business hours.

"I'm at lunch," Liz said, and as if to prove it, Rosie heard the crinkle of a paper bag through the phone. "I went to my twenty-fifth reunion last weekend. Can you believe we're that old?"

Liz was three years older than Rosie, but Rosie decided not to point that out. "Some days it's not that hard," she said.

"Most days," Liz said with a full mouth. "I saw Derek Johnson. Do you remember Derek?"

Did she? Silly question. Liz knew full well Rosie had a passionate crush on him when they were kids. He'd dated Liz their senior year of high school when Rosie was a lowly freshman. Whenever he came to the house, Rosie would hover, trying to catch a glimpse of him. He was tall, athletic, blond, and everything a fourteen-year-old dreams of. She'd been acutely and painfully aware of Derek Johnson, but he could never remember her name.

Liz swallowed. "Anyway, he's a lawyer now—corporate. Small world, huh?"

"Yeah. Small world." Rosie wondered why Liz had called to tell her about Derek, but she knew better than to ask. Liz built her conversations the way she built her cases, methodically. If Rosie interrupted, she'd have to listen to the whole thing over from the beginning.

"He asked what you were up to, and I told him you own an interior design business in Laguna Niguel." The sound of a straw sucking more air than liquid came through the line.

"He knows I exist?" Rosie said.

Liz ignored her sarcasm. "Anyway, he just got divorced. And guess what?"

"He asked you out."

"You're no fun. Yes, he asked me out." Liz had too many boyfriends over the years to count, but she'd never married. Not that she hadn't been asked. She had. At least three times, but she'd always said she was married to her career.

"That's great. Hope you have a good time."

"So, you're not mad?"

"Why would I be mad?"

"Because he was rude to you when we were kids."

Rosie laughed. "Is that really why you called?"

"I wanted to make sure you approved."

"Since when?"

"I think he has potential."

"Really? That's an un-Liz-like thing to say."

"Yeah, well, how are the brats?"

"My *wonderful* children," Rosie said with emphasis on the word "wonderful," "are fine."

"And Peach?"

"She's fine too." Rosie noted that Liz did not ask about Eric. It wasn't an oversight. Liz didn't like Eric. Rosie didn't know all the reasons, and she didn't ask. She assumed it was because they were too much alike. Both type A personalities—there wasn't enough oxygen in any given room for the two of them to coexist.

"Good." Liz's mouth was full again. Rosie decided to take advantage of the opportunity.

"You'll never guess who moved to Laguna—"

"Damn. Rosie, sorry babe, but I'm getting another call. Gotta blast." Liz hung up before Rosie could say goodbye. She stared at her dead phone for a moment, then threw it in her purse. Some things never changed.

She parked a block away from the gallery and walked along the highway to the front entrance. She got there just as asymmetrical hair lady was opening up. The woman flashed her a tight smile. "You're here early."

"I want to make sure the painting is delivered as soon as possible."

Rosie followed the woman to the desk and held her breath while she ran the bank card through the swiper. It was Rosie's business card, not a personal one, but you never knew. Maybe the hacker had gotten into all their accounts. She hadn't needed to worry. The card went through, and the painting was purchased.

The bell on the front door sounded as she was stuffing the paperwork into her purse. She heard the muted tread of footsteps on the industrial carpet behind her. Asymmetrical hair lady looked past Rosie and beamed. "Mr. Rinehart, what can I do for you today?"

Rosie froze, her hand on the zipper of her purse. A yellow butterfly batted in her stomach, which made no sense. The decision about whether to pitch the man her services had been taken out of her hands. He wasn't a potential client. He was just a man with a temperamental dog.

She plastered on a pleasant look and pivoted. "Hi."

The look of surprise on Rinehart's face was so comical, her own smile broadened into a genuine one. "How's your dog?" He said.

"Fine."

"Really?"

"Yes, no problems."

"You'd tell me?"

"Of course."

"It's Rosie, right? Rosie Ring?"

"Good memory."

"Your name has a certain ring to it, no pun intended." But, of course, the pun was intended. It always was. Jacob grimaced. "I'm sorry. You've probably heard that a hundred times."

"Closer to a thousand," Rosie said lightly. "How's the move coming along?"

"I'm in a mess. I hate moving."

"It's high on the stress meter. Right under death of a loved one and divorce."

He gave her an absentminded nod. "Do you know anything about art?"

Asymmetrical hair lady spoke up. "I can answer any questions you might have."

"Yes, I'm sure you can. But I'm looking for a layman's opinion." His tone was friendly, but pointed.

An annoyed expression crossed the woman's face, but before she could argue Rinehart turned to Rosie again. "Can I show you something?"

"Sure," Rosie said. She knew where he was taking her before they got to the painting of the tower.

He stopped several feet away. "It's my house."

"It certainly is."

"Do you like it?"

Rosie stared at the piece for a long minute before answering. "It's really well done," she finally said.

"You don't like it."

"*Like* is the wrong word. I think it's powerful, captivating, and a little disturbing, but it's good. It's very good."

He crossed his arms over his chest and took a step back. "I saw it last night during the Art Walk, and I thought about buying it. But I wasn't sure if I wanted it in my living room. You know what I mean?"

"I do. I had the same reaction."

"I couldn't stop thinking about it, though."

"It has a magnetic quality."

"How do I decide whether to buy it or not?"

He seemed to be speaking more to himself than Rosie, but she gave him the answer she generally gave clients when they asked that question. "Can you visualize it in a certain space in your home?"

"Yes. On a wall between two picture windows that look out on the ocean."

"Will it complement the rest of your furnishings? Or, if you buy it will you have to completely redecorate?"

He scratched his chin. "I'm not sure, but I was planning to redo things anyway."

"If you love it, it could be an inspiration piece."

He glanced at her. "An inspiration piece?"

"Yes. Something that dictates the feel of the room. The colors you choose. The furniture."

"You sound like you know what you're talking about."

Rosie couldn't have orchestrated a better business introduction if she'd tried. Too bad it was too late. "I'm an interior designer," she said.

Rinehart slapped his thigh. "I knew it. I knew you were a creative.

It's that kindred spirit thing. I can always tell if someone is an artist, or a musician, or a writer. I bet you paint, or throw pottery, or sculpt, or something on the side."

"I used to paint. Now I only paint walls."

"I tried it for a while. My shrink said it would be good for me to have a hobby, but I was terrible." Jacob Rinehart pulled a cell phone from his pocket and checked the screen. "Are you available Monday morning? I'd love it if you'd come by and look at my place. I need help." Rosie paused. Twila wouldn't like her butting in. His forehead furrowed. "I'll pay you for your time."

"Oh, no. That's not . . . I was wondering about Twila."

His forehead furrowed. "Twila?"

"Twila Wilkes." The furrows deepened. "The woman who showed you this painting last night. I thought you were her client."

"She's an interior designer?"

"Yes."

"I thought she worked for the gallery." His gaze shifted to Rosie's face. "Where were you? I didn't see you."

Rosie pointed to the other room.

One side of Jacob's mouth turned up in a half grin. "Hiding." It wasn't a question. It was a statement.

Rosie shrugged. "She's not my favorite person."

"Hey, I'm not judging. I hide from people all the time. Trust me. I'm a pro. So, Monday. Can you come by?"

"What time?"

"Is ten too early?"

"No, ten is perfect."

They shook on it, and Rosie watched him walk to the front door of the gallery. "Did you make a decision on the painting?" Asymmetrical hair lady called after him.

"I'll run it by my interior designer after she sees my house," he said.

The woman looked at Rosie with a quizzical expression. "Are you his decorator?"

"I'll let you know on Monday." Rosie left the shop with a lighter step than she'd entered with. She'd call Liz tonight. Tell her about Rinehart before she hung up on Rosie again.

# 4.2.4

The weekend and been long and quiet. Eric was gone to a conference in Texas. Generally, Rosie didn't like it when he was away, which happened more and more of late. Eric had traveled to Fort Worth, Boise, Boulder, and Seattle in the past four months trying to stop the hemorrhage Skandalis had started. This weekend, however, she was relieved to have him gone.

She hadn't wanted to tell him about meeting with Rinehart until she knew if she had the job or not. If he wasn't around, she wouldn't be tempted. He'd gotten home late Sunday night and left early for work on Monday morning. She'd hardly seen him. It was perfect.

Rosie held up two dresses. "This, or this?" she said to Peach. The dog thumped her tail. "That's what I thought." Rosie laid the blue dress on the bed. "Blue builds trust. Besides it'll look nice with the ocean view."

An hour later she pulled up to the curb outside the tower, and the insecurity she'd fought on the weekend disappeared, replaced by excitement. She felt like a kid at the gates of Disneyland. The house, impenetrable and mysterious, had toyed with her imagination for years. She was about to enter the forbidden city.

Rosie straightened her shoulders and her skirt and walked toward the front door. Unlike many expensive homes, the door of the fortress was visible from the street. Only a short path and low hedge separated it from the public, yet it seemed as private as if it were surrounded by iron gates.

The house, constructed entirely of stone, loomed over the sidewalk like a castle. The closer she got to it, the smaller she felt. She raised a hand to ring the brass bell embedded in the stonework, but the door flew open before she had a chance. A dark shape rushed forward with a volley of yelps and leaped at her.

Jacob was close behind. "Fury, no."

Today Fury was a bundle of wriggling joy, nothing like the attack dog she'd met before. "It's okay," she said attempting to pet the moving target.

Jacob grabbed the dog's collar, pulled him off, and Rosie got her first real glimpse of the tower's interior. A hall stretched before her. Sunlight shining from the rooms opening onto it made patches of pale gray along its length. A rectangle of sunlight and blue ocean shimmered like a mirage at its far end.

"Come in," Jacob said.

The front door closed behind her, and the hallway was submerged in shadows. The dim light didn't feel gloomy or oppressive. Instead, it accentuated the bright space that beckoned ahead.

She followed Jacob through the long building, catching glimpses of wide rooms devoid of furniture. In one was a fireplace topped with a marble mantel and flanked by empty floor-to-ceiling bookshelves. In another, an impressive chandelier dangled over nothing. Halfway through the house, a staircase rose from an alcove on her left.

She'd lost count of the number of rooms they passed. The house was bigger than it appeared from the street. Rosie felt a tingle of apprehension. A job like this could take a year, or longer, without a staff to help her.

They finally came to a set of French doors leading into the bright room she'd seen from the front door. Jacob spread his arms wide. "This is where I've been living. I call it 'my apartment.'"

It was a beautiful space that ran the width of the house. To the left was a kitchen, modern and well-appointed enough to make Honey happy. On the other side of its stainless-steel counter in the dining area,

Jacob had placed an old, scarred hardwood table surrounded by mismatched chairs.

To her right was a sitting room. A couch and easy chairs with deep, midnight blue cushions were grouped around a green-tarnished brass topped coffee table. The French settee she'd seen the day Jacob moved in was nestled in a corner with a floor lamp next to it.

It would have been a comfortable but unremarkable room if it wasn't for the wall of windows that surrounded it on three sides. The house commanded a panoramic view. To the left, horseshoe shaped coves scalloped the shore all the way to Dana Point. To the right were miles of coast land. Directly in front of her was the ocean and San Clemente Island.

"Wow." It wasn't a very literate comment, but it was the one that came to her mind.

"Yes, wow. This is why I bought the place. Spectacular right?"

"It's amazing."

"The problem is I have all these empty rooms I don't need and have no idea what to do with."

The empty rooms were wonderful from a designer's perspective. Lots of opportunity; blank canvases for her paint. However, she couldn't actually imagine living with all those dark, hollow corners so perfect for hidden things. "You could close most of them up," Rosie offered.

He shrugged. "I could. But Cecily, that's my publicist, wants me to start having parties. Entertain the Hollywood types."

Rosie raised her eyebrows in question.

"The next step in my career, in her opinion, is a movie. My agent has been pitching, but you know what they say."

Rosie, having no experience with that world, didn't know. "What do they say?"

"Oh, it's all who you know. Cecily wants me to break out of my introverted ways and invite the hordes over."

"How many rooms are there?" Rosie asked.

"You know, I've forgotten. We could count. I believe there are six bedrooms. Maybe seven. Want to take a look?"

Jacob led her through the kitchen to a door she'd assumed was a pantry. It wasn't. Behind it was a narrow flight of stairs that led into blackness. "This is the servants' stairway," he said. "Since I don't have any servants, I use it."

She followed Jacob up the stairs to a small landing enclosed by two doors. He opened the one on the right. It led onto an upper hallway in the middle of which was the grand staircase Rosie had seen from below. Circling the staircase like the petals of a flower were six doors.

They walked from room to almost identical room. Each was painted a plain beige. Dark shapes on the walls revealed where furniture had once stood—ghosts of times past. There was a small private bath attached to each. A bit of the overwhelming feeling that had come over Rosie when she'd realized how large the house was disappeared. These rooms wouldn't be difficult to decorate. She would come up with one plan and replicate it six times.

After viewing the last guest room, they returned to the door leading to the servant stairs. To its right was another hallway, a shorter one. "I apologize in advance," Jacob said, leading her down it. "It's just me here. No one sees my bedroom but Fury."

The master suite was directly above the kitchen and sitting room, but had an even more spectacular view. Rosie walked to the north facing windows. She could see all the way to Newport Beach.

"I don't know what to do with all this space," Jacob said.

Rosie hadn't noticed the interior of the room, she'd been so drawn to the world outside the windows. Now she turned and glanced around. Jacob had a bed on the windowless wall. It was a California King but looked like a child's bed in the huge open room.

There was a long low bureau on another wall, an antique tallboy between two windows and a recliner near the fireplace wall that separated the sleeping area from what she assumed was the master bath and closet. As nice as the pieces were, they looked lost.

"This is it," Jacob said.

Rosie meet his eyes, gray-green today, and she thought he looked lost as well, swallowed in too much house. It would be a challenge to bring enough color, enough warmth to make it feel like a home.

"No more?" Sarcasm played over her words. You could fit three or four homes the size of hers inside the tower's walls.

Jacob led her out of the bedroom to the servant stairs. "Well, there is the morning room, the library, the formal living room, a dining room, a laundry room, butler's pantry, and a three-car garage I haven't shown you yet."

When Rosie stepped into the stairwell, she noticed the door she'd seen on the way up. "Where does that lead?"

"The attic. There's nothing up there but spiders."

When they reached the lower level again, the apartment felt almost cozy after the echoing expanse of the second floor. Rosie couldn't imagine sleeping in this house. It was the perfect setting for a modern ghost story.

"So what do you think?" Jacob said.

"I think there's a lot to do," Rosie said.

"What I meant was, will you take the job?"

Rosie should have jumped at the offer. Twila would have. But Twila had assistants. Rosie worked alone. She hesitated. "What's your deadline?"

Jacob shrugged. "The longer you take, the longer I can put off Cecily's parties."

Rosie laughed. "Then I'm your girl. Since there's only me, it will definitely take longer to get the work done than if you hired someone from a larger firm."

Jacob pulled a face. "I'm not a big firm kind of guy."

"I prefer to work alone myself."

"Like I said, kindred spirit."

"Can I look around and make some notes?"

"Of course." Jacob disappeared into the kitchen to make coffee.

Rosie pulled her iPad from her purse and toured the lower floor snapping pictures and taking measurements. She needed to get a handle on the house, understand the layout. By the time she'd finished, two mugs, cream and sugar, and a plate of cookies sat on the scarred table.

"So what do you think about that painting?" Jacob said as soon as she sat.

"I think it would be beautiful between the picture windows, just like you imagined. This room is so bright, its stormy mood would make a striking contrast."

"Not too gloomy then?"

"I don't think you could make this room gloomy."

"Good." He blew on his coffee and took a sip. "I tend to be attracted to the dark side. I wasn't sure if I was taking things too far with that painting."

"I don't think so. We can pick up its gray-blues and violets and go for soft, subdued tones. The stormy weather in the piece will make this room seem like a cozy haven."

"As if it were a window, you mean?"

"Exactly."

They chatted about how Jacob would like to use the different rooms of the house, his preferences in furniture styles and colors, and the budget. Rosie had to tamp down a rush of anxiety when they discussed the last. She was so used to clients who watched every penny, she was afraid to mention her financial estimates. But Jacob named a figure exponentially larger than she'd planned.

In the end, they decided she would start with the space they were seated in, and use the painting as an inspiration piece. The kitchen had been recently remodeled, and Jacob liked its industrial, minimalist appeal. It would remain as is, except the little bit of visible wall between the cabinets. That would be painted to match whatever color they chose for the rest of the apartment.

When this was finished, she'd tackle the master suite, then the guest bedrooms, and finally the library, formal dining room and living room, and the morning room. The last would be transformed into Jacob's office.

Rosie packed up her things. Jacob walked her to the front door, the noise of their footsteps bouncing off the naked walls. "I didn't think it was possible, but I'm actually getting excited about this," he said as she stepped into the warm autumn sunshine.

She put out a hand. "I'm thrilled. This house has always fascinated me." Jacob took her hand, and they shook.

On the way home, her mind churned with ideas. She couldn't wait to share the news with Honey. And Eric. Of course, Eric. Guilt nudged her. She should tell Eric before she told Honey. And she would. If he came home on time. He'd been staying at work so late. That's why she hadn't thought of him before Honey. Honestly, though, she'd like the first person she told to be happy for her.

She stopped at a red light and drummed her fingers on the steering wheel. By the time the light turned green, she'd decided. Whoever got home first, Honey or Eric, that one would be the first to know. The compromise made her feel better.

# 4.2.5

After a salad, Rosie got to work on the schematic of Rinehart's apartment. She opened the design program on her laptop and began creating virtual rooms with the measurements, windows, doorways, and stationary structures of the actual rooms. She placed the kitchen counters, cabinets, the fireplace, and so on. Next, she played around with mock-ups of the furniture Jacob already had, putting the pieces in various locations. She put a JPEG of the painting he planned to buy on the wall between the windows and pondered its colors.

Building a virtual room was the professional approach to interior design these days, but she enjoyed making an old-fashioned mood board as well. She didn't always, but a client with Jacob Rinehart's artistic nature might enjoy a more tactile representation of her plans.

When she made a mood board, she glued fabric, carpet, paint samples, and pictures of furnishings onto foam core creating a collage of color and texture. She loved that part of her job. It gave her some of the satisfaction she used to have when she painted.

After several hours, she glanced at her clock. It was 3:10 and time for a coffee break. She stood and stretched and wandered to her front window. Honey's car wasn't on the street. Not that she expected it to be. Honey didn't usually close the shop until five.

Rosie made a cup of coffee. Before taking it into her office and getting to work, she walked to the window again. She was rewarded with the sight of Honey's van pulling into the driveway next door.

Peach beat her to the front hall. Her doggy sixth sense kicked in whenever someone was about to leave the premises. "Sorry, baby. I'll walk you after dinner." Rosie patted her and hurried next door.

Honey was lifting grocery bags out of the van as Rosie rounded the corner. "Can I help?" Rosie said.

"Could you get that last one and close the door?"

Rosie did as requested and followed Honey through the garage dodging piles of laundry, a bike with no wheels on a bike stand, the bike's wheels, empty delivery boxes, and a large bag of dog food. The dog food gave Rosie a pang. Honey's boxer, Bruiser, had died eight months ago at the ripe old age of eleven.

The inside of the house was only marginally neater than the garage. It was clean, but couldn't be called tidy. Every table was covered with stacks of mail, magazines, cookbooks, and odds and ends.

On the way to the kitchen, Rosie stepped over several pairs of shoes, two Nordstrom Rack shopping bags, and a set of twenty-five-pound dumbbells. Honey's husband worked out at the fire station in between fires and on his days off. He believed fitness saved lives, a sentiment Honey didn't subscribe to.

The kitchen stood out like a pearl in the sandy mess of an oyster shell. It was an oasis of pristine order and cleanliness. The stainless-steel counters and appliances gleamed. The natural stone floors were swept and polished. A circle of white cabinets beamed from coffee and cream-colored walls like a movie star's smile.

Rosie set the bag she carried on the counter next to the ones Honey had deposited. "You're home early."

"I have a dinner tonight. I had to shop and make appetizers," Honey said. "Coffee?"

Rosie nodded. She'd left a half-drunk cup at home. Honey's cafe au lait, like everything else she made, was delicious. "I saw the inside of the tower today," she said.

"That's right. You had that appointment. How did it go?"

"Terrific. I got the job."

As Honey busied herself with coffee making, Rosie filled her in. She told her about the vast empty spaces, the almost identical guest rooms, the large living-dining area she'd started work on today. Honey set out two steaming mugs, complete with heart designs in their foamy interiors.

"This job is gonna be a game changer, Rosie. My first big gig was in Coto de Caza. It was for a bank president's wife. After that, I got so many requests I had to start turning people away. That party is the reason I was able to open Sweeter."

Honey leaned her elbows on the counter, took a sip of coffee, then set her cup down. "Jacob Rinehart is your bank president's wife."

"I hope so," Rosie said. "It's certainly the biggest job I've ever had."

"So that means you're in a good mood, right?"

"Sure. Why?"

Honey exited the kitchen, returned a second later, and slapped a magazine onto the counter. It was the most recent copy of *Orange County Lifestyles*. Leering up at Rosie from its glossy cover was Twila. The headline read "TW Designs Does It Again."

Twila leaned against a whimsical iron lampstand topped by an eye-catching blown glass shade. Behind her a fairyland of colorful glass glowed from the trees and bushes of a lush garden.

"Sorry to be the bearer of bad news, but I knew you'd see it as soon as you got the mail."

While Honey unpacked bags and organized ingredients on the kitchen counter, Rosie leafed through the article. There were pictures of Twila at the Chihuly Museum and Gardens in Seattle, supposedly getting inspiration for the Monarch Beach backyard.

Rosie's jaw tightened. She recognized that backyard. She'd seen it on her appointment with Gayle Conrad, a local orthodontist who was married to a judge. Gayle had loved Rosie's plans for her new home for at least a week. Then, when Rosie called to make a second appointment, she told her she'd found another designer.

"I'm so sorry, Rosie. Your ideas were lovely, they really were. But Twila gets us, you know?" Rosie didn't know, so Gayle explained. "She came up with the most stunning plan for Kurt's sports memorabilia collection, right there on the spot. It's been a bone of contention between us for years." She trilled a laugh. "I do believe she may have saved our marriage."

How could Rosie compete? She only decorated homes and redesigned spaces. She didn't offer family counseling sessions.

"It's beautiful." Rosie said through tight lips.

"Did you read the part where she says she travels up and down the West Coast looking for unique things for her clients? It's such a puff piece. Makes her sound so dedicated."

"The garden is nice." Rosie cleared her throat. She didn't like the waspish tone of her own voice.

Honey laughed. "You sound so sincere."

"I am. It is nice."

"You could have done that in your sleep."

"Thank you, but you're not exactly unbiased." Having Honey tell her she was talented was like having her mother tell her she was pretty.

"When you're done with Jacob Rinehart's place, you'll get a spread like that. He's a celebrity. The house is a Laguna icon."

"I don't know," Rosie said. Honey raised her eyebrows in question. "He probably doesn't want anyone to know where he lives because of..." She didn't want to talk, or think, about the murder.

Honey began chopping garlic with more force than necessary. "That's okay," she said between slams of knife on wood. "He'll still have people over. People in his social circle. People he trusts. Those are the people you want to meet anyway."

Honey was a perpetual optimist. It was one of the things Rosie loved about her.

"And," she blew her bangs out of her eyes, "I've seen magazine spreads that don't name the home owners, and none of them give the address."

Rosie shrugged. "I'll be lucky if I can take pictures for my portfolio."

Honey pushed the garlic into a blender, added a handful of spinach, a dollop of sour cream and turned the machine on. Rosie was thankful for the break. Honey's heart was in the right place, but the conversation was starting to erode today's excitement.

It seemed no matter what she achieved, Twila was always one step ahead of her. Rosie signed a famous author. Getting the cover of a magazine, maybe even a national publication, seemed like a no-brainer, but her famous author wouldn't want the publicity.

She shouldn't compare herself to Twila. She knew that. She should just be happy with what she'd achieved, with her own gifts and talents, but Twila seemed to suck up all the air in the industry leaving Rosie gasping for breath.

When she was a child, she'd had terrible asthma. The first attack came when she was five. In the grand scheme of things, it wasn't that traumatic. She'd had friends in high school and college who'd suffered at the hands of abusive boyfriends, been date-raped, and had parents die tragically. An asthma attack was a small thing in comparison, but it was emblazoned in her memory.

Her ballet school was having a recital. They'd rented an auditorium with a stage and an orchestra pit and movie theater seats that folded by themselves when you stood. The space terrified and excited her in equal measures. It seemed so grown-up to dance in a room like that.

As the night of the performance drew closer, the excitement began to dwindle leaving only jangling nerves. She tried to bow out, claim she was sick, which wasn't entirely untrue. She was sick. Every time she thought about it, she wanted to throw up. Her Grandma Bea saw the truth though.

"Look out in the audience, Rosie," she'd said. "You find me, and dance only for me. Then you'll be fine."

That well-intentioned advice had backfired. When Rosie stepped onto the stage that night, it was worse than she'd imagined. The audience was in darkness and the spotlights blinded her. She searched for Grandma Bea, for her mom and dad, for Liz, but it was like trying to see into the bottom of a well with a flashlight shining on you.

Panic tightened her chest. She became confused and disoriented. As the music ended, Rosie, thinking she was following the other dancers, pirouetted right off the stage and into the orchestra pit.

On YouTube, it might have looked funny, but in real life, it wasn't. Rosie lay on the floor of the orchestra pit, leg twisted underneath her at an odd angle, her eyes blinded by green spotlights. She gasped for air;

sure she was dying. Her sister Liz did all the performing in the family after that.

When the blender switched off, Rosie said, "The Laguna Niguel home is done. I found a painting the night of the Art Walk. I spoke with my clients, and they would love to throw a party." Time to change the subject. Get Honey thinking about food. "They don't want to do dinner though. Just appetizers. Can you do a cooking class around appetizers?"

"Sure. I've done it before. When?"

Rosie pulled out her phone. Honey wiped her hands on a towel, grabbed her calendar, and they set a date. "They want it to be a couples event, so invite Booker if he's home." Rosie said.

"Booker will only go if Eric goes," Honey said. "He's been persnickety lately."

"Why? What's the matter?" Persnickety wasn't a word Rosie would apply to Booker. He was a big, bold man with a big, bold personality. Persnickety sounded small and peckish.

"I honestly don't know. He's not talking. Just sulking and slinking around. I thought it was Bruiser. He was Booker's dog, you know that. But Bruiser's been gone for months now."

"It's hard to lose a pet."

Honey didn't agree or disagree. She focused on picking up imaginary crumbs off the counter with a fingertip.

"I'll tell Eric about the party tonight, and let you know," Rosie said, gave her a hug, and headed outside.

The shadows had lengthened while she'd been in Honey's kitchen. Eric would be home soon. She didn't know how he'd react to her news. He should be happy for her, for them. The tower was a spectacular job. But she didn't think he would be. He'd been so high-centered on his problems at Pacific, she feared all he'd hear when she said "Jacob Rinehart" would be "murder" and "scandal."

Whatever his reaction, she wouldn't let him ruin her excitement. She wouldn't let Twila's magazine spread put a damper on it either. She told herself that, but envy threaded through her like a fault line.

4.2.6

On her way to Laguna Beach on Wednesday morning, Rosie flipped on the radio. A local show featuring two of the most annoying talk radio hosts in the world, Hank and Frank, blared into her car. Eric must have put the station on the other night when he'd driven it.

Hank's voice was aggressive, yet whiny. It grated. "You're so friggin' gullible."

Frank's voice was calm and controlled. "I don't agree with you, so I'm gullible?"

"Come on, man. It's obvious," Hank whined.

Rosie reached toward the radio to switch it off but stopped at his next words. "Jacob Rinehart's publisher is in this up to their skeevy eyeballs. He's got a new book coming out and what happens? All the gossip rags are talking about the *Pillory* murder again."

Frank snorted. "I'm the gullible one? What, you think this is a made-for-TV movie?" His voice lowered half an octave, apparently to make him sound like a news anchor. "This just in: Trammel Publishing accused of hiring a hit on a flight attendant to increase book sales."

Rosie's hand dropped into her lap. She hated Frank and Hank's shtick, but she couldn't turn it off.

"Hey, the book hit number one on the *New York Times* list *after* that woman was killed," Hank said.

"Rinehart's books usually hit the list, don't they?"

"His first one, *Crate*—"

Frank's guffaw interrupted Hank. "*Crate*, what's that a horror novel for dogs? It was *Cage. Cage* was the first book."

"*Crate, Cage*, whatever, the point is that book did okay, but he's crashed and burned since."

"If an author stops selling, publishers move on. They don't kill people. There's plenty of writers in the sea."

The light at the corner turned red, and Rosie slammed on her brakes. She hadn't noticed it was yellow.

"I'm just saying."

Hank never got to say it, though, because Frank was on a roll. "I can't believe a big publishing company—"

Hank interrupted. "Okay, forget the company. Did you see the face that publicist chick made when she said Jacob Rinehart's name? Huh? Did you?"

"Sure. I saw her face. So what?"

"She looked like she was totally obsessed with the guy."

Frank laughed derisively.

Hank said, "I'm not kidding. You think I'm kidding. Check out the YouTube video."

A thump came through the radio sounding like Frank slapped the desk. "Just because the woman has the hots for Rinehart—and I'm not saying she does—doesn't mean she'd kill for him."

"Somebody did."

"She's a publicist not a gorilla." Papers shuffled near the mic. "I don't think a woman could've pulled off a hit like that, anyway."

"That stewardess—," Hank said.

"Flight attendant—geez. You say stewardess one more time, and we're going to start getting calls." Frank was priming the pump, hoping for calls. Outrage was their bread and butter.

"*Flight attendant.*" Hank's tone was mocking. "Anyway, the *flight attendant* was whacked over the head from behind. She was dead before the head and hands thing."

"Really?"

"Yeah, came out in the autopsy. Which means it didn't have to have been a guy who did it."

Frank paused, like he was considering Hank's point, then said, "Yeah, yeah, but you know what they say about dead weight. I still think it was the husband Marianne Kennedy was cheating on."

"He was in Puerto Rico," Hank said.

"He could have hired someone."

"On a pilot's salary? No way."

"Or somebody who didn't like Marianne Kennedy killed her. Maybe one of the guys she was messing around with. The husband has the best motive, though." Frank was sticking to his guns.

"Then why do the whole *Pillory* act? Why leave the book?" Hank argued.

"I don't know." Frank exhaled loudly. "Maybe because a person who decapitates someone and leaves them in a park is just a little deranged."

"I think—"

"Shut up. We have to go to a break," Frank said. "Okay, folks, don't go anywhere. We're going to solve the *Pillory* crime right here after José brings you the traffic."

Rosie shut off the radio and sat in silence, her heart hammering in her chest. Why was she letting Hank Trent, of all people, get her upset? She didn't like Frank Cantrell any better, but at least in this case he made the more rational argument. The woman's husband was the most likely suspect. She'd been cheating on him. Or it could have been one of the creepy guys the woman was sleeping with like Frank said. Either way, Rosie wasn't going to solve the crime any more than Hank and Frank were. If Jacob or Cecily were suspects, the police would be talking to them.

Rosie pulled up to the curb in front of the tower, grabbed her laptop, and marched to the door. Jacob Rinehart was her client, a nice man, a man who rescued dogs and liked fine art. After listening to that show, she could understand why he'd run away from Seattle. It must be horrible to have the world dissecting your private life like that, using tragic situations to get listeners.

She knocked firmly. She was glad she got this job. Not just for the money, or the prestige, but so she could be a friend. Jacob Rinehart could use one.

Several long seconds passed and no one came to the door. She checked her watch, 10:32. Their appointment was for 10:30. She rang the bell and heard chimes cascading behind the thick wood door. A hum she hadn't noticed before stopped. A moment later, there were footsteps. The door opened. It wasn't Jacob.

A petite woman probably mid-forties with dark hair, dark eyes, and light brown skin that glowed against a startlingly white blouse stood in the doorway. "Yes?" she said.

"Hi, I'm Rosie Ring. Mr. Rinehart's interior designer. We have an appointment."

"I'll tell him you're here."

The door closed in Rosie's face. A servant? Really? Rinehart didn't seem the type. Footsteps sounded on the other side of the door again. It opened. "You can come in," the woman said. Her accent was light, but there. Spanish of some kind.

Rosie followed the woman the length of the building to the windowed room at the back. Jacob lounged on his couch, a laptop in his lap. "Hi. I've got that schematic to show…" her words died on her lips.

Jacob glanced up from his computer, his face a blank.

"I've got the right day, don't I?" Rosie stammered the words, suddenly unsure of herself.

He stared at her, seemingly not comprehending her words.

"I can come by another time." She placed one foot behind the other, ready to pivot.

His expression cleared, and he smiled. It wasn't quite his usual charm-the-socks-off-you smile, but her unease dissipated. "No, no. Stay." He closed his laptop. "I get in this writing zone and forget what's going on around me sometimes. I'm back in the real world now. What have you got?"

Rosie sat next to him on the couch and took her computer from her bag. "I did an initial plan, but we can change anything you don't like. It's just a starting point."

She pulled up the schematic and began talking Jacob through it. She clicked on the three possible paint colors she'd chosen from the painting: a soft gray, a warmer taupe, and a gray blue. "I think any of these would work. I lean toward the taupe, but—"

"The gray. I like the gray," he said.

"Great. Gray it is," she said. "If you like the gray, what do you think about this rug? It's a handmade, wool, oriental. A really beautiful complement to the cool wall color."

"I'm not big on red. Not after Seattle." Rosie looked at him with curiosity. "There was a lot of red thrown at my house. Someone painted "killer," in red spray paint. I got that cleaned up and the next day someone tomato bombed it. More red. The worst was a group of pick-eters. Their signs were pictures of the woman who was killed with big red slashes across her neck."

"That's terrible. I didn't know," Rosie said.

"I loved Seattle. Lived in the area my whole life."

"Maybe you can go home when they catch the killer," Rosie said.

"Yeah, maybe, but once people make up their minds the facts don't always sway them."

Rosie didn't know what to say. He was right. Pacific Financial went through the same thing. People heard about Seb Skandalis and even though neither Eric nor Bob had any knowledge of the trafficking of women from the Middle East, despite the fact they would have turned him into the police if they had, they were being punished. "How do you like this rug? It's the same pattern with a charcoal background."

They went through the rest of her design scheme. Jacob chose darker colors and coarser fabrics than they'd originally discussed, but he had good taste. She could make it work. "I'll bring you something next week. Monday morning?"

"That works. Lupe will show you out." He nodded to the woman who was dusting the sparse furniture in the room.

"No need. I know my way," Rosie said. She walked over to the woman and extended a hand. "Hi, Lupe. Nice to meet you officially."

Lupe switched her cleaning rag to her left hand, and shook.

"Are you here every day now?" Rosie asked.

"Mondays and Wednesdays and some Saturdays," she said.

"I'm sure I'll see you again then." Rosie turned to go, but stopped. She looked at Jacob. "Where's Fury?"

Jacob paused long enough that Rosie began to worry he'd say he'd sent the dog to the pound. "He's crated at the moment. He was getting under Lupe's feet while she cleaned. Hates the vacuum. Kept attacking it." He turned to Lupe. "If you're done vacuuming, you could let him out."

She nodded and disappeared into the kitchen and up the servant staircase. Rosie saw herself out and was happy to close the door behind herself today. Jacob's story about the harassment in Seattle was disturbing, and it hit a little too close to home.

4.2.7

She left the tower with a new compassion for Eric. He hadn't been happy last night when she'd told him she'd signed the contract with Rinehart, and they'd argued. She'd said she wasn't about to refuse the project because of Eric's paranoia. Not very nice words, but that's how she'd seen it at the time.

The anger in Jacob's voice as he told her about the events that had driven him from his home in Seattle had been a like a sucker punch. She'd known what Eric and Bob had gone through, intellectually and certainly financially, but the emotional aspect had never hit her before.

Eric and Bob hadn't had picketers outside their homes. They hadn't been tomato bombed. Their office hadn't been spray-painted. But they'd paid a heavy price for Seb's crimes. It's no wonder Eric was a little paranoid.

Rosie wanted to see him, say she was sorry. Not for taking the job, but for being less sympathetic than she should have been. She seemed to be saying she was sorry a lot these days.

It was almost noon. She started the car and headed south on the Coast Highway toward Dana Point and Pacific Financial. She knew he didn't have any lunch plans because he'd made himself a brown bag that morning. She'd surprise him. Take him out.

She wouldn't dwell on the apology, on the negative. She'd focus on the positive, try to reassure him that everything would be okay. There were no angry mobs outside the tower. Jacob was a nice guy, and he'd given her a large check. That should cheer him up.

After parking in the office building's lot, she climbed the stairs to the second floor. She pushed open the heavy metal door at the top and entered Pacific Financial's lobby. Blue industrial carpet ran under the receptionist's desk and down a hallway of glass doors.

Barbara, the office manager, phone pressed to her ear, waggled her fingers at Rosie. She looked tired and drawn. She'd always been a bright spot in the office. Gray curls, big smile, she'd reminded Rosie of a lean Mrs. Claus. Not today.

"Yes, I'll tell him. I'm sure he'll get back to you this afternoon. I understand. Right. Right." She hung up the phone and sighed audibly. "How're you doing, Rosie?"

"Great. Since when are you at the reception desk?"

"Since they let Natalie go."

"I didn't know she was gone."

"There aren't many of us left."

"You must be swamped."

"Yes, but not as swamped as I would have been in the past. We've lost a lot of clients, but I'm sure you know that."

Eric had talked about almost nothing else for the past three months. Rosie realized now that in some ways it hadn't seemed real. "Is he in?"

Barbara waved toward the hallway. "Yeah, he's back there."

Rosie headed in, glancing right and left. The normally busy space was deserted. All that was left in the glassed-in offices were phone and computer cables stretched across empty carpeted spaces, and here and there a cardboard box.

She heard Twila's voice before she saw her. "That depends. How handy are you?" She laughed, seductively. There was a mumbled response Rosie couldn't make out. Twila laughed again.

Rosie turned the corner. She could see Twila now at the end of the hallway. She'd slipped one foot from her expensive spiked shoe and rubbed it along the calf of her bare leg.

There was something intimate in the gesture that unsettled Rosie.

Especially because she was doing it in Eric's office. Honey's words about Twila's penchant for other people's husbands echoed in her mind.

Twila leaned toward Eric, a hand on his desk to balance her one-legged stance. Her discarded shoe had fallen on its side. The sole was blood red.

Maybe the rumors were true. Twila was a driven career woman with no time for outside commitments. Other women's husbands were perfect for her. They came without the distractions a man of her own would bring.

Rosie walked faster. She'd never worried about Eric. They had a solid marriage, and apart from that he was the most responsible man she knew. He was a great dad, a good provider, and a stellar son.

Now, however, she found herself examining his face, gauging his response to Twila. Both were focused on a file that lay open on his desk. He wasn't smiling. She found some comfort in that.

Rosie cleared her throat when she got within a few feet of the door. Their heads jerked toward her. Twila's expression was calm and condescending. Eric's was harder to read. The man she thought she knew better than she knew herself was suddenly a mystery.

She leaned into the doorway. "Hi."

Eric closed the file. "Hi, babe."

"I hope this isn't a bad time."

"No. Of course not." One side of his mouth lifted, a partial smile.

"I came to take you out to lunch."

"Oh." His eyes shot to Twila as if asking her permission.

"I was about to leave," she said.

Eric's face cleared. "Great. Just let me straighten up."

Since when was taking her husband to lunch such an awkward experience? In the past, he'd have jumped to his feet as soon as he saw her. Even when he was busy, he'd always had time to give her a kiss. Could he still be angry with her about taking on Rinehart as a client? She'd assured him that Jacob didn't want publicity any more than Eric did. He'd seemed mollified, if not happy. "Should I wait outside?" Rosie's tone was sharp.

Twila flipped the scarlet sole of her shoe to the floor and slipped on the pump. Eric gathered up the file and handed it to her. "No. Just give me a sec," he said.

"See you Saturday," Twila said. It sounded like a command.

"I'll be there."

"Eight-thirty? I want to get an early start."

"Right. Eight-thirty."

What were they talking about? Eric didn't normally work on the weekends unless he was traveling. But nothing was normal these days.

Twila disappeared. Eric stood, came around the desk and gave Rosie a peck on the cheek. His lukewarm reception left her feeling off-kilter. She wanted to ask why he was meeting Twila on Saturday, but if she asked now, she'd sound like she didn't trust him. She bit her lip. "You sure you're not too busy?" She tried to keep the edge out of her voice.

"No. I need to get out of here." He gave her shoulder a squeeze. The warmth from his hand made her feel a little better.

They didn't speak as they walked past the empty offices. Embarrassment and sadness were in the set of his shoulders, fatigue in his gait. She hadn't realized how bad things had gotten at the company until this walk down the empty corridor.

Eric and Bob had founded the business together eight years ago. They'd become friends while working for the same large accounting firm. Starting their own company became a dream. One they'd planned over hundreds of lunches and cups of coffee. One they'd saved up for years to make real.

Pacific Financial had grown rapidly, and five years ago they'd taken on another partner. Seb Skandalis came with money to invest and a group of clients. Eric hadn't liked him, but Bob was impressed and the infusion of cash would allow them to move into a larger office and hire more staff.

Eric acquiesced. Bob and Eric's relationship, so good for so long, was strained now. Eric was as angry with himself for not taking a stronger stand against Skandalis as he was with Bob for pressuring him to hire the man.

Twenty minutes later, Rosie and Eric sat at their favorite sushi place on the Coast Highway with iced tea in front of them. "This is a nice surprise," Eric said. For the first time since she'd cleared her throat in the hallway at the office, he seemed relaxed and pleased.

"I got my first infusion of cash from Jacob this morning. Thought we should celebrate."

Eric frowned but lifted his cup. "Congrats."

She tapped it with hers. "Thanks."

"Tell me all about it. I need a diversion."

"There's not much to tell. I brought him my initial schematic. He had more opinions than I thought he would."

"He's the artistic type, right? Don't they all have opinions?"

Rosie stirred her iced tea with a straw. "I guess. He wasn't as easy going as I'd thought he was."

"See, temperamental. That's what I'm talking about. Trust me, I live with one."

She pulled a face. "Funny."

"I'm not joking." He said the words with a comically straight face.

"You're probably right. About Jacob, not me. I interrupted him while he was writing."

"Oh, so it's Jacob now?"

"What am I supposed to call him? Mr. Rinehart?"

Eric opened his mouth to respond but at that moment a server placed a California roll, a rainbow roll, plates, and chopsticks on the table. Rosie took the opportunity to ask the question that had been niggling at her. "So why are you meeting Twila on Saturday?" She kept her voice light.

The smile Eric had been wearing since they'd sat slid from his face. "We're trying to save money."

Rosie took a slice of rainbow roll and dipped it into soy sauce. "You and Twila?"

"No. Me and Bob. We need to modify the new office. Twila could hire a crew, or we could roll up our sleeves and do some of the work ourselves."

"By ourselves, I assume you mean yourself?" Rosie couldn't imagine corpulent Bob, whose idea of exercise was walking his equally corpulent English bulldog around the block, rolling up his sleeves and doing any kind of manual labor.

Eric nodded, his mouth full.

"Isn't the landlord responsible for that kind of thing?"

"I'm assembling partitions and putting up shelves. Nothing that effects the structure of the building itself."

"Oh." A wave of relief was followed quickly by a backwash of guilt. She didn't doubt Eric. Not really. She doubted Twila, and in that she might be justified. "So, I talked to Becca yesterday before you got home." She hadn't mentioned it the night before because as soon as he'd arrived, she'd told him about the Rinehart job, and then...

On to happier topics. She and Eric chatted about their children for the remainder of their lunch. It felt like pre-Seb days.

When the server brought the check, Eric glanced at it then laid a credit card on top. Their accounts must have been cleared by the bank. "You got the new credit cards?" Rosie was surprised he hadn't mentioned it.

"Ah, no," he said picking up the bill and glancing over his shoulder for their server. "It's a company card."

"So what's going on with our account?"

"The bank said they're going to issue new cards. We should get them soon." Rosie frowned. It seemed to be taking a long time. "Soon in red-tape bureaucracy speak, probably means in a few weeks," he added.

"You're not paying anyway, remember?" She reached for the tray. Slapping her own card on the bill sent a happy glow through her. She, Rosie Ring, had bagged the tower. Even if she never got a spread in *Orange County Lifestyles*, or anywhere else, she had bagged the tower. Twila could eat her heart out.

Rosie was ahead in their unacknowledged rivalry. Finally.

**MOLLY:** Congrats to Rosie. Her eat your heart out comment might not have been in the best taste, but I can't blame her. Twila does seem like a piece of work.

I have to say, one of the things I love about

all the women I've interviewed for this podcast is how vulnerable they've made themselves. Every one of them has stated that if their story could possibly help someone else out there, they're happy to tell it. Even the parts that don't show them in the best light.

Before we end for the day, however, let's get into the next patient excerpt.

# patient zero

EXCERPT OF RECORDED PATIENT INTERVIEW
FROM THE FILES OF DR. LEWIS CARVER:

Mom was pretty free with her hands. She slapped us. A lot. It bothered my brother more than it bothered me, so sometimes I stepped in and took it for the both of us. Dad would stop her if he was home, but he wasn't home all that much. I think he was as afraid of her as my brother was.

One day when we were in third grade, we got home from school and smelled something burning. Smelled it as soon as we opened the front door. We ran into the kitchen. Black smoke was coming through the cracks around the door of the stove. My brother isn't good in those kinds of circumstances. He panicked and didn't know what to do. I've always been the clear thinking one.

I grabbed a potholder and took the tray of burning cookies out of the oven. I walked outside, holding the flaming thing in front of me like I was in one of those stupid egg-on-a-spoon races and set it on the grass.

When I was sure the fire was out, I went inside and opened all the windows. Then I thought I'd better go find Mom, see if she was okay. She was where I expected her to be, passed out on the couch. She never could cook without a drink, not even cookies. It seemed best to let sleeping dogs lie. If I was lucky, she'd stay like that until Dad got home, then he could deal with her. My brother and I went upstairs and started our homework.

A couple of hours later, I heard Mom banging around. I didn't like it. It made me nervous, but my brother got so scared he hid. Mom was always at her most cranky when she woke up from a drunk. Now that I'm older, I realize she must have still been buzzed. Not enough to be out cold, but enough to keep her inhibitions at bay.

I heard her footsteps on the stairs. I'll be honest, I thought about getting in the closet, but that's not my style. It isn't now, and it wasn't then. I'm an action-oriented kind of person. So she came into the bedroom and started slapping me around, yelling at me for eating all the cookies. I tried to tell her I didn't eat anything. They weren't edible. I told her if she didn't believe me, she could check the backyard. But she wouldn't listen. Shocker.

When she was good and done, she went downstairs. I lay on the bed, licking my wounds until the sun went down. It must have been late when Dad finally got home, because my stomach was growling like it hadn't been fed all day. When he came up to see us, my brother finally came out of hiding.

Dad hugged us and said how sorry he was. He got a wash cloth and cleaned the blood off my face. I think he even cried a little. But he didn't say anything to Mom. He went to the kitchen and cooked up a pot of hot dogs and beans. She ate dinner with the rest of us like nothing had happened.

When I went to bed that night, I made a decision. Things were going to change. I didn't know when. I didn't know how. But I wasn't going to put up with it anymore. Not for me. Not for my brother. We were going to have the kind of home the other kids at school had. It would be nice if there was a mom in it, a cookie baking, soccer mom, kind of mom. But if we couldn't have that, the next best thing would be no mom at all.

In looking back on that day, I realize now how pivotal it was. Until then, I think I labored under the delusion that Dad would fix things. That he'd send her packing. That he'd protect us. I understood something that day I'd never understood before. Dad wasn't a bad guy, but he was weak. And weakness can kill you.

**MOLLY:** Weakness can kill you. I'm sure that's true, but just as we discussed last season, sometimes the traits we think of as strengths are merely reactions to fear. They're weaknesses in disguise.

This leads to my question of the week: Do you think Rosie's envy of Twila is a positive or a negative in her life? Will it inspire her to push out of her comfort zone? Or is it a distraction? Something that might cause her to make unwise decisions.

Let me know what your thoughts on the Facebook page. And join me next time for more *Murders Under the Sun.*

**(cue music)**

**VO:** This episode is brought to you by St. Barnabas Academy in Dana Point, a caring, educational community. *Murders Under the Sun* is edited by Jim Wilbourne, theme music is by Eclectic Blends, and I'm your host, Molly Shure.

# part four

# MURDERS UNDER THE SUN
## SEASON FOUR; EPISODE THREE

**MOLLY:** Welcome to episode three of *The Tower*. This is Molly Shure, your host.

Wow, there were a lot of varying opinions on the Facebook page this week. Some of you felt envy in any form was completely detrimental to emotional health and happiness. Others viewed it as a great motivator. This week, we'll find out more about how it affected Rosie.

Thanks, also, for your interest in our back-story about the CSU students. Your confidence in me and Abby is heartwarming. I hope it's not misplaced. We're still digging around, just not sure what, if anything, we'll find.

We have a lot of ground to cover in this episode, however. Not only does Rosie get started on the remodel of the tower, but she also gets a new client, and does the decor for a truly strange Halloween party. So, let's get into it.

## 4.3.2

Rosie adjusted Eric's collar while they waited for John and Carol's front door to open. "Remember, try to talk to as many people as you can. This is about sales." The night of her showing-off party, as Honey called it, had arrived and Rosie was nervous. She shouldn't be. She knew the house looked fantastic.

"You've told me fourteen times."

"That's because I know what happens when you and Booker get together. You end up in a corner arguing about sports."

"We don't—" The door flew open.

"Well, look who finally decided to show up." Booker's face erupted into a grin.

"Speak of the devil," Eric said.

"Everybody's always talking about me. I'm just that fascinating. Come on in. How are you Rosie, darling?" Booker gave her a bear hug and kissed her cheek. "I still can't figure out what a gorgeous thing like you is doing with this loser."

Booker was an unrepentant flirt, but it was all an act. His love for his wife was obvious to everyone who saw them together. Booker had been captain of his high school football team in a small town in Kentucky that Rosie had never heard of. Honey had been the homecoming queen.

They'd married before they were twenty-one and neither had ever looked back.

"You beat us here," Rosie said.

"Honey had to get things going in the kitchen. You know her. I'm her beast of burden." He flexed a well-muscled arm.

"Is she in the kitchen?" Rosie said.

"She is, along with the hosts."

Rosie left Eric and Booker in the hallway and hurried toward the kitchen. She took in her work in quick satisfied glances on her way: The ash flooring was dotted with rich oriental rugs. The white walls showcased framed art and an antique plate rack. Dark wood end tables and elegantly upholstered furniture were set in welcoming groupings. It looked great. She was proud of the work she'd done.

She passed the large drop-leaf dining table surrounded by hundred-year-old ladder-back chairs and entered the modern kitchen. Honey stood at a pale granite counter placing bacon wrapped dates onto a cookie sheet while John and Carol, Rosie's clients, watched.

"Sorry I'm late," Rosie said.

Carol's intelligent blue eyes found hers, and she smiled. "You're not. None of the guests are here yet."

"I wanted to help," Rosie said.

"There's nothing to do," John said.

Honey wiped her hands on a dishtowel. "She can pour me a glass of wine."

Carol moved toward the case of wine on the counter. "I'll get you one."

"Let Rosie do it. It'll make her feel useful. I have another job for you. I need the chives cut."

"Got it," Rosie said.

"Choose your poison," John said. "I have to set the rest up in the dining room."

Rosie pulled a bottle of pinot noir from the case, uncorked it with an elaborate electric cork remover sitting by the toaster, and poured three glasses. "The house looks beautiful," she said, handing a glass to Carol.

"It does. Thanks to you. I can't believe what a difference the walls and the flooring made. Everything looked as old as the antiques before. I'm so happy with it."

Rosie's cheeks grew warm. This was what she loved about her chosen profession. Often people believed they had to move to have their dream home. That had been the case with John and Carol. They'd hired her to give them advice about staging their home to sell it. By the time she was done explaining the updates they could make, they'd decided to stay put.

"People are going to start showing up any minute," Carol said. "I think you should be out there."

"No," Rosie said. "You need to great your guests. I'll stay and help Honey." Although she knew this event was in part planned to help her get her more clients, she struggled with the idea.

Most of her business came through people like Honey, and Peter, and her landscape architect friend, Carlos, who referred people to her. If she was going to be really successful, to have the kind of success Twila had, she had to become more proactive. Knowing that didn't make it any easier.

Honey popped the cookie sheet into the oven and turned to face Rosie and Carol. "Both of you, get out of here. I've got this under control."

They exited the kitchen as John ushered the first arrivals into the living room. Their reaction made Rosie flush all over again. Everyone raved. They loved the new layout, how Rosie had made the antiques feel inviting instead of like museum pieces. They admired the art she'd chosen.

The first half hour slipped by in a seeming matter of minutes. John stood in a clutch of men by an early twentieth century sideboard that was being used as a bar. An occasional guffaw erupted from the group, and Rosie heard the names of football players being bantered about.

The women followed Rosie and Carol through the rooms that had been redecorated and commented on the details. An attractive blonde, who Rosie learned was an OB-GYN, examined the painting of black-eyed Susans. "Where did you find this?"

"In a Laguna Beach gallery. I really like this artist's work."

"I need something like this."

"What we need is an overhaul." A man came up behind her and put his hands on her shoulders. He smiled at Rosie. "My wife, who is constantly sleep deprived and overworked, seems to think she can purchase things she likes and throw them at our house and somehow they'll arrange themselves. Our office is filled with things she's picked up on vacations or trips to galleries. They sit in piles waiting for the day she'll have the time and inclination to do something with them."

The woman stiffened. Rosie was concerned she was about to witness a marital spat, but the doctor's shoulders relaxed under her husband's massaging fingers. "He's right. I keep buying nice things in the hopes they'll somehow magically find their place in the house."

"Rosie could be our magician, Anne."

"I love the idea of doing it myself, but you're right. It won't happen. At least not until I retire."

"In thirty years?" her husband said.

"Do you have a card?" Anne asked, and Rosie handed one to her. They promised to call within the next two weeks.

The group of men had broken up, and the guests had rearranged themselves by the time Rosie extracted herself from the conversation. Honey circulated the room with a tray of appetizers. Rosie found Eric with two couples and Booker near the dining room table. He stretched out an arm when he saw her. "Here she is."

"So this is the famous Rosie Ring." An older man, early seventies probably, but very fit and handsome, put out his hand.

Rosie took it. "I don't know how famous I am."

"Around here you are. John has talked about nothing else at work for the past two months. And, I must say, you achieved quite the transformation. It's nothing short of wonderful."

Rosie was sure her cheeks were glowing, but it had happened so many times tonight she hardly felt the blush. "Thank you."

Eric put an arm around her shoulders and squeezed. "I was telling Sid, here, about your skill with beach homes. Sid lives in San Clemente."

"Oh, really? Where in San Clemente?"

Sid rattled off an address that made Rosie suck in her breath. The homes in that area all had spectacular ocean views and spectacular price tags to go with them. She'd love to get her hands on one of them.

"We had someone in when we first moved into the place, but that was, what twenty-five years ago?" He directed the question to a tall, elegantly dressed woman Rosie assumed was his wife.

"Twenty-seven," she said.

"We could probably use an update."

"Crab puff, anyone?" Honey slipped into their group. "They were made by my first lovely group of students. I'll be starting on the stuffed bacon wrapped dates next if you want to roll up your sleeves."

The elegant woman ignored her. "I find it difficult to find a decorator for beach homes. If it's one's primary residence one expects a certain level of sophistication. It's not a cottage, after all. My neighbor had a designer come in. The results were abysmal. The man filled her house with kitschy ocean things, flip-flop wallpaper, driftwood furniture. I've been a little hesitant to hire anyone since I saw his place."

"This is my wife, Lillian, by the way," Sid said.

Lillian's face cracked into a brief and frigid smile.

"I—" Rosie planned to say she always tried to take her client's tastes and desires into consideration, but Honey interrupted her.

"Rosie wouldn't dream of doing that kind of thing. She only works with high-end clientele. Like right now, she's doing an ocean front home in Laguna for Jacob Rinehart."

Rosie's heart missed a beat. She and Jacob had never discussed it, but she was sure he didn't want anyone to know he'd moved to town. She'd told Honey that when Honey showed her Twila's magazine spread.

"The author?" Lillian raised her eyebrows.

"The very one." Honey gave the group a smug smile. "You know that big house—"

He definitely wouldn't want people to know the address. "I'll take one of those." Rosie reached for a crab puff and jostled the tray knocking most of them to the floor.

Honey let out an exclamation and dropped to her knees. "Here let me help you with that." Rosie squatted beside her. "Don't say any more about Rinehart." Her words were a harsh whisper.

"But they won't—"

"Yes, they will."

"I don't think—"

Rosie stood. "Let's take this mess into the kitchen." She gave Honey a small shove in that direction. "Are you trying to get me fired from the biggest job I've ever had?" she said when the door slapped shut behind them.

Honey stared at the counter. "Rosie, I think you're overreacting."

"You haven't met Jacob Rinehart. I have. He's a very private person." His aversion to the color red rang through her mind.

"He's a public figure."

"A public figure who's been accused by some in the press of murdering a woman to increase book sales." Rosie's voice rose. "He's been traumatized. Do you remember when your brother-in-law was under suspicion for embezzlement?"

Four years earlier Booker's brother was accused of siphoning money from the mission fund of the church he worked for. He was eventually exonerated, but life had been miserable for his family in the meantime.

Honey's eyes met Rosie's, but she didn't respond. "When someone threw that rock in the window with the nasty note, and his wife was afraid to go out after dark, remember that? That's what it was like for Jacob in Seattle, only worse."

Honey inhaled and exhaled sharply before she answered. "I'm sorry. I didn't realize."

Rosie placed a hand on her arm and softened her tone. "It's okay. But, please, for my sake, don't do it again."

The door to the kitchen swung open. "We have a date with some dates," a woman in a royal blue dress called out. A man, middle-aged and stout, and another woman who looked enough like him to be his sister, entered giggling. Apparently, the party had started in earnest.

The stout man looked at Rosie. "Are you staying?"

She picked up the tray with the remaining crab puffs. "No. I'm going to take these out."

All three of Honey's new students snatched a puff as Rosie passed them.

The volume in the living room had increased while she'd been in the kitchen. The music had turned from classical to jazz. The conversations were brighter, the laughter shriller. Everyone had been drinking, and there hadn't been much food going around.

She circulated through the crowd, offering the appetizers, and looking for Eric. The crab puffs disappeared, and so had he. He wasn't anywhere. She found Booker in a corner of the family room talking to a rapt audience about the last round of firestorms to hit Southern California. Firestorms were a subject that concerned everyone, but especially those who lived in some of the wealthy equestrian communities on the outskirts of more developed areas.

"It's all about creating good burn barriers. If there's nothing to feed the fire, it'll go somewhere else," Booker said.

"Yes, but how do you get the neighbors on board?" a tanned, athletic looking brunette asked.

"Excuse me," Rosie said before he could answer. "Sorry to interrupt, but do you know where Eric is?"

"He got a phone call. I think he went outside to get away from the noise," Booker said.

"Thanks."

She headed to the front door. The night seemed blissfully quiet as she closed it behind herself. The moon had risen and painted the yard in blue tones. The red roses bordering the house were deep purple in its light. The grass had become the color of the ocean on a stormy day. It was surreal and lovely.

She crossed the yard to the street. They'd parked up the block when they'd arrived to leave more spaces for the guests. She saw Eric, his pale blue shirt glowing in the moonlight. He leaned against their car, a phone pressed to his ear.

As she walked toward him, she heard bits and pieces of his conversation floating on the moist night air. "I said I would. Thirty maybe. Does it really matter?"

His voice was low and didn't hold much expression, but she got the feeling it was a private conversation, intimate even. Her steps slowed. Should she let him finish his call before announcing herself?

"No," Eric said. "She doesn't know. I'm sure." Rosie stopped under the deep shade of a crepe myrtle tree. *She?* She, who? A client? An employee? "I don't want her hurt."

Rosie amended her thoughts. This didn't sound like a business call. There was a tenderness in Eric's voice when he spoke about the mystery woman he didn't want hurt. "I know what you want, and I'm doing my best. But I have to be careful."

There was a long pause, and Eric sighed, a sound filled with such resigned fatigue, her heart squeezed. He'd been under so much pressure. Seeing the empty offices on Monday had made her realize she hadn't been as compassionate as she should have been. She'd been acting like a self-absorbed school girl, more worried about what it all meant to her than what he was going through. That had to change.

And here she was hiding, spying on her husband. She should step out of the dark, reveal herself, let him know she was there for him. She pushed off the trunk of the tree.

"I have to get back. Rosie is going to wonder where I am." Could she be the woman he didn't want hurt? Warmth radiated through her at the thought. For all his seeming distance and preoccupation, he was concerned about her. She took a step in his direction. She wanted to wrap her arms around him. Tell him it would all be okay if they tackled things together.

"Okay. I'll see you tomorrow morning, eight-thirty."

Rosie stopped short. The warmth in her chest froze over. She slipped into the shade of the tree again.

He'd been talking to Twila. Talking to Twila about her. A vision of Twila's naked foot rubbing the calf of her other leg, such a sensual gesture, played through her mind. She turned and hurried into the party.

Rosie plastered a smile on her face. She waded through the rest of the evening doing her best to stay afloat as waves of small talk washed over her. Eric and Booker set up camp near the fireplace. Every time she glanced at him, Eric had a drink in his hand. She would find out the details on the way home. She repeated that to herself as she shook hands at the door, promised phone calls, and helped to tidy up the house.

When the kitchen counters were wiped down and the dishwasher was humming, she and Honey went to find the men. They were seated in the living room under the painting of black-eyed Susans, and they were drunk. She stared at them in surprise. Rosie hadn't seen Eric drunk for at least a decade, and she'd never seen Booker drunk.

They weren't loud or boisterous. They weren't aggressive or argumentative. They'd each slipped into a sullen stupor, eyes narrow slits. Depression hung heavy in the air around them. She and Honey steered their husbands outside in an attempt to shield them from John and Carol.

When they reached the street Eric fished his car keys from his pocket. Rosie snatched them away. "I'll drive." He didn't argue.

Five miles later Rosie said, "You're going to feel good tomorrow." Her words were biting and sarcastic, but he didn't seem to notice.

"What do you mean?"

"You have to get up early, right? Go work on the new office?"

His answer was a groan.

"I can't believe you drank so much."

He shrugged and sank into himself. Rosie's fingers began to tingle from gripping the steering wheel too tightly. She relaxed them and breathed deeply, tightening her jaw.

She wanted to punish him with silence. Punish him for embarrassing her in front of John and Carol and who knows how many guests. Punish him for the phone call. However, she wasn't going to be able to sleep without finding out who'd been on the other end of that call. "Is Bob going to be at the new office tomorrow?" she blurted out the words.

"Bob?" Eric laughed. "Are you kidding? Can you imagine that man with a hammer in his hands? No, Rose. Bob will not be there tomorrow."

She paused for a long moment. "Are any of the other staff going to be there? Or just you?"

"Just me."

*See you Saturday.* Twila's words from earlier in the week played through Rosie's mind. It had been her on the phone. She was the only other person planning to be at the office tomorrow.

Rosie pulled into her driveway. Honey and Booker had beat them home. Their van was parked next door, and their house was dark and quiet. She was glad. She couldn't face anybody else tonight.

She pondered what Eric had told her while she brushed her teeth and put on her nightshirt. She crawled under the covers next to him and stared up at the ceiling. Sleep evaded her.

Eric flipped onto his side and bunched up his pillow. He was awake too. "Eric," she said.

"Yeah?" His voice was thick with alcohol and sleep.

"Where did you go tonight?"

"What do you mean?"

"During the party. I was looking for you. I couldn't find you anywhere." She held her breath, waiting for him to answer. Would he tell her the truth? Would he tell her he'd taken a call from Twila?

"I stepped out for some fresh air. It was getting kind of close in there."

"That's it?"

"Yeah? Why?" There was a defensive edge in his voice.

"Nothing. Just wondered where you went."

That was it then. He'd lied. On the grand scale of things it wasn't a huge lie, but it was a lie. There was no getting around it. And it wasn't a lie like the kind you used to hide a birthday surprise or anniversary trip. He'd lied about Twila.

## 4.3.3

The next morning, Rosie watched Eric drive away with a sinking heart. He'd never lied to her before. At least not that she knew of. Now she wondered. Lies were like keys. So small, but able to open the door to a world of distrust.

Rosie stood in the window and stared at the place his car had once occupied. What did this mean? She couldn't, wouldn't, believe he was seeing Twila. Not Eric. It was something else. It had to be.

She pivoted on her heel. There was no time to stand there and wonder. She'd promised Peter she'd meet him at the Nightshade by nine.

Traditionally, Rosie looked forward to Peter's Halloween party. It was a time to show off her decorating skills for the local glitterati. She always ended up with at least one new client from the event. Often they wanted her help with a party or a wedding, but still, work was work. Her enthusiasm was missing this morning, however. She stood in her closet staring at her clothes, forgetting why she was there.

*Shake it off.*

She wished Honey hadn't put thoughts about Twila and other people's husbands into her mind. They were a distraction, a waste of time and energy. She grabbed a pair of jeans and a long-sleeved t-shirt, ran a comb through her curls, put lipstick on, and was out of the house in twenty minutes.

Peter's eyebrows drew into a concerned line when he saw her. "You don't look good."

"Thanks."

"Coffee?"

"Please."

He put the coffee into mugs this morning instead of the usual fragile china, presumably so they could walk around the gallery while they sipped. He handed one to her. "Do you want to talk about it?"

"Talk about what?"

"Whatever is bothering you."

"There's nothing bothering me. Too much wine last night."

He squinted at her for a long minute, then said, "Okay, then let's talk Halloween. The theme this year is Grade B Horror flicks. Like it?"

Rosie nodded. "Like the old Dracula, Frankenstein movies?"

"No." He waved a dismissive hand. "Those are classics. I mean the low budget ones, *The Blob, Them, The Fly.*"

Interesting choice. "Have you ever seen *The Monster That Challenged the World*?"

"No, but it sounds perfect."

"It's about a giant sea slug that slithers around eating people." She and Eric had watched it together last Halloween between groups of trick-or-treaters. It had been a fun night. They'd roared at the horrible special effects, but that had been before Seb's death.

"Let me show you what I've got so far." Peter led her to a worktable in a backroom. On it were brochures from poster companies, artists, and other galleries. He liked to bring in both fine art and less expensive prints to match the mood of the night. He'd found it was the one time of year people other than his usual patrons purchased more darkly themed art.

Rosie always wondered if they were sorry after the party was over, and the costume came off. It was one thing to gravitate toward a demon portrait when you were dressed like a zombie, and another when you were in your jeans.

"What do you think about these posters?" Peter had drawn circles around several in one of the brochures.

Rosie helped him decide between them, then they moved on to

more creative things. After a half hour of brainstorming they came up with a plan that included a movie projection onto the steam from dry ice, the use of funeral urns for punch bowls and serving dishes, and frayed black satin coverings for the furniture.

"Wonderful." Peter rubbed his hands together like a delighted gnome. "I think this will be the best party yet."

"You say that every year," Rosie said.

"And every year it's true. We get better and better at this, Rosie, my dear. Now, let's discuss the guest list." He pulled up a spreadsheet on his computer. "I've already sent the invites to everybody who came last year."

Rosie leaned forward and read the list of usual suspects. Most were local gallery and business owners, or patrons of Nightshade. She noted the names of a few Laguna restaurateurs. "Who is doing the food?"

"I don't know. I don't want to ask Phillipa again. How about your friend Honey?"

"I could ask her. If you allowed her to market her cooking classes, she'd probably do it."

"Of course. That's what this party is all about—networking. You know that."

Rosie pulled out her phone to text Honey, and realized she'd never said goodbye or thank you for the night before. She'd been too preoccupied with Eric. She returned the phone to her purse. She'd call, or better yet, go into Sweeter and talk to her. She wanted to make amends, see how Booker was before they talked business.

"Speaking of networking," Peter said. "What do you think about inviting Jacob Rinehart?" He looked at her with a hopeful expression.

Rosie didn't have to think about the answer. "He won't come."

"Don't think he'll want to get to know people? He's new in town."

She shook her head. "He moved here to hide. It was pretty rough in Seattle. If the press gets wind of his new address, things could heat up here."

"Why don't we let him decide?" Peter said. "I'd like to meet him."

Rosie tensed. She wasn't Jacob's social secretary. "I can mention it, but no promises."

"Let's keep you out of it. I'll send an invitation, and I'll mention it to Cecily. She might think it's a good move for him."

Rosie was relieved. She'd rather not be involved.

"We're done," Peter said, shutting off his computer. "We earned our breakfast. My treat."

At the thought of food, Rosie's stomach growled. Peter stood. "Let me put a few things away, and we can go."

She watched him walk into the kitchen area, then turned her gaze to the table. She leafed listlessly through the fliers and brochures littered there. While she'd been lost in the flow of creativity, she'd forgotten about the phone call and Eric's lie. Now the heaviness she'd felt earlier crashed on her again.

She toyed with the idea of stopping by the new office after lunch, but she didn't know the address. Besides, she didn't want it to seem like she was spying on him, or that she didn't trust him. But did she? How did you trust someone who lied to you?

A movie played in her mind; Twila's bare foot rubbing her leg. A red-soled shoe. *Don't think about that.*

Without noticing, Rosie had picked up one of the brochures and was bending it between nervous fingers. She set it down hastily and began to smooth out the creases. When she saw the painting displayed on its cover, she gasped.

It was a woman's face, pale and drawn, dark hair in tangles around her head, lips twisted into a grimace. *The eyes.* She shuddered. It was the eyes that had made her gasp.

Black stitches between the lids and cheek sewed them shut. Rosie's hand retreated. She didn't want to touch the paper the image was printed on.

"That's awful, isn't it?" Peter said as he entered.

"You're not acquiring this artist's work?" Her voice trembled a little.

Peter took the brochure from the table and flicked a fingernail at the photo. "No. I'm not opposed to making a statement, but that's just sensationalism. It's not even good sensationalism." He stared at it a moment longer, then met Rosie's gaze and smiled. "Let's go."

The painting haunted Rosie all through breakfast, on her drive home, as she did her Saturday chores, and into the evening. It wasn't until Eric got home, tired and achy from physical labor, that it was driven from her mind. The woman in the painting was replaced by visions of Twila working side by side with her husband in the empty office.

## 4.3.4

Rosie whacked the edge of the mood board she'd done for Jacob on the door of her car as she loaded it. She swore under her breath. It looked okay though, only a small dent. She was nervous about their appointment, and it made her clumsy. His reaction to the digital schematic she'd presented the week before wasn't what she'd expected. He was a hard man to figure out.

Rosie saw people as colors. Honey, for instance, was brown—stable, warm, reliable brown. Eric was blue—tranquil and sure like the sky. But she was struggling to find Jacob Rinehart's color.

She'd thought at first he was purple—that combination of honest blue and energetic red whose offspring was creativity, introversion, and self-awareness. Last Monday, however, he was overshadowed by a gray filter.

She saw Jacob before she pulled up to the curb in front of his house. He and Fury were approaching from the direction of Heisler Park. He must have taken the dog for walk. He waved and smiled that charming smile. Today he was purple. Definitely purple.

"What have you brought me?" he said when he reached her.

"The mood board. I really liked your suggestions from last week. I can't wait for you to see it."

He unlocked the front door. "Let's do it then."

"No Lupe today?" Rosie asked.

"No, she had to take her son to the doctor. Poor kid has diabetes. I guess he had an episode over the weekend."

Jacob unleashed Fury who trotted toward the sunny apartment at the end of building. Rosie and Jacob followed. "I see Fury has made himself at home," Rosie said.

"He seems to be settling in. Every once in a while I have to crate him, but that's happening less and less often. It takes him a while to warm up to new people." He laughed. "Kind of like me."

When they reached the apartment, he walked into the kitchen, picked up the dog's bowl and took it to the tap.

Rosie set the mood board on the table and turned toward the windows. Every time she looked at the ocean from this vantage point, she saw something different. It was a living thing, constantly changing and had to be taken into consideration when planning the decor of the home. That understanding was the reason her reputation with beach homes was a good one.

Today the water was flecked with whitecaps. Dark clouds blew across a bright sky occasionally covering the sun. Patches of deep blue and gray in the otherwise brilliant color of the water reflected them. Perhaps blue wasn't as trustworthy and peaceful as people thought. It seemed to her now that blue was a capricious color, one moment calm, the next reckless.

"Beautiful, isn't it? I never get tired of looking at it." Jacob put a cup of coffee into her hand.

"That's what I was thinking."

"See those rocks?" He pointed to an outcropping that separated two coves. "When the tide is high water rushes in and out of a big crack there. Kids call it the washing machine. I've watched them paddle around in it. It looks like fun, but it's dangerous."

"We think we're indestructible when we're young."

"A surfer drowned there last year."

Rosie couldn't imagine a worse death. She knew the sheer panic of running out of oxygen. The helplessness of trying to inhale when the body had shut down its airways. When it felt as if every useless breath was another blow to the chest. Consciousness would fade. Sea water would burn its way into places it was never meant to go. Bright blue would turn to black.

Jacob broke the silence. "Didn't mean to get moody."

Rosie shook herself. "Speaking of moods, let's take a look at that board." She led him to the table. Jacob felt the fabric swatches. Tilted the board under his standing lamp. Carried it around his apartment looking at it in different lights. "I like it," he finally said. "It's a bit darker than I thought we'd go, but I like it."

She was confused by the comment. The board reflected what he'd asked for last Monday. "We can lighten up."

"No. No, this is good. It's just not what I expected."

Rosie didn't want to sound argumentative, but she needed clarity. There was a lot of house to decorate. They had to be able to communicate. "It's what we talked about last week. When I showed you the digital schematic."

Jacob stared at her for so long, she grew uncomfortable. She couldn't read his expression. Was he angry?

When his face cracked into a smile, relief washed over her. "That's right. I forgot. I'm finishing up a new book."

"A new book?'"

"When I'm deep in a story I lose touch, forget things. It can be embarrassing."

Rosie nodded. She understood. Creativity took her out of the real world from time to time. "You're sure you like it?"

"Yes. Besides, I have news. News which means a slight change of plans."

"What's that?"

"I've been invited to a Halloween party in town. It's at your friend's gallery—Nightshade."

"Right, I help Peter with the decorations every year."

"I was hoping you'd be there. At least one friendly face. Anyway, Cecily is coming for it. She wants to see my new digs, and strategize now that things have settled a bit."

"So you need me to get a bedroom ready for her," Rosie said.

"Exactly. You can take a pause on this room. It's functional, if not beautiful."

"When is she coming?" The party was in two weeks. That didn't leave her much time.

"She'll be here next Friday night."

Five days. Rosie's chest tightened. She wanted to do a stellar job for Jacob, and not only because he was the highest paying client she'd ever had. There was something about his personality, his quiet reserve, that made her want to please him.

"I'd been planning to do each guest room the same, but I won't have time to—"

Jacob waved a hand. "Don't worry about the other ones. Not now. Besides, I'd like Cecily to have her own room here. She'll be here a lot. Let's do something special for her."

Some of the tension left Rosie. She couldn't do six bedrooms in five days, but she could do one. "Have you picked a room for her?"

"No." His eyes brightened like a child's at Christmas. "Let's do it."

Rosie had to trot to keep up with him. He chattered as they climbed the central staircase. "I want her to have the best view. I think that would be one of the two bedrooms at the rear of the house."

He made a sharp left at the top of the stairs and entered a guest room. The view wasn't panoramic, but it showed much of the coastline to the north. "This?" he said gesturing out the window. "Or—" he darted across the hall and into the bedroom opposite. "This?"

The second window yielded a view of town and the Laguna coves. They were equally pretty. Rosie pondered the his question, then asked, "Is she a peaceful, sunset sort of person? Or would she like the vitality of sunrise in the morning and city lights at night?"

Jacob, one hand on his low back, one on his head, pondered the question. "She's a city girl," he finally said. "She's not much on sunrises —likes her sleep too much—but she'd like the action out this window."

"This is the winner then. We can use room darkening shades so she can sleep in," Rosie said. "Now tell me more about her."

"High energy. She hardly ever sits still. Lives for social occasions. She's basically the opposite of me."

If Jacob was purple, yellow, or gold would be the contrasting color. "We'll go with muted golds and yellows, and temper them with pale sea greens and blues."

His eyes widened with surprise. "Those are the colors she has in her house. How did you know?"

"It's my superpower."

Jacob left her to her work. Rosie took measurements, checked the bathroom's fixtures, and made notes. Twenty minutes later, she joined him in the apartment. He was seated on the couch. Laptop in his lap. Fury at his feet.

"I'll do a quick schematic. I can get it to you tomorrow," she said. "I'm thinking a nice neutral sand for the walls. I should be able to get a painter in on Wednesday, and as long as he's here I'll have him do all the bedrooms if that's okay with you. It'll save money. The bathroom fixtures may need to be replaced down the road, but they'll do for now. Do you need me to order bed and bath linens?"

"Please. I didn't even think about that."

"How about art for the walls?"

He pursed his lips. "I have some paintings and things from my old place in the attic. You could take a look. Art is a big decision. I'd hate to rush into buying new pieces."

Rosie turned toward the kitchen stairs, but paused. "How many spiders are in that attic anyway?"

"Not that many, but they're big ones." He separated his hands about three feet.

"Ha. Funny," Rosie said.

"Try banging on the door before you go up. Scare them into hiding."

"Hidden spiders sound even worse."

He set his laptop onto the couch and leaned forward as if to rise. "Want me to go with you?"

"No. I'm a big girl," Rosie said, but as she ascended the stairs, she wished he would have come. She'd hated spiders ever since she'd opened her eyes in the middle of an asthma attack at eight years old to see one descending toward her face, swinging on its silk. She'd been paralyzed by fear and lack of oxygen. It had been a terrifying moment.

When she reached the attic door, despite feeling silly, she did as Jacob suggested and banged on it several times. "Okay, I'm coming in," she said to any arachnids that might be within earshot.

The door opened smoothly—no haunted house creak—onto another flight of stairs. She flipped on a wall switch and a bright electric light popped on. Nothing scary about this attic.

She climbed into a huge, raftered space. The first twenty feet or so were illuminated by a bare, hanging bulb. The rest was in shadow, lit by the soft light from a small window at the far end of the room. It looked as if the attic ran the length of the house. Happily, she wouldn't have to go exploring. Jacob had stored his things in the lit area in front of her.

Paintings and mirrors leaned against the bottom half of a dormered wall. Boxes were piled in its center. Three table lamps were perched on top of them. An old-fashioned coat rack, a faux-elephant foot umbrella stand, and a floor lamp stood nearby.

She was surprised to see so much stuff when the living spaces downstairs were all but empty. Why hadn't Jacob filled as much of it as he could with things he'd brought from Seattle?

She was glad he'd vanquished the umbrella stand, though. Using elephant's feet for furniture, popular in the Victorian era, was both illegal and repugnant. This one was made of plaster, but still... Bad taste.

She walked across the plain, plank floor to the stacks of pictures and began looking through them thinking not only about Cecily's bedroom but also the larger rooms of the main level. She tilted each forward until she could see it clearly. Jacob had good taste in art. She could use many of these.

Rosie pulled a landscape—a sunrise over a field dotted with scrub oaks—and a still life—a bowl of citrus fruit—out of the stack. She blew dust off the frames and carried them downstairs. "You have some beautiful things up there," she said when she emerged into the apartment.

He glanced up from his work and smiled. "Thanks. One day soon we'll have to haul it all down and figure out what we want to use. Did you find something for Cecily's room?"

"These." Rosie showed him the paintings she'd chosen. "What do you think?"

"I approve."

Rosie snapped photos of the pictures and collected her things. "Okay, I'll be by tomorrow." Jacob and Fury walked her down the long hall to the front door. She gave the dog a farewell scratch. "He doesn't let you out of his sight, does he?"

Jacob looked at him with affection. "No. He's a good friend. He calms my nerves."

The wind whisked her hair into her face as she exited the house. Clouds skittered across the sky. Rosie loved the beach. Her last two jobs had been farther inland, but now she had the fortress and tomorrow she had an appointment in San Clemente. She was meeting with Sid and Lillian Rawlinson, the couple from John and Carol's party.

She took Coast Highway south before turning up Crown Valley Parkway toward home. It was a beautiful drive, a beautiful day. How quickly life could change. Only three weeks ago, she was finishing up the last of the jobs on her schedule and had no new prospects on the horizon. Today she had a seven-bedroom oceanfront property to redecorate and four appointments on the calendar.

Despite her worries about Eric, life was good. She needed to focus on that. She and Eric had weathered other storms together. Maybe not storms with the gale-force winds of this one, but there'd been many. You couldn't raise three kids without facing a hurricane or two, especially during their teen years.

Yes, Eric had lied to her. But when he was talking to Twila on the phone Friday night, he'd said, *I don't want her hurt.* Sometimes people lied for altruistic reasons. Rosie should think the best, believe the best, hope the best. Wasn't that what love did?

*Twila's foot, her calf, her red-soled shoe.* Rosie pushed that thought firmly away.

# 4.3.5

After dropping off paint samples and pictures of furniture and bedding with Jacob on Thursday morning, Rosie drove to San Clemente. She parked on the street and surveyed the Rawlinson's property. Prior to getting the tower, it would have seemed large and daunting. No longer.

It was a good-sized house, but she was sure the square footage was at most half of the tower's. The front yard was deep and well-landscaped. Queen Anne palms sheltered red impatiens and white roses on either side of a walkway leading to double front doors. She rang the bell and listened to a cascade of tones tinkle behind them.

A moment later the door opened. Rosie blinked in surprise. So did Lupe. "What are you doing here?" Lupe said. Then seeming to realize how rude that had sounded, she added, "I didn't know you knew the Rawlinsons."

"I could say the same," Rosie said. "What are you doing here?"

"I work for the Rawlinsons on Thursdays."

"I hope to be working for them soon too." Rosie held up her portfolio.

Lupe stepped out of the doorway. "I'll let Mrs. Rawlinson know you're here."

Rosie waited in the entryway while Lupe's brilliant white blouse disappeared through an open doorway. The foyer was round and had four doorways leading from it. A circular staircase rose directly in front of her, the gesture seemed too grand for the home. A crystal chandelier hung in the center of the circle. Another grand gesture.

She could already tell by the marble tile and flamboyant silk flower arrangement atop an elaborately carved side table that her taste and Lillian's weren't in the same ballpark. That was okay. A good designer could work with any style.

She heard footsteps clicking on hard flooring, and a moment later Lillian, swathed in a gray sweater and matching slacks, emerged from the same doorway Lupe had disappeared into. "Rosie." Her hand was outstretched. Rosie took it, and Lillian gave her fingers a gentle squeeze. "I've been looking at your website. You've done some beautiful work. Smaller homes, generally, but lovely."

Lillian was friendlier today than she'd been at John and Carol's party. She'd must have had a chance to digest the fact that the famous author Jacob Rinehart was Rosie's client. As if on cue, she said, "I'm sure if you can handle Jacob Rinehart's home, you can handle this one."

"I've done several beach homes. My clients were happy." Rosie said, unsure how to respond to the comment.

"There's tea in the library." Lillian turned and led Rosie through a doorway on the right. The library turned out to be a glorified office with a couch and easy chairs around a small fireplace and a desk in the far corner. You could fit three of these rooms into the library at the tower. It should have been cozy and would have been if it wasn't for the attempt to make it look like a classic British library. The room was a collage of browns, Kelly green, and plaids. Rosie half expected to see a painting over the mantel of dogs playing poker.

Lillian gestured to the plaid couch. Rosie sat. Lillian perched on the edge of an easy chair. "We can walk through the rooms we'd like help with after we have tea," she said.

Rosie didn't like hot tea, but accepted a cup. "That would be great. I brought pictures to show you." She moved her teacup out of the way to make room for her portfolio on the coffee table.

"What is the square footage of Jacob Rinehart's house?" Lillian asked.

"The square footage?"

"Yes. I was wondering because... " Her words trailed off. She sipped her tea.

"Because?" What was she driving at?

"Well." She set her teacup in its saucer and folded her hands in her lap as if she was about to recite a poem. "I want to be sure our home won't be too much for you."

Rosie stiffened. "If you don't have confidence in me—"

Lillian flapped a hand in the air. "No. No. It's not that. Of course, it's not that. It's just a home of this size—if you're not experienced it's hard to estimate how long things will take to complete. How expensive they're going to be." She coughed. "I canceled an appointment with Twila Wilkes."

Twila's name hung in the air like a bad smell. Trying to understand Lillian was like trying to understand someone speaking a language you studied in high school. The words were familiar, but Rosie was sure they held more meaning than she comprehended. Why bring up Twila? Was it a veiled threat? Do what I want, introduce me to Jacob Rinehart, or I'll work with your competition?

Rosie asked, "What is the square footage of your home?"

"Thirty-five hundred." Lillian gave her a humble smile.

"Jacob Rinehart's is probably twice that," Rosie said in a monotone. "Now, let me show you—"

"That large?" Lillian's eyes opened wide as if to accentuate the statement.

"Yes." She set her portfolio on the coffee table and opened it to a photo spread of a home in Corona del Mar. It was a remodeled bungalow with a peek-a-boo ocean view. She was proud of the work she'd done on it. It managed to be relaxed and elegant at the same time —something this home didn't achieve.

"So where exactly is it?"

"This home is in Corona—"

"No, not this one. Jacob Rinehart's."

Rosie soothed the irritation rising in her chest with a deep cleansing breath, something she'd learned to do in Pilates. "I really can't—"

"It's not like I'm part of the general public. I'm a potential customer."

"And you wouldn't like it if I gave out your address, I'm sure." Although the Rawlinson's address was probably a matter of public record. Rosie guessed Jacob had done some legal maneuvering to hide his. She gestured to her portfolio. "This home may be smaller than yours but smaller is often more difficult."

The woman's mouth tightened into a tight line, but she allowed Rosie to lead her through the photos. She made a lot of comments on the things she did and didn't like. She was blunt. Very blunt. Rosie hoped they'd be able to work together.

"Are you ready for the tour?" Lillian glanced pointedly at Rosie's full tea cup. She hadn't touched it. She downed the tea in three gulps and hid a grimace. "Ready."

The home hadn't been updated in twenty years. Sid Rawlinson said that at the party, but Rosie had thought he was exaggerating. He wasn't. There was a lot of work to be done if they were going to bring it into the twenty-first century. Rosie made notes on flooring and furnishings she'd like to keep, and those she'd like to get rid of. Money had been spent on the home; nothing was cheap, but it lacked personality.

They returned to the library and negotiated a budget. That done, she folded her portfolio, picked up her purse, and stood. "Will you be at the Nightshade party?" Lillian asked.

"Yes. I help Peter with it every year." Rosie couldn't keep the surprise from her voice. She hadn't seen the Rawlinsons' names on the guest list.

"We'll be there as well. I heard one of the editors of *Orange County Lifestyles* is attending this year. They're looking for stories."

The Rawlinsons would have to be better connected than Rosie thought they were to bag that. *Orange County Lifestyles* didn't usually do feature stories on tract homes in suburban neighborhoods, even expensive neighborhoods like this one.

"We could mention this little redecorating plan of ours and, who knows, maybe they'll come in and take pictures when we're done."

"Maybe." Rosie tried to keep the skepticism from her voice, but Lillian narrowed her eyes. Rosie was saved from an awkward moment by Lupe's appearance in the doorway.

"I'm leaving, Mrs. Rawlinson."

"Have you finished upstairs? The guest rooms? We have company coming this week."

"Yes." Lupe nodded.

Lillian looked at her watch. "You don't leave until 2:30. It's only 11:45."

Lupe's jaw jutted forward, a tiny but definite movement. "My son is home from school today. We spoke about this last week, remember?"

"Oh, yes, that's right." Lillian sounded annoyed. "Next week you can stay a little longer to make up for it."

"I have to pick up Luis at three o'clock every day."

"Well, we'll have to adjust your pay then. Makes the bookkeeping so complicated."

Lupe stood still and quiet, but a veil seemed to drop over her eyes. Rosie had the feeling this was a practiced posture.

"I'd better get going," Rosie said breaking the tension in the room.

"Lupe will show you out," Lillian said.

The house wasn't that large, regardless of what Lillian thought. Rosie could find the door on her own, but didn't mind walking out with Lupe. She'd like to commiserate with her. Say something to show she respected Lupe even if Lillian didn't.

When the door closed behind them, she put a hand on the house-keeper's arm. "How is your son? Jacob told me he had an episode over the weekend."

"He's doing much better, thank you."

The two women walked up the path to the street. "When I was a kid, I had asthma. I was always missing school, disrupting my mother's schedule. It's tough on the family when one member has health issues."

Lupe stopped in front of a blue Honda Civic parked directly in front of Rosie's SUV. "Do you still have asthma?"

"No, I outgrew it. Some kids do."

Her face grew serious. "Luis can't outgrow diabetes."

"He can learn to manage it, can't he?"

"That's the plan, but he is only eight."

Rosie remembered her own children at eight. They weren't responsible enough to stay home alone, never mind take care of something as volatile and hard to comprehend as their blood sugar. "Will I see you at

Jacob's tomorrow? I'll be by in the afternoon to check on the painter. He's doing the guest rooms. We're trying to get one ready for Jacob's publicist by Friday."

"As long as it's before 2:30."

The women said goodbye, and each got into their own cars. Rosie started her engine, but waited for Lupe to pull away from the curb. It was a small gesture, but one she hoped conveyed respect.

Lupe was an enigma. She wore a respectful, subservient shell that hid a woman Rosie would like to get to know. Pink. Sensitive, tender, nurturing pink. That's the color Rosie thought she'd find under the armor.

Lillian was less of a mystery. She was neither black, nor white. She matched the clothes she'd worn that day. Lillian was gray, the color of compromise.

4.3.6

"The cobwebs were hung by the chimney with care, in hopes that Jack the Ripper soon would be there," Peter said.

Rosie surveyed the stretchy netting she'd strewn all over the Nightshade. "Cute," she said. "They're last year's cobwebs, but I think they still work."

The week and a half leading up to the party had flown by. Rosie felt like she'd been in constant motion, and so had Eric. The problem was they'd winged past each other with hardly a word exchanged between them, and she was worried. He'd spent more time with Twila getting the new offices ready than he had with her. As much as Rosie shoved aside the thought that there was anything between them, it still rankled.

"Ratty is better when it comes to cobwebs. Come check out the video."

Rosie followed Peter through the gallery to the room he used for an office. Tonight, it would house the food and drinks. The conference table had been covered with shattered black satin, and the walls adorned with horror movie posters. In order to reach the bar set up at the far end of the room, you had to walk through a wall of fog onto which *Bride of Frankenstein* was being projected. At the moment, the title character was hissing menacingly at Rosie.

"Thought it might help people avoid overindulgence," Peter said.

"You may have invented a whole new approach to addiction recovery."

Peter stepped behind a black curtain at the other end of the room. Rosie heard a click, the projection disappeared, and he reemerged. "Are you done?"

"Am I ever?"

The two of them wandered toward the main gallery. They stopped in the doorway, Rosie, hands on hips, Peter, chin resting on a fist. Her gaze traveled around the space taking in the dark art draped with black and gray gauze, tall candelabras—their misshapen candles covered with the warts and tumors of melted, re-hardened wax—crematory urns brimming over with chocolates and nuts, and cobwebs everywhere. Neither said anything for a long moment, then Peter broke the silence. "I think you outdid yourself, Rosie."

"I didn't do it alone."

"True. We outdid ourselves."

"It's a whimsical nightmare."

"That's going to be the name of my next gallery." Peter spun on his heel and disappeared behind the black curtain again. He returned a moment later with a bottle of wine. "I have one bottle of Red Ravish left, the stuff Gwen Bishop turned me onto. You deserve a glass."

"Do we have time?"

"Plenty."

They collapsed into Peter's uncomfortable Victorian chairs with glasses in their hands. "I heard *Orange County Lifestyles* will be here," Rosie said.

"Yes. Genevieve Cabot, the society editor, is coming with a photographer." He held up his glass for Rosie to clink.

"How did you manage that?"

"I didn't. She contacted me. Said she'd heard about the party, asked if they could come and cover the event."

"How did she find out about it?"

He shrugged one shoulder. "One of our guests, I assume." He sipped his wine and closed his eyes. "I'm going to have to make a trip to Paso Robles to get more of this."

"Can't you buy it locally?"

"No. The Leaky Barrel used to carry it, but I haven't been able to find it anywhere else since they went out of business. Have to go to the vineyard now."

"It's a nice vineyard."

Peter changed the subject. "This will be a good night for us, Rosie, my dear. I feel it here." He thumped his chest.

Rosie felt it in her stomach. Nervous excitement whirled there like a dust devil—happy, yet a bit anxious. The goal was to dance her dance, promote her business, but stay out of the orchestra pit. She drained her wine, adding its warmth to the mix in her gut, and stood. "I'd better get dressed."

"You can have the bathroom first. I'll stay here and wait for Honey."

Rosie walked into the parking lot. A blast of wind hit her as soon as she left the shelter of the building. There was moisture in it, not uncommon at the beach, but tonight seemed wetter than usual.

She glanced at the darkening sky. Deep, charcoal colored clouds gathered around a rising moon. It looked like rain. She hoped it would wait until after the party, after the guests were safely home in their beds. A storm would add lovely atmosphere, but Southern Californians didn't drive well in weather, especially after a few drinks.

She opened the trunk of her car, took out the stuffed gorilla she'd borrowed from Becca's room, her dress, and a makeup bag. She'd found the dress, a plain cream-colored shift that fell to mid-calf, at a thrift store. She'd added a few buttons and shredded the hem line. That, sandals, movie star makeup, and her gorilla, would transform her into Ann Darrow, King Kong's girlfriend. She got the inspiration from a movie poster depicting Fay Wray, the actress who played the part, dangling from the big gorilla's hand. Eric, who was coming later, would wear a safari outfit.

The wonderful aromas of Honey's cooking hit her as soon as she emerged from the bathroom. Honey and Peter had set up chafing dishes, platters, and bowls of food on the conference room table. "Smells heavenly," she said when she saw her friend.

Honey wore a white chef's jacket and hat, a stark contrast to the black trappings of the gallery. "Or, devilishly delicious." She added a basket of baked treats to the table. "The place looks perfect. Not sure I'm gonna like working with Frankenstein's wife stalking me all night though."

Peter had turned the movie on. The male monster stood in a high vaulted room gazing with longing at a female monster reclining on a table.

"Is Booker coming?" Rosie said.

"No. He went into the station for a meeting. On his weekend off. Seriously, I don't know what's going on with that man."

"And they say women are hard to understand."

"They are," Peter said.

Rosie looked down her nose at him. "Ten minutes until party time. You'd better change, Peter."

The guests began arriving twenty minutes later. Within an hour the gallery was full and buzzing with conversation. Rosie made the rounds, greeting and making small talk, a task that didn't come naturally to her. But since Peter had no wife, she played the part of hostess to his host each year. She was getting better at it.

Each time the doorbell jangled, she glanced that way looking for Eric, or Jacob. She hadn't seen either yet. Eric had left early that morning to do the final touches on the new office space. Monday was moving day, and he was under the gun. She hadn't asked if Twila would be there. Not because she didn't want to know, but because she couldn't figure out how to ask without sounding like a jealous wife. And because they'd come to a place of relative peace. At least she thought they had.

His mood of late made her wonder if she was wrong. She tried to attribute it to the fatigue and strain of moving, but he'd thrown darts at her all week. She'd been ridiculously busy and had never made it to the grocery store. Instead of offering to pick something up for the two of them, he'd asked if she was eating at Jacob's. If he should take care of his own meals. When she fell asleep in front of the TV, he accused her of being bored with her home life.

Eric wasn't a demanding husband. He'd always been understanding when she was under a deadline or lost in a creative void. She could tell the tower job bothered him, and she didn't know why. What she did know was she was nervous about Jacob and Eric meeting for the first time.

By 8:15, she began to worry about Eric in earnest. He'd guesstimated his arrival at 7:30 the latest. Her phone was in her purse, which had been tucked into a cupboard behind the bar. She headed in that direction, but made terrible progress. Every few feet she was stopped by someone who wanted to compliment her on the decor, or introduce her to someone else, or ask how business was going.

It was 8:35 before she retrieved her phone and stepped into the parking lot. The damp wind of earlier was now cold and blustery. It plastered her dress to her thighs. She huddled against a brick wall and punched in Eric's number. As it rang, a car pulled into the lot. It was him. She hung up.

She couldn't see his face as he hurried toward her, head down. "Hey," she said when he drew close. He jumped.

"You startled me." He reached for her and gave her a kiss. "You're like ice. What are you doing out here?"

She held up her phone. "Calling you. I was starting to worry."

They hurried inside. It was a relief to get out of the wind and into the warmth of the gallery. Eric raised his voice to be heard over the noise. "Yeah, sorry. It took all day to get everything done for the move on Monday. I guess I could've gone back tomorrow, but I really wanted Sunday off." He had gone to the old office, the new one, or both every day for the past week.

"Not a problem. Just hoping you were okay."

"Fine." He didn't look fine. Lines of exhaustion creased his forehead and radiated from his eyes.

She smoothed his hair, disheveled from the walk across the parking lot. "Want me to get you a drink while you fix yourself a plate? The food is amazing."

He put the hat in his hand onto his head and gave it a tap. "I can do it. You're busy." She pointed to the bar, and he disappeared through a wall of Dr. Frankenstein's castle.

Rosie ran to check on Honey who enlisted her to refill chafing dishes and bread bowls. When she was done, she dodged guests on her way to the main room to find Eric. He stood alone by a candelabra, drink in hand. She touched his shoulder when she reached him. "Having fun?"

"This place looks amazing."

"Thanks." She slipped an arm around him.

"No, seriously. I mean it." The word "seriously" slurred ever so slightly.

"Have you eaten anything?" Drinking on an empty stomach was never a good idea.

"Not hungry."

"You have to try Honey's corn fritters. They're wonderful." Rosie tugged him toward the food.

"I will. In a bit." He waved his drink. "So, which one of these characters is Jacob Rinehart? I want to meet the man who's changing my wife's career."

Rosie scanned the room. "I don't see him. I'll ask Peter if he's heard anything." She found Peter deep in conversation with an overweight restaurant owner wearing a skeleton costume. "Are Jacob and Cecily coming?" she said as soon as the restaurateur paused for a breath.

"They're here."

"Here? Where?"

Peter pointed to a man in a black hat, sunglasses, and raincoat, his face covered in white bandages. "The Invisible Man." A short, round Bride of Frankenstein stood next to him.

Rosie laughed. It was a perfect costume for Jacob. He twiddled his fingers at her as she crossed the room. "I was wondering when you were going to come and say hello."

"I didn't recognize you," she said. "Great costume."

"You look great too." He leaned close and kissed her cheek, the rough bandages scratching her skin. "But who are you?"

"Ann Darrow, King Kong's girlfriend." Rosie pointed over her shoulder to the stuffed gorilla she'd left on a shelf.

He nodded with appreciation. "Clever."

"I thought so, but if I don't carry King Kong around, no one gets it. Speaking of not knowing who people are…"

"Sorry." He gestured to Mrs. Frankenstein. "This is Cecily. Cecily, Rosie, my amazing interior designer."

"Love, love, love, the bedroom." Cecily stuck out a hand and Rosie shook. "The colors are fantastic. I may never leave."

Rosie laughed. "Jacob deserves a lot of the credit."

He shook his head. "All I did is tell her about you, and she knew what colors you'd like. It was kind of spooky."

Rosie felt an arm encircle her waist. "She is kind of spooky." The arm pulled her close. "I'm Eric."

"Rosie's husband. I've heard a lot about you." Jacob didn't offer to shake hands. Eric's were full, a drink in one and Rosie in the other.

"I bet I've heard more about you."

There was an antagonistic tone to Eric's voice that Rosie had only heard on two occasions in their twenty-plus years of marriage. The first time had been at his parents' home in Colorado. They were newly married, no children yet, and they'd decided to spend a Christmas with his family.

Things were going great until his brother, Mathew, arrived, stoned and silly, and sucked up all the peace on earth and goodwill toward men. Eric's response was to get drunk. She'd never seen him drunk before that day. It wasn't pretty. He and Mathew hardly spoke for the rest of the evening.

The second time was the year before he and Bob started Pacific Financial. Granite, their old firm, made the announcement that a man Eric had trained had just been promoted. It was a nepotism thing and totally undeserved, but that man was now his direct supervisor. Eric came home and cracked open a bottle of Jack Daniels. That wasn't pretty either.

"Have you two eaten?" Rosie asked in a bright voice. "I was telling Eric how wonderful the food is."

"We have," Cecily said.

"I'm not hungry," Eric said, his voice too loud. "I want to talk to the man who is single-handedly turning my wife's career around."

Embarrassment skittered over Rosie's skin. "Eric, that's not—"

"Seems to me, your wife's career was headed in a fine direction. I saw her portfolio." Jacob's voice was quiet.

"Oh, she's talented. Don't get me wrong. But her clients..." He pulled his arm from Rosie's waist and rubbed his thumb and middle finger together. "Not much money."

"Eric." The word shot from her lips. "You need to eat." She threw an apologetic glance at Jacob.

"This is a great opportunity for her. That's all I'm saying. You know?" He swayed a bit on his feet.

"Smile." A photographer snapped a picture of the four of them before Rosie had a chance to react. "How about another? A little closer together." He had to be from *Orange County Lifestyles*. Rosie glanced around wondering who the editor was.

"I'm going for seconds. Why don't you come along?" Jacob reached for Eric's arm. "I'll tell you all about your wife's plans for the house."

Eric let himself be led away. Worried, Rosie started to follow after them, but Cecily put a hand on her arm. "Let them go. Jacob's a writer."

Rosie furrowed her brow, not understanding.

"Conferences. The bar is a popular spot. He doesn't drink, but he's good at sobering people up."

The photographer held up his camera. "One more?" Rosie and Cecily smiled, he snapped, then moved on to the next group.

"Eric doesn't drink hard liquor, ever really. This is an anomaly."

"He'll be okay once he gets some food into him," Cecily said.

"How was your flight?" Rosie didn't want to talk about Eric anymore. She was angry at him for making a scene at her event, especially in front of Jacob.

She and Cecily chatted about the flight, the weather in Seattle, and the tower. Everything but the thing hanging over Jacob's head. She wanted to ask if there was any news on the murder? Had the city of Seattle moved on to the next big story and forgotten about Jacob? But she couldn't figure out how.

When the conversation flagged, Rosie said, "Maybe we should go find the men. I don't want to saddle Jacob with Eric all night."

She and Cecily walked toward the back room and bumped into a corpse bride. The woman wore a tattered white dress, her face a painted skull. "Rosie," she said.

The costume was so professional, so well done, it took a moment for Rosie to recognize her. "Twila. Didn't know who you were."

"Who are you supposed to be?" Twila said.

"Ann Darrow."

Twila wrinkled her bone-white forehead in confusion.

"King Kong's... Have you seen Eric?" Rosie said.

"I did. He was with the Invisible Man, but I don't know where they went."

Cecily glanced at Rosie. "Maybe he and Ja—"

Rosie cut her off before she could say the name. "They're probably at the bar." She took Cecily's arm and pulled her through the smoke screen. "Sorry. I didn't want that woman to know Jacob was here. She's a complete media hound. She'd have made sure the magazine got a picture of the two of them and that they knew who he was."

Cecily looked alarmed. "Oh, thanks."

The men weren't at the bar, nor were they by the food, but Honey was. "Do you know where Eric went?" Rosie said.

Honey pointed to the door that led to the parking lot. "He went outside with some guy dressed like a mummy."

"He's the Invisible Man." Rosie corrected her without thinking.

"I could see him."

"No. From the movie... Never mind. We'll watch it sometime. I'm going to find them."

Cecily turned toward the gallery, and Rosie exited the building. The parking lot was empty. Empty and cold. She hugged herself. She was about to go inside again, when she heard her name.

"Rosie." It was Eric. He leaned from the passenger window of a car she didn't recognize.

Rosie fought the wind to reach him. "What are you doing?"

"Sobering up," Eric said and gave her a lopsided grin.

She bent over and peered into the car. Jacob sat behind the steering wheel. They both had plates of half-eaten food in their laps. Jacob hoisted a cup filled with what looked like water.

"Jacob, quite correctly, realized I needed food and water and to lay off the booze for a bit." Eric didn't sound entirely sober, but the angry edge was gone from his voice.

"Thank you," she said to Jacob.

"I've been enjoying your husband's company."

Rosie patted Eric's arm. "Are you ready to come inside?"

"In a minute. You go."

Rain spit in her face. She decided not to argue.

Cecily was talking with Sid, Lillian, and Twila when Rosie reentered. Rosie had seen the Rawlinsons from across the room several times but hadn't had a chance to greet them. Truthfully, she hadn't been in any hurry. She didn't like Lillian's superior attitude, or the way she'd talked to Lupe the other day. Sid and Lillian were clients now, however. She had to play the game if she didn't want to lose them to Twila.

She joined the group, and Cecily turned to her. "Did you find them?"

"I did. They'll be in soon."

Lillian widened her eyes, but was too polite to ask who they were talking about. Rosie didn't say. They'd figure it out when the men returned.

"I was looking for you," Lillian said.

"You were?" Rosie said.

"Yes. I was talking to Genevieve, the *Orange County Lifestyles* editor, she wants to get a picture of the three of us together." She threaded her arm through her husband's.

"Really?" Twila said, her voice dripping with skepticism.

For once Rosie agreed with Twila. She knew Lillian had hoped for an article about the decorating project, but for the life of her, she couldn't see why the magazine would be interested.

"Don't sound so surprised. Everything the next mayor of San Clemente does is of interest to the public."

"Mayor?" Twila said.

"Now, Lil, we don't know I'm going to win." Sid's words were humbler than his tone.

"Of course you are." She lifted her chin and searched the crowd. "Where is that photographer anyway?"

"I'll find him," Twila said. Rosie saw Eric and Jacob enter the room as Twila spun away. Her ghostly gown swept the floor as she moved toward them. Eric stiffened when he saw her. Why? Was it guilt? Did he feel awkward being in the same room as his wife and his...*interior designer*?

She watched his mouth tighten as Twila spoke. Although Rosie couldn't hear his response, it seemed forced. She longed to move closer, to listen to their conversation. How to extract herself from Lillian and Sid gracefully was an issue, however.

When Cecily saw the group in the doorway, she excused herself and walked their way. A moment later, Eric was at Rosie's side. Tension crackled in the air around him.

Sid didn't seem to notice. "Eric, my man, I hear your business is moving out of Dana Point and into San Clemente."

"Yes. Monday morning."

"I'd love to see you at the next Chamber meeting."

Sid's mayoral campaign explained a few things, like Lillian's hunger for publicity. Rosie hoped Cecily got the message earlier about letting people know who she and Jacob were. Lillian would insist on taking a picture with the famous Jacob Rinehart if she hadn't.

Lillian returned with the photographer and a woman Rosie assumed was Genevieve Cabot. The woman had a mass of hennaed hair pinned into a tight bun and wore a fitted black dress and blood red lipstick. A vampire maybe? "Genevieve, this is Rosie Ring, the interior designer I told you about. Genevieve is the society editor for *Orange County Lifestyles*."

Genevieve smiled revealing very straight, white, expensive teeth, and a set of fangs. Vampire it was. "Nice to meet you." She put out a hand. "Lillian and I talked about doing some before and after pictures of their place."

"That would be wonderful." As Rosie shook, she glanced around the room looking for Twila. She wished she was present to hear this. Of course, the Rawlinsons' home might not get the cover like Twila's client had. Their placement would probably be dependent on election results.

"I'd like to interview you about your process, as well. When do you expect to be done?" Genevieve said.

"Early next year—"

"Before the holidays—" She and Lillian spoke at once. "I know we talked about dates, but I was hoping we could move things up a tiny bit. We're planning a big Christmas party for the city council members and staff." Lillian's words were sweet, but there was steel in her tone.

That wasn't going to happen, but the photographer saved Rosie from having to say so. She and Lillian would have to have a conversation about this next week. The photographer arranged the group and took several shots of Sid, Lillian, Eric, and Rosie, then a couple of Genevieve with the women. Genevieve said she'd be in touch and she and the photographer wandered off.

"Your career is taking off, Rose. I'm proud of you." Eric whispered into her ear.

That's what she'd wanted, wasn't it? To be as influential and affluent as... Well, to be influential and affluent. So, why wasn't she more excited?

Because she couldn't share the joy with Eric. The reason came to her as soon as the question entered her mind. She might pretend his problems were his problems and act as if they didn't affect her, but it wasn't true. They were a team, a couple, a family. When he hurt, she hurt.

She knew there was something more than Pacific's failing business bothering him. The exodus of clients had actually slowed, so why the sudden heavy drinking? It couldn't be that he was envious of her success in light of his own bad luck. Could it? Could that be why he'd been so caustic about the tower job? She hated to think that about him. Eric had always made more than she had. Always been the primary bread winner. Was he afraid to lose that status?

That he wouldn't be honest with her, wouldn't tell her what was going on with him, left a hole in her no amount of personal success could fill. Anxiety, undefined and amorphous, nibbled at the edges of her mind.

# 4.3.7

Eric flew into the gallery, and the door slammed shut behind him. His hair hung in his eyes in wet ribbons. "It's really coming down."

As if in agreement, a clap of thunder shook the night. Peach must be terrified. Rosie had an image of her dog, head beneath the bed, shivering. She was too large to get all of herself under, so she hid ostrich-style. "We should go."

"I'm leaving too," Peter said.

Rosie's gaze traveled around the gallery, now empty of guests. This was the earliest a Halloween party had ever broken up. It was 11:00, but the shop had begun to empty at the first crack of thunder. By 10:15 the only people left were her, Eric, Honey, and Peter.

They'd cleaned up food and helped Honey load her van, but the gallery was a mess of dirty dishes, abandoned lipstick-rimmed glasses, and crumpled napkins.

"You should follow Honey home. Make sure she gets there okay," Peter said.

"But the mess," Rosie said.

"I have a cleaning service coming on Monday morning."

"What about tomorrow?" The Nightshade was usually open on Sundays.

"I'm closed for four days starting tomorrow," Peter said.

Rosie raised an eyebrow.

"Have to make another trip to Seattle. Now, please leave."

"You're sure you don't need help?"

Peter placed hands on Rosie's shoulders and turned her toward the door. "Go. I'm right behind you. Just going to lock up."

Eric fished his keys from his pocket. "I'll drive. We can get your car tomorrow."

Rosie examined his face. It was flushed, from cold or alcohol, she wasn't sure. He'd lost the antagonistic tone of voice after his trip to Jacob's car, but she'd seen him at the bar another time or two.

"I'm fine. I've been drinking soda water," he said as if answering her thoughts.

She was too tired to argue, besides going back and forth to Honey's van through the storm must have had a sobering effect—kind of like a cold shower. She hugged Peter goodbye and hurried to Eric's car.

They pulled onto the Coast Highway in the pelting rain. The street was all but deserted. Lightning flashed over the ocean, making the sky bright as day for a split second before darkness fell again. Eric drove slowly and carefully, riding the waves of the storm. The skin on Rosie's arms tingled with nerves. She hated driving in bad weather.

"So what did you and Jacob talk about?" Rosie was curious, but she also wanted to get her mind off the conditions outside.

"You, mostly. He's pretty impressed with you."

"All I've done is one bedroom."

"He really likes your plan for his, what did he call it, his—"

"Apartment?"

"Right, apartment. He's awed by your sense of color, your artistic eye." Eric drew out the word "awed" and waggled his eyebrows when he said "artistic." He was teasing her, but he was proud. She could hear it in his voice.

"Listen, Rose." He grew serious. "I'm sorry about earlier. I shouldn't have acted that way. I didn't know what my problem was until I was sitting in that car with Jacob." He paused.

"What was it?"

"I was jealous of the man."

"Jealous?"

"Envious. Jealous. Yeah. I wasn't worried you two were having a fling. Just haven't felt like much of a provider lately. I used to be the one paying the bills. Your income covered the extra stuff. It felt like that got turned around. Like Rinehart was paying the bills. I didn't like it. Didn't like him."

"What changed?"

"It was the way he talked about your work. Made me realize how talented you are. That you deserve some time in the sun. And, he's a nice guy."

Despite the cold night, a warm ember glowed inside her. She still had a hard time believing she was doing the interior design of the tower. To make everything even more surreal, her client was a famous author. And he loved her work.

"He is, isn't he?" Rosie said.

"I only hope he isn't handsome. I couldn't tell with all those bandages on his face. If he's handsome, I may change my mind."

Rosie glanced at Eric's profile. She reached out a hand and stroked his cheek. "You're handsomer."

Eric snorted. Neither spoke for several long minutes. The steady *swop-swop* of the windshield wipers and the patter of the rain were the only sounds.

"Were you alone at the new office today? Did anyone come to help?" Rosie was sorry she'd asked as soon as the words left her mouth, but she was too tired to edit her conversation.

"Only Twila. She's a hard worker, I have to give her that."

Rosie turned up the car heater. "Is everything ready for the move on Monday?"

"I think so. I'm not going in tomorrow either way."

They stopped at a red light. Rain drops raced across the blacktop like tiny birds before a wave. Thunder crashed, and another bolt of lightning lit the sky. Eric dropped a hand on Rosie's thigh. "I'm glad we drove home together. I'd have worried about you the whole way."

Rosie squeezed his fingers. She'd been more worried about his driving than her own, but soda water, food, and time seemed to have done the trick. Eric was navigating the roads well.

The light turned. They made a left onto Crown Valley Parkway, and the wind buffeted the car as they headed inland. Eric removed his hand from her leg and gripped the steering wheel with both fists.

She studied his profile again in the passing streetlights. He'd aged in the last six months. Her husband, the fit, athletic man who never seemed to get any older, had aged. New lines had formed near his mouth and across his forehead. They made him appear sullen, especially when his face was in repose.

"I think the move will be good for you and Bob." She spoke without thought. They'd come from a place of compassion, not logic.

Eric frowned. "I hope so."

"I'm sure it will. A fresh start in a new—"

Tires screeched. The car swerved right and into a cacophony of sensations: Ground thudded under her feet. Head, rag doll-like, bounced off leather. Streaks of light blinded her eyes. Then stillness. Nothing but the thrumming of rain on the roof.

"Rose."

She opened her eyes and closed them again. She inhaled, but not deeply. Something seemed to press against her chest.

"Are you okay?" Eric said.

She licked her lips. "Okay. That was close."

"It was a cat. Or a possum. Or something," he said. "I didn't see it until the last second."

Her face cracked into a smile. "Did you hit it?"

One side of Eric's mouth turned up. "I don't think so."

"Possum, one. Rings, zero."

Eric hit the gas, cautiously at first then with more pressure, but the car didn't move. He opened the door and stepped outside. Rosie watched him walk to the front of the vehicle, then disappear as he bent down. A long moment later, he reentered with a wet gust. "Car looks okay, but we're stuck in the mud."

Several metaphors popped into Rosie's mind, but she resisted the urge to say them. Instead she said, "I'll call Triple A."

An hour, or hour and half later—Rosie had lost track of time—a tow truck pulled up in front of them. Eric got out to talk to the driver. She closed her eyes. The adrenaline rush from the near crash had worn off, leaving fatigue in its wake.

"We're lucky. If we'd have been going any faster… " Eric had said while they'd waited for Triple A. Apparently, they'd missed a telephone pole by a few feet.

Luck was a funny thing. They were stuck in the mud, which didn't seem very lucky, but neither she nor Eric were injured, and the cat-possum was safe. They were lucky it was raining, because it had slowed them down. Of course, if it hadn't been raining Eric might have seen the cat-possum, and they wouldn't have had to swerve to miss it. If they'd been really lucky, Eric would have been more alert, because he wouldn't have been drinking, because he wouldn't have been upset about work. Luck was relative.

She'd won the lottery three weeks ago, she knew that. She'd stumbled into the tower job and that had led to Sid and Lillian's job. Then she found out Sid had a good chance at becoming the next mayor of San Clemente, and because of his wife's need to appear better than the neighbors, Rosie might end up with a spread in *Orange County Lifestyles* like Twila had.

Twila. Rosie had watched her career for years and had concluded that Twila was luckier than she was. That Lady Luck had smiled on the woman but wouldn't smile on Rosie. Oh, she'd gone through insecure phases where she'd felt her talent was lacking, or Twila's was exceptional. In her saner moments she knew their gifts were different but not unequal. It had driven her nuts. Why had Twila's career skyrocketed while Rosie's plodded?

*You make your own luck.* That's what Lizzie said. "I can tell you before I even look at the books which of my clients have handled their affairs well and which have messed them up royally. Foolish people let life lead them around by the nose. Smart people make their own luck."

Rosie had also been convinced Twila was smarter than she was. She had to be, or she wouldn't be so much luckier.

Eric opened the driver's side door and stuck his head inside. "We have to get out while he pulls the car onto the road."

Rosie tugged her coat more tightly around herself and stepped out into the rain. She and Eric huddled together and watched as the tow truck driver hooked up their car. Eric jutted his chin in the man's direction. "He says we're really lucky. It could've been bad."

Luck. There was that word again. Standing there in the rain, hair plastered to her head, fat drops of water cascading off the end of her nose and into her mouth, looking, she was sure, more bedraggled than Ann Darrow had after being slung around by a giant gorilla, she didn't feel very lucky.

Feelings weren't facts. That was what her father had always said. Her luck *had* changed. Maybe the Lady had shifted her favor from Twila to Rosie. She didn't know, but she did know she planned to take advantage of this new turn of events. You never knew when a cat-possum would run out in front of your car, and you'd wind up in a ditch. Make hay while the sun shines. That was another one of her father's favorite expressions.

An engine roared, chains clanked and the car was pulled from the mud. Ten minutes later, Rosie was on the road again and counting her lucky stars.

**MOLLY:** Close call. I enjoyed all of Rosie's musings on luck. We'll be revisiting those in our question of the week. Before we get into that, though, I have another patient interview for you.

# patient zero



I'm a patient person. I keep myself to myself, as they say in England. And, I watch. You can learn all kinds of things by watching. For instance, I learned that Mom was actually a very regimented person for a drunk. She had an unchanging meal plan for every night of the week. I hadn't realized everybody's mom didn't run their kitchens the same way until my brother told a kid at school that we always had meatloaf on Wednesdays. The kid made fun of him.

The revelation was so interesting to me, I never put the kid in his place for mocking my brother. I was grateful to him. He taught me something about my mom, something unique. Knowing unique things about people is good. It's a kind of power.

My dad was old-school Catholic and wouldn't eat meat on Fridays. Mom, being no Julia Child, made frozen fish sticks. She also baked cookies or brownies on Fridays. I'm not sure what the two had to do with each other except maybe she thought as long as she had the oven on, she might as well kill two birds.

About six months after the burned cookies incident, I came home from school and Mom was passed out with her head on the kitchen table. I saw an opportunity.

I climbed on a stool, got her Betty Crocker cookbook out of the cupboard, and opened it to the chocolate chip cookie recipe that was my favorite. I pulled flour, sugar, eggs, all the things the recipe called for, out of the cupboard and poured the right amounts into a mixing bowl. I made it look kind of messy. Shook some flour on the floor. Sugar on the table. I even held a spoon in her hand, and she and I stirred up the batter together. I let the dirty spoon drop on the floor.

She almost woke up then. I bolted to the kitchen doorway, ready to run if she came to. But she didn't. She made these smacking noises with her lips, groaned a couple of times and was quiet again.

I waited for a couple of minutes just to be on the safe side. Then I walked around the room to make sure I hadn't missed anything. I noticed the kitchen window was open. That was a close call. I closed it tight, then put the oven on three-hundred and fifty degrees.

I didn't light the pilot light. You know what I'm saying?

Our stove, like most things in that house, was old and only halfway worked. You had to light it with a match or it would leak gas. My brother and I weren't allowed to use matches unless we were supervised. I didn't see anyone around to supervise me, so I left. I closed the kitchen door and went outside to play.

I stayed out until the streetlights came on. That was my curfew. When I rounded the corner onto our block, I stopped cold. I don't know what I'd been expecting, but it wasn't this. It was beautiful. Red and white blinking lights. Men in uniforms. All the neighbors out on the street. It was like the Fourth of July.

Dad saw me from a half a block away, and opened his arms. He had tears streaming down his face. When I reached him, he hugged me hard and said, "I was so worried about you." That's when I knew it would be okay. He wasn't crying about Mom. He'd been worried about me.

After a while, life settled into a new routine. We didn't eat the same things every night, and we had pizza a lot, but there was no more screaming and yelling. I think Dad was as relieved as me and my brother that Mom was gone. He came home from work earlier, took us places on the weekends, and smiled a lot more.

I never told anybody I was the one who turned on the oven, not even my brother. He'd have told Dad, and Dad would have felt like he had to tell the police. Besides, I liked keeping it a secret. I felt like a fairy godmother, or a good elf, or something.

A year after Mom died, Dad married again. It was okay. She made nice meals, and never got drunk. Everything was good for a long time. It wasn't until high school that we started having problems again.

MOLLY: Okay, then. Whoever this person is, he or she definitely believes in making their own luck. Patient Zero has progressed from dumping a handicapped kid's wagon in the water to matricide. That's a pretty big leap. I wonder what's to come.

Now to the question of the week. How much of our success is circumstantial, due to things outside of our control? How much is based on our efforts?

Do you fall on the side of Liz, Rosie's sister, and believe we make our own luck? Or do you lean more on the Lady? Let's talk about it.

Join me next time for more *Murders Under the Sun*.

**(cue music)**

VO: If you enjoyed this episode, please leave us a five-star review on your favorite podcast service—it really helps. Murders Under the Sun is edited by Jim Wilbourne, theme music is by Eclectic Blends, and I'm your host, Molly Shure.

# part five

# MURDERS UNDER THE SUN
## SEASON FOUR; EPISODE FOUR

**MOLLY:** Welcome back to *The Tower*, Episode Four. This is Molly Shure, your host.

Last week we waded deep into the murky waters of luck. Is it real? Or is luck simply an illusion created by people who work incredibly hard behind the scenes? In other words, ten-year-overnight successes.

Obviously, it isn't something we can solve in one discussion, but I thought I'd add a little insight from my research into the mix.

According to *Psychology Today*, the way we view luck has a lot to do with our personalities. Optimists tend to see positive outcomes as something within their control. Pessimists lean more on luck or fate. They believe success just sort of happens to some and not to others. That it's random.

How does this view impact their lives? Several studies show that optimists are, in fact, generally more financially successful, more productive, and happier than their pessimistic counterparts. Apparently, Rosie's sister is right. We make our own luck.

And, speaking of luck, we had an interesting development in the CSU-Fullerton student mystery. Last season, I told you something very curious that Camilla Jimenez wrote to me. Several months after Raphael disappeared, she received a check from a life insurance company. This seemed weird for several reasons. Raphael was in his early twenties. She'd never taken out a policy on him, and she couldn't imagine that he'd taken one out on himself.

Also, when we researched it, we found that life insurance companies do pay out in missing person's cases but—and it's a big but—the courts must declare the person dead first.

There are four requirements for a missing person to be declared dead. They must be gone for a significant time period, typically seven years. There must have been no communication from them in that time. There must be no reasonable explanation for their absence. For example, they can't be a felon running from the law. And, finally, there has to have been a diligent search for them.

Obviously, none of these criteria had been met when Camilla received her check. So, this seemed odd enough for us to do a little more digging.

Our first thought was to contact the payer. But Camilla no longer had the name of the company, and she'd changed banks since then. She's digging through old records, but it might take a while. Next, we decided to see if either Melissa's family or Ariana's family received checks.

I learned that Melissa's father died of cancer shortly after she disappeared. I knew that. What I didn't know was that her mother got a life insurance payout on him from a policy she wasn't aware he'd had.

Now, this isn't as strange as Camilla getting a payout on her 20-year-old missing son, but it is odd that no one knew about the policy. Melissa's mother never looked into it, though. She was grateful for the money. It had been an extremely difficult time, as you can imagine, and she wasn't able to work for about a year. She accepted the windfall with no questions asked.

I attempted to get in touch with Ariana Blackstone's family to see if anyone there received a payout, but haven't had any luck as yet. I'll let you know when I learn more.

Now, let's get into the episode. It's a big one, people. Things are beginning to spiral out of control in Rosie's world.

## 4.4.2

Monday was moving day at Pacific Financial. Eric left early, despite the pain in his back. He'd strained it while putting together a bookshelf at the new offices on Saturday. Careening off the road Saturday night had been the final straw. Watching him wince as he dressed gave Rosie more resolve than ever to work hard and work smart. It was her turn to carry some of the family burdens since his luck had, apparently, run out.

She decided to go to Laguna Beach and install the curtain rods and swags in the guest rooms. While she was there, she'd begin exploring the idea of using tower pictures for publicity purposes. If she promised to protect Jacob's identity, maybe he'd go along with her plans.

Haze covered the sun muting the day's colors. Even the air seemed thick and hard to breathe. The closer she got to the beach, the heavier the haze became, turning the world into a pastel painting.

She rang Jacob's bell and listened to Fury's barks grow in volume. Jacob held the dog's collar as he opened the door but released it when he saw Rosie. Fury leaped around her in happy circles.

"Come in. We're still breakfasting." Jacob gave her a sleepy smile. "It's impossible to wake up in this kind of weather." Rosie followed him through the house to the apartment at its end.

Cecily sat at the big table, glasses perched on her nose, laptop open, and a half-eaten plate of eggs in front of her. Her hair was down today, a halo of brown curls, and she wore no makeup. She looked much more approachable than she had as the bride of Frankenstein.

She glanced up from her screen and grinned. "Good morning."

"Are you hungry?" Jacob asked.

Rosie said no. She took a cup of coffee and headed upstairs. As she drilled holes and leveled rods, the conviction that she ought to hire someone else to do this kind of work grew inside her. She could be making appointments, working on PR, and running ads, maximizing her new opportunities.

The idea made her a little sad. She enjoyed working with her hands, liked watching what she'd envisioned come in to being. It filled her with a peaceful satisfaction. Maybe she could find a compromise. Hire an assistant for some of the more mundane tasks, and cherry pick those she enjoyed.

She stepped away and surveyed the last swag. She'd chosen a sunny gold for all the guest rooms. The color went well with the sand tone of the walls. A bright color outside the window caught her eye. It looked unnatural in the white gloom of the day.

She moved closer and looked toward Cliff Drive. A van with bright letters painted on its side was parked at the curb in front of the house. A chill ran over her.

She snatched up her tools and trash, and jogged to the main staircase. She heard Jacob's deep voice and Cecily's laughter echoing from the French doors of the apartment. She thought about calling out to them, but instead dumped her load on the floor and ran to the library. Its windows faced the same direction as the bedroom she'd just left.

She could read the van's letters from the doorway. They were the call letters for a local news station. They'd found him. They'd found Jacob.

She sidled up to a window and peered out. Only one camera man and one reporter adjusting her hair in a handheld mirror. That was good. Not a mob out there.

She stepped away, and chewed a thumbnail. But reporters were like ants. If you saw one, you could be sure the entire anthill wasn't far behind.

What would she say? How could she break the news to Jacob? She paced the library as if she might find the answers in one of its corners. His reasons for fleeing Seattle played through her mind, the red paint, the picketers, and she felt ill.

Cecily.

Cecily would know how to handle this. Rosie ran toward the apartment but slowed her steps as she drew close. She needed to calm herself. Her anxiety would make things worse.

The scene before her was so cheerful, so warm, she hated to disturb it. Jacob peered through a telescope trained out a south facing window. Cecily leaned on the windowsill watching him, the expression on her face adoring. That was one thing Frank and Hank got right anyway. Cecily was in love with Jacob. He straightened when Rosie entered. "Did you see my new toy?"

"No. Where did you get it?"

"Cecily gave it to me. A housewarming present. It's perfect, isn't it?" His face was almost childlike with delight. She was about to destroy his happiness.

"We have a situation," she said.

Two sets of eyes, Cecily's earthy brown, Jacob's intense green, fixed on her.

Rosie paused for a breath, then said, "There is a news van out front."

Jacob's face went white. A long silence followed. Finally, Cecily said, "It was going to happen sooner or later. I was hoping for later."

Jacob sank into a chair. "Why can't they leave me alone?"

Cecily placed a hand on his arm. "It's their job to make people miserable."

"What is so fascinating about me?"

Cecily began tapping on her laptop which lay open on the table. "This." She slid the computer toward Jacob. Rosie crossed the room so she could see the screen.

"Hiding Behind the Mask" the *Orange County Register's* headline read. Under it was the tagline, "New information links dead flight attendant and Jacob Rinehart," and a picture of Jacob, Cecily, and Rosie in their costumes.

"What new information?" Jacob said.

"Give me a sec." Cecily's lips moved slightly as she read. "It says you both grew up in Lacey, Washington, went to the same high school."

Jacob's face went white. "What?"

"It says—"

"I know what it says, but it doesn't make sense. I never met that woman in my life." Jacob stood and walked to one of the windows.

Nobody said anything for a long moment, then Cecily said, "Don't worry, Jacob. Lacey is a big town. Makes sense both of you would end up in Seattle at some point. The police aren't knocking at your door. This will go away like everything else has."

He spoke without turning to face her. "You think so?"

"I'm sure of it. Honestly, what I really want to know is where that picture came from."

"It's from the Halloween party," Rosie said, stating the obvious.

Cecily's mouth tightened. "Right. That magazine photographer took it."

"He was there working for *Orange County Lifestyles*. How did it end up in the *Register*?" Rosie said.

"He must have heard the news, figured out who Jacob was, realized he could make some money, then sold the picture to the paper."

Rosie was shocked. "Can he do that?"

"He did."

Jacob turned away from the window, his mouth hard, his eyes slits. "The question isn't whether he can or can't sell the photo, but how did he know? How did he know it was me? I wasn't recognizable."

"Someone told him, obviously," Cecily said.

"Who?" The single word held such suppressed rage, Rosie took a step backward. Fury, who'd been dozing under the table, jumped up and ran toward the stairs, tail tucked.

Who at the party knew Jacob had moved to Laguna? Rosie ticked off people in her mind: Peter and Eric, but she doubted either of them had said anything. Both understood the need for discretion. Eric, especially, knew what it was like to be hounded by the press. Honey had learned her lesson at John and Carol's party when she'd let the cat out of the bag to Lillian and Sid. It couldn't be her.

Lillian and Sid. Their names lit up like a neon sign in Rosie's mind.

She took a sharp breath. Cecily and Jacob turned to her. "What?" Cecily said.

"I might know."

"Who?" Jacob repeated the question.

If it had been Lillian who'd told the photographer, it could come back to bite Rosie. After all, it was her friend, Honey, who'd told them. And it was Rosie who'd told Honey. Rosie pulled out a chair and sat, her legs felt weak. "It doesn't matter, does it? What matters is what we do about it."

"It matters to me."

"I don't want to say anything until I'm sure."

"Eric?" Jacob said.

Rosie shook her head. "No. Definitely not."

"I didn't think so. He told me a bit about what he'd been through. We commiserated." Jacob and Eric had talked about more than Rosie that night. She'd thought so.

"It wasn't Peter," Cecily said. "He and I discussed the need for anonymity. In fact, it was his idea for Jacob to come as the Invisible Man. But knowing who leaked to the press isn't our immediate problem."

Jacob clenched and unclenched a fist as if trying to release the idea. "You're right, you're right. First things first."

"I'll get dressed and talk to the reporter," Cecily said.

"What are you going to say?" Jacob asked.

"I'm going to answer the questions I can and ask them to respect your privacy."

He snorted.

"I have another appointment," Rosie said, her voice subdued. She was supposed to meet with a woman from John and Carol's party in a half hour.

"You'd better postpone it," Cecily said. "We have to go over talking points."

"Talking points?"

"Right. You're in this photo too. There will be more media attention coming our way, I can guarantee it."

A wave of nausea coursed through Rosie. She was now part of Jacob Rinehart's story. That was exactly what Eric had been afraid of.

Cecily had been talking, but Rosie hadn't been listening. She latched onto the woman's words like they were a lifeline now. "We'll be upbeat, positive. Jacob had no idea Marianne Kennedy was from Lacey. He never knew her. He didn't run away from Seattle, he'd been thinking about moving closer to LA for some time. That's the future for a best-selling novelist, right? Film. And LA is the place to be."

Cecily pulled a legal pad from a briefcase under the table and began jotting notes onto it.

"What do I say if they bring up the murder?" Rosie said.

"Nothing. You don't know anything about it. They know more than you do. You talk about the house; how great it is to work with Jacob on a creative project. Maybe we say when the place is done, we'll showcase the home in *Better Homes and Gardens*, or *Architectural Digest*, or someplace."

Rosie sat very still. She couldn't believe what she was hearing. She'd been planning to pitch that very idea to Jacob. Now because of this, the idea was being put forward by Cecily. If it turned out Lillian was the one who'd talked to the *Orange County Lifestyles* photographer about Jacob, it would look like Rosie had maneuvered the entire thing for publicity.

Cecily stood. "Let me do the talking. You smile a lot and say what a great client Jacob is. Can you do that?"

Rosie nodded. Jacob reached for his phone.

Cecily's eyes narrowed. "Who are you calling?"

"My lawyer."

"Your lawyer?"

"I'm going to put this place on the market."

"That's the worst thing you could do. It'll look like you're running. Like you're guilty of something. They were going to find you, Jacob. You know that. It's sooner than we'd hoped, but… "

He stared at her. "Sooner or later, what difference does it make?"

"New atrocities wipe out the memory of old ones. There hasn't been anything as sensational as the flight attendant in the past six months, but there will be. Sadly, it's inevitable. It would've been better if your address hadn't been made public until after a terrorist attack, or major plane crash, but we have to deal with what is. It could be worse. It could be national news people out there."

Cecily marched from the room, back straight. Rosie and Jacob sat in silence. Her thoughts were churning. A vision of Eric, the pain on his face as he dressed that morning played through her mind like a movie. He was still suffering from the scandal that had rocked their lives earlier that year, and she had just embroiled them in another. How would she tell him?

When Cecily returned, dressed in a suit, hair as neat as a helmet, Rosie still had no answers. The two walked the length of the house and through the front door into the haze of the day.

4.4.3

Rosie checked her rearview mirror all the way home. Silly, she knew the press didn't care about her. They'd made it clear they were interested in Jacob. All their questions had been about him. What was he like to work with? What kind of man was he? Did he have a temper?

She'd pasted on a smile, and answered everything in an upbeat, positive manner just as Cecily had instructed. She hadn't needed the encouragement. Everything she'd said was true. Jacob was a great client, easy to work with. She wasn't in the least bit afraid of him. He was more complicated than she'd first thought, most people were, but she didn't say that.

Her home embraced her like a hug. The familiar furnishings, saturated hues, nothing muddled or unclear, these things unified to calm her jangled nerves. After greeting Peach, she made herself a cup of coffee and retreated to the sun porch—her safe place.

When she was a child her safe place was her bedroom. She'd filled it with a crayon box of colors: a brilliant green, pink, and orange floral bedspread, peach-colored walls, her own artwork tacked up everywhere. The clarity of the colors untangled her mind and helped her sort through the confusions of childhood.

The front door opened and closed, and Peach's claws skidded across the hardwood floor of the entryway. Rosie glanced at the grandfather clock in the hall. It was only 1:30. "Eric?"

She heard his footsteps and a moment later he leaned against a wall of the sunroom. "Hi." He looked terrible, his face lined and gray. "I couldn't stay."

Rosie set down her pillow and went to him. "What can I get you? Have you taken anything?"

"Nothing stronger than an aspirin."

She walked with him to the living room. He collapsed on the couch, and she continued on to the kitchen for an icepack. After bringing it to him, she sat on the coffee table next to him. "You shouldn't have gone in."

"I had to."

"Have you eaten?"

"Not hungry." He closed his eyes. "Tell me about your day. Get my mind off my pain."

"I'm afraid it'll make it worse."

"Couldn't," he said.

So Rosie told him about the news van outside Jacob's house, and her fear that it was Lillian who had informed the press. "What makes the whole thing worse is that Cecily told the reporter we'd be working with a national home decor magazine once the house was done."

"How does that make it worse? That's great for you."

"Right, it'll look like I engineered the whole thing?"

Eric snorted, then groaned. "Don't make me laugh. It hurts."

"I wasn't trying to."

"Even if you told Lillian about the tower job, how could you know she'd talk to someone in the media? And, then, how could you know what Cecily's response would be? You're spooky smart about people and color, but you're not psychic."

"I guess." Rosie heard the doubt in her own voice.

Once, shortly after the orchestra pit incident, she'd awoken with the knowledge that she would have an asthma attack that day. She knew it was imminent, waiting for her, the way a dog knows when an earthquake is on the way. She told her mother, but her mother felt her forehead, examined her tongue, and pronounced her fine.

Rosie had gone to school and sure enough, right in the middle of a spelling bee, it hit. She'd been given the word "schedule" to spell. She knew how to spell schedule, but the letters became a dancing hodge-podge before her eyes. She couldn't corral them, bring them into any kind of order.

Her breathing grew labored with the effort. Within moments she was on the floor of the room, twenty pairs of eyes glued to her gaping mouth as she gasped for air. It was terrifying and humiliating. She stayed in her room for the rest of the week, only venturing as far as the bathroom.

She felt a little like that now. Although she'd outgrown the asthma, anxiety sat on her chest making it hard to breathe. She picked up an orange throw pillow and hugged it to herself trying to soak in the warmth and encouragement of the color. What should she do? *Nothing,* her mind screamed. She knew that was the wrong answer.

"Even if you'd told the media yourself," Eric interrupted her thoughts, "you couldn't have known the outcome. It could just as easily have backfired on you. Jacob might have decided to sell the house and run."

"That was his first response." Rosie said dully.

"Doesn't surprise me. That's all I can think about these days."

"What do you mean?"

He opened his eyes and stared into hers. "Do you ever think about moving, Rose? Getting out of Orange County?"

"Where would we go?"

"I don't know. We could move to Massachusetts, be near your family."

"What about your business?"

He massaged his forehead. "What business?" His words were a mumble. She sat quietly waiting for him to say more, but after several minutes she heard his breathing become slow and steady.

She'd never thought about moving. Rosie loved her home. It was the place her children grew up. It was where they came on school breaks, holidays, and when they needed to soak up family love and support.

Eric loved living here, too. At least, he used to. He used to say he felt sorry for people who had to put up with winter. Californians may have firestorms and earthquakes, but we can surf and ski on the same day.

This would pass. She was sure of it. He was discouraged. Of course, he was, but she'd help set things right. Rosie was making better money now than she ever had in her life. They'd weather this storm together, and when Eric's business was on track again, they'd be that much farther ahead.

She rose and went into her office. She'd get to work on the schematic for Lillian and Sid's place. She'd take it to San Clemente tomorrow, and she'd find a way to question Lillian about the photographer from *Orange County Lifestyles*.

Maybe Eric was right. Maybe Jacob wouldn't be angry with her if he found out it was another one of her clients who'd caused the problem, but Eric hadn't heard Jacob's voice. He hadn't seen the anger in his eyes. No. She needed to know if she was responsible for this, even if inadvertently. She couldn't risk losing the tower. Not now.

# 4.4.4

Lupe opened the door to Lillian and Sid's house the next morning. Her face was solemn, and Rosie's thoughts immediate went to her little boy. Before she could ask if he was okay, Lupe said, "I'll tell Lillian you're here," and spun away.

Alone in the dramatic entryway with the gaudy chandelier and overly large staircase, Rosie rehearsed her lines in her mind. *Lots of fun at the party wasn't it? Some wonderful costumes. Jacob Rinehart's was really clever wasn't it?* If Lillian didn't know who he'd been that night, it would mean she hadn't been the one to tell the press Rinehart was there. Wouldn't it?

Maybe not. Perhaps Lillian told Genevieve Cabot and the photographer that Jacob had moved to the area. Maybe the photographer recognized Cecily and put two and two together. Rosie exhaled. This was so complicated. Eric was right. Who cared who'd said what to the press? What mattered was what happened moving forward.

Moving forward. That was another problem. She'd have to address the project timeline with Lillian. Rosie had mulled it over and thought she may have found a compromise. She'd work to get two of the big rooms completed before the holidays, but the rest of the rooms would have to wait. It would cost Sid and Lillian more money. Painters and other workmen would have to come twice, but if they were willing to pay the price it could be done.

"Rosie." Lillian's smile was tight as she crossed the foyer. "Come into the library."

Rosie followed her into the plaid room and sat on the couch where she'd sat last week. The same tea things were laid out on the coffee table. She moved them to one side to make room for her laptop. "The Halloween party was so much fun this year wasn't it?" she said, attempting to keep her tone bright and casual.

"Yes, lovely," Lillian's response sounded distracted.

"There were some wonderful costumes."

Lillian's lips curled up and released to their original position so quickly it could hardly be called a smile. She wanted to get down to business, not socialize, obviously.

Rosie complied, and took her room by room through the plans. A frown formed on Lillian's brow and deepened as much as her Botox injections would allow. Rosie couldn't tell if it was from concentration, or distaste. When she was done, she sat on the couch and waited for Lillian's reaction.

Lillian scrolled between rooms for several long moments, then said, "It's too informal. Sid will be the mayor, after all."

Rosie had been prepared for that reaction. She leaned over and took the latest edition of *Architectural Digest* from her bag and handed it to Lillian. "Check out the spread that begins on page thirty-two."

The article featured the home of a senator and was decorated in a similar style to the one Rosie had outlined. As Lillian leafed through, Rosie tried to think of a way to reopen the conversation about the party. She was a blank.

Lillian dropped the magazine to her lap. "I don't like mixing antiques and modern."

Rosie's phone rang. She checked the screen. It was Eric. She'd get to him later. She declined the call and returned her attention to Lillian. "It's done all the time."

"Is this the kind of thing you're doing at Jacob Rinehart's house?"

As annoyed as Rosie had been with Lillian for constantly bringing up the tower the last time she was here, she was grateful for the woman's obsession this time. "Actually, we're going a bit more eclectic, but definitely casual and comfortable."

Lillian's gaze moved to the ceiling as if searching for answers from above.

"Speaking of Jacob Rinehart, did you get a chance to meet him at the party?" Rosie went on.

Lillian's eyes snapped to Rosie's face. "Was he there?"

That answered one question anyway. She hadn't pointed him out to the photographer. "Yes. He was dressed as the Invisible Man," Rosie said.

"That was him?" Lillian's eyes widened. "I wish you would have introduced me."

Rosie's phone rang again, but she ignored it and took a sip of tea. It was lukewarm and bitter. She set the cup down. "He didn't go as the Invisible Man for nothing. He was trying to stay incognito." Now how to ask her second question: Did you tell Genevieve he'd moved to Laguna? There didn't seem to be any other way to phrase it.

Lillian gave a small shrug. "Maybe we can have him to dinner when the house is done."

"I'm sure he'd enjoy that." Rosie wasn't sure about that at all.

"I have something to tell you." Lillian switched topics. "I've decided to use Twila Wilkes. I spoke with her at the party and told her I wanted to give you a chance to present your plans. I'm sorry, Rosie, but I think our styles are just too divergent."

Rosie stared at her. "But—"

Lillian held up a hand. "Twila and I are more..." Her gaze traveled the room, then returned to Rosie's face. "*Simpatico.*" She must have been happy with the word, because she repeated it. "Simpatico."

"Right. Well." Rosie didn't know what to say. Twila? The woman was plague. Why wouldn't she just go away?

Rosie's phone rang for a third time. It was Eric again. "I'm sorry. I'd better get this." She accepted the call. "Hi honey, can I call you b—"

"Rose, I need to talk to you."

"It's not a good time."

"Something has happened to Twila."

"Twila?" Rosie was confused. What did that have to do with her? With Eric?

"The police are here at the office. They've questioned everybody. I told them you knew each other, were in the same business, and now they want to talk to you."

"Me?"

"It's crazy, but I get the feeling they think I had something to do with it."

Rosie heard her own pulse in her ears. "With what? What's happened to her?"

Lillian closed Rosie's laptop and began to clean up the tea things.

"I don't know. I guess she's missing."

"Why would…" Rosie felt eyes on her, and glanced up. Lillian stood with the tea tray in her hand staring at Rosie with a quizzical expression on her face.

"Rose, I can't talk now. I've got to get back. Just come, okay?"

"I'll be there in fifteen minutes."

"Is everything okay?" Lillian said after Rosie hung up.

Rosie began gathering her things. "I'm sure it's fine." She left the house in a hurry to get to Eric, but also to get away from Lillian.

Her thoughts spun into dark circles as she drove to the office. She'd wished Twila would go away. Only minutes ago. Now she was missing.

It was a strange coincidence. As ridiculous as it was, Rosie couldn't shake the feeling that she was in some way responsible. Rivalry, envy, resentment whatever you wanted to call it, she'd harbored it toward Twila. Held the emotion in her heart. At times she'd worried it would poison her, but she'd never imagined it could curse someone else.

# 4.4.5

Rosie threw open the door of Pacific Financial's new office and rushed inside. In a quick glance, she took in the tiny lobby, and row of glass front workspaces behind it. The size caused her a pang, but other worries crowded out the emotion.

"Hi, Barbara. I'm looking for my husband."

Barbara's eyes were bloodshot and tired. "He's in the conference room with the police."

"Where is the conference room?"

She pointed out the door Rosie had entered through. "We share it with the other businesses on this floor, but I would wait. They asked not to be interrupted. I could get you some coffee."

"No, thanks." Rosie turned toward a grouping of chairs against two of the lobby's walls. They didn't look comfortable. They had metal arms and sparsely padded blue fabric seats. Apparently, Twila wasn't going for comfort when she'd designed the space. Rosie sat. Barbara returned to her paperwork.

Rosie glanced around the room as she waited. It was nondescript, as if Twila had tried to be as bland as possible. The colors: oatmeal, smog-sky blue, and dirty white, were strikingly boring.

Was that the point? Were the muted colors supposed to have a soothing effect, calm high emotions? They engendered the opposite reaction in Rosie. They gave her nothing to hang onto, nothing to focus on, and allowed her mind to run wild. Which it did.

Why were the police more interested in Eric than the other staff members? *A naked foot.* What did they know that she didn't? *The foot massaged Twila's naked calf.* Did they believe Eric and Twila were close? *A red-soled shoe lay on its side.* Closer than their business relationship would imply?

She stood abruptly and began to pace. Barbara watched her for a long second, then began shuffling papers again.

What had happened to Twila? Was she dead? Missing? Injured? Had someone attacked her? Had she accused Eric of something?

She had no answers to the questions circling in her mind. She paused before Barbara's desk. "What's happening?" Her tone was strident. She cleared her throat and softened it. "Do you know anything?"

Barbara turned her palms up. "I don't. I'd tell you if I did. Want me to see how much longer they're going to be?" She pushed out of her chair. She wasn't gone long, and when she re-emerged, a woman followed her.

The woman was petite; Rosie would say thin, but that would have been incorrect. She was lean, but strong looking, athletic. Her skin was a beautiful shade of mahogany, a brown so deep it verged on black. She didn't wear a uniform, but her posture said cop. "Rosie Ring?"

"Yes."

"Investigator Sylla. Would you follow me?" Her accent was British. Surprising for a California cop.

Rosie followed her along a corridor and into a room, empty but for a long table surrounded by chairs. She pulled one seat out for Rosie, rounded the table and sat on the other side. She placed a tablet onto the table, tapped it, then looked at Rosie with a smile that was more feral than friendly. "So, you're Rose Ring, wife of Eric Ring?"

"Actually, my name is Rosamond. Most people call me Rosie."

"Very good, then Rosie. How do you know Twila Wilkes?"

How did she know Twila? That was a complicated question. They'd met for the first time at a neighborhood barbecue. Before Twila's business had taken off, she'd lived in a modest two bedroom not far from

Rosie's house. They'd hit it off that night, both with degrees in interior design. Twila had made a couple of disparaging remarks about their host's choice of furniture. Rosie had laughed about the wall color, and the floral ruffled shower curtain in the guest bathroom, and they'd become friends. Sort of.

"We're in the same industry."

"Decorating houses?"

"Interior design. Homes and commercial properties."

"That's right. Twila did this office, didn't she?"

Rosie nodded.

"Funny," Sylla said.

"What's funny?"

"That Pacific Financial didn't use your services instead of Ms. Wilkes. I'm assuming you'd have given them a friends and family discount."

Rosie stared at the detective. Her eyes were brown, the color of earth, overshadowed by enigmatic black. Rosie had the feeling they didn't miss any more than they revealed.

"Bob, ah Robert Thompson, was afraid the staff would see it as nepotism, but really what does this have to do with anything? Has something happened to Twila?"

Detective Sylla pursed her lips. "That's what we're trying to discover."

"What do you mean? Is she missing?"

Sylla ignored her question. "Since you two are in the same line of work, you must know much of the same crowd."

Rosie shrugged. "She works with more upscale clientele."

"More upscale than Jacob Rinehart?"

Rosie's jaw tightened. How would— Oh, the *Register* article. "He's my first client in that income bracket."

Sylla tapped onto her tablet. "So, you don't know any of her clients other than your husband?"

"Not current ones." Lillian and Sid came to mind, but she didn't say anything. Were they really Twila's clients now that Twila was missing?

"And the last time you saw Ms. Wilkes?"

"Saturday night. We were at a party together."

"Not since?"

"No."

"Okay." She handed Rosie her card. "Please let me know if you think of anything, or hear anything you think I should know about."

"Since I don't know what's going on, I don't know what you need to know." The subterfuge irritated Rosie. Twila must be missing, but why wouldn't the woman say so.

Sylla bowed her head. "I'm not at liberty to discuss the case, you understand?"

"Can I assume she's missing?"

"We can't assume anything at this point."

Rosie took the card the investigator held out to her, and turned to leave.

"One more thing." Sylla's words stopped her. "Your husband went to work on Monday?"

"Yes."

"Would you say he's a dedicated employee?"

"He's not an employee. He's a co-owner of the company. And yes, he's very dedicated."

"What time did he get home on Monday?"

"Early. One-thirty maybe."

"And he was home the rest of the day?"

"Yes."

"You were there with him?"

"I went out for a few hours. In the evening."

"From..."

"From about six to when the stores closed. Nine, I guess."

"Okay. Thanks then." She gave Rosie a smile and nod. Rosie felt like a grade school student who'd been dismissed by a teacher.

When she got to the lobby Eric was there, seated in one of the uncomfortable chairs, his head cradled in his hands. She hurried to him. "Are you okay? What did they—"

He took her arm abruptly. "I'm hungry. Let's go to Enzo's."

Rosie followed Eric and parked next to him. They walked through the business lot, past a florist shop, and into Enzo's, best pizza in Laguna Niguel. The lunch rush was over. It wasn't crowded.

Enzo, a New York transplant with a wide smile and an even wider mid-section, greeted them like they were long-lost family. He seated them in a booth near the rear of the restaurant, handed them menus, and bustled away.

Rosie picked up the menu. "What did they ask you?" She set it aside. "What's going on with Twila?" She wasn't hungry. "Do you think she did something illegal and skipped town?"

"One question at a time. My brain isn't fully firing," Eric said.

"Why did they keep you in the conference room for so long?"

"That's another question. And I don't know the answer. As to your first question: they asked me when I saw Twila last, and what my relationship to her was."

"What did you say?"

"The truth. The last time I saw her was on Saturday at the Halloween party, and that our relationship was professional."

"They questioned everybody at Pacific?"

"Yes. That detective, Sylla, talked to each one of us but grilled me for an hour."

"An hour? What about Bob?"

"In and out in fifteen minutes."

"Why focus on you?"

"I don't know. Maybe because I've been working the most closely with her."

A middle-aged waitress dropped off two glasses of water and asked if they needed another minute. They did.

"Something is going on," Eric said after the server walked away. "She didn't show up for the move on Monday, which was strange. She'd said she'd be there, and she's been on top of things."

"A missing person doesn't usually warrant a full investigation unless the person is a child."

"Or rich," Eric said.

"She's neither." Which meant there had to be another explanation.

"That's why I think it must be more. That and the saw."

Rosie froze. "The saw?"

Eric rubbed the thumb of his right hand along the top of the left. "The police had my saw in a plastic bag. Asked if it was mine. I said it was, but they wouldn't give it to me."

"A saw?"

"Yes, which makes me wonder if they found blood at her house, or in her car, or someplace."

"A saw?"

"Why do you keep saying that? Yes, a saw. I brought it to the new office to trim shelving and must have left it there."

"But why bag it and ask you about it?" Her mind flitted to a grisly movie she'd watched between her fingers once.

"To confirm it was mine I guess." His voice sounded tired. "Maybe Twila took it home with her, they found it at her house and jumped to conclusions."

The server returned, pen poised over a pad. Eric ordered a small pepperoni pizza. Rosie ordered an antipasto salad. She lowered her voice even though the waitress had walked away and was out of earshot. "What kind of conclusions?"

He leaned toward her. "That I'd been over there."

"Had you?"

His blue gaze fixed on her. "Had I been to her house?"

Rosie couldn't meet his eyes. She dropped her gaze to the red Formica table and nodded, afraid to hear the answer.

"No, Rose. I've never been to her house." The fatigue in his voice deepened.

The phone call on the night of John and Carol's party trotted into her mind. *I don't want her to be hurt.* That's what he'd said. It had sounded so personal, so intimate. She tried to shove the thought aside, but it wouldn't budge.

"I overheard a phone conversation." She paused. The air grew still between them. "That night at John and Carol's." Eric didn't move.

Rosie inhaled, then exhaled the story about how she'd gone outside to look for him and heard his half of a phone conversation.

"What made you think I was talking to Twila?" He said when she'd run out of words.

"Because you said you'd see whoever you were talking to the next morning. Twila was the one planning to be there."

He shook his head slowly. "I wish you'd have said something at the time. It's not what you think."

"Who didn't you want hurt?"

"Not you," he said.

"Who?"

He didn't say anything for a long moment then said, "Beth. One of the assistants. We were planning to let her go. I didn't want her to hear the news from Twila."

"How did Twila know?"

"She overheard me and Bob talking about it. She and Beth know each other outside the office. I didn't want her to say anything." Eric leaned away from her. "Are you done grilling me? I feel like I'm still talking to that cop."

The food came, but neither of them ate. Rosie pushed an olive around her plate with a fork. Eric sat with forearms on either side of his.

Rosie broke the silence. "I'm sorry. I should have asked you, but I didn't want to sound like a suspicious wife. You've got enough problems without me heaping more on you."

He put a hand on hers and squeezed her fingers. "It's okay. Look, Twila is probably away on a long weekend with a carpenter half her age. She's the least of our worries."

Rosie wasn't so sure. She speared the olive and ate it rather than disagreeing. Yesterday all she could think about was protecting her position with Jacob Rinehart. Today that seemed like ancient history. What mattered was her husband, her marriage, her family. Business concerns paled in comparison.

That's why she'd never be as successful as Twila. Twila didn't care about anything but business. Why had she been envious of the woman? Twila was missing and the only people the police questioned were clients and professional associates. She had no husband, no children.

Nobody was home wringing their hands waiting for news. Her success suddenly seemed empty.

Why were the police investigating Twila's... Twila's what? Her disappearance? And, why had that investigator thought Eric's saw was significant enough to bag?

A lump formed in Rosie's stomach. She pushed her salad away. She couldn't eat anymore. She wished she was comforted by Eric's words, but she wasn't. She didn't believe Twila was the least of their worries.

## 4.4.6

On Wednesday morning Eric left for work at the usual time as if nothing had happened the day before. Rosie wished she could compartmentalize the way he did. He'd always been able to lock up family dramas and focus on the tasks of the day. Not her.

When Ryan was being bullied, when Becca didn't get invited to the popular girl's birthday party, when Conner's grades tanked, Rosie was a basket case. Her family life and her professional life were a homogeneous blend, inseparable.

She hadn't even remembered to get Halloween candy despite the fact that it had been upfront and visible in the stores for weeks. She and Eric had sat in a darkened house the night before to hide from the trick-or-treaters. She was embarrassed. He didn't care.

Maybe it was too important to her to maintain the image of the perfect home, the perfect family. Eric had accused her of competing with the neighbors and the other PTA mothers in the past. She liked to think it was love, not rivalry.

This morning, she putted around her office, pulling things up on her computer but staring out the window instead of at the screen. She wandered into the kitchen and forgot why she was there. She opened the refrigerator but had no appetite. At 11:30 she decided to take Peach for a walk. She wasn't getting anything accomplished anyway.

Peach was delighted.

It was a lovely day, warm not hot, with a gentle on-shore breeze. She lived six miles inland and could smell a faint tang of salt in the air. This was her favorite kind of weather, but she hardly noticed it. Her mind and emotions were trapped in the bland lobby of the new Pacific Financial Offices waiting for news.

Less than a mile from her house, her cellphone jangled in her pocket. It was Jacob.

"Hi. You sound out of breath," he said.

"I'm walking."

"Ah. Hope I'm not interrupting—"

"No. Getting Peach out for some exercise."

"I won't keep you then. Just calling to let you to know all the guest room furniture arrived this morning. I had the delivery guys assemble it and set it up in the rooms, but I'm not sure it's the way you want it."

"How does it look?"

"I like it."

"Good. I can come by after lunch if that works for you."

Jacob didn't answer immediately, and Rosie heard the shuffling of paper. Then he said, "I'm leaving for LA in a couple of minutes, but Lupe will be here until 2:30."

"I'll be there well before 2:30."

"That works. If you need more time, she can show you how to lock up."

They said goodbye, and Rosie made a U-turn. The new furniture would distract her, and she needed a distraction today. Forty-five minutes later, she was in the car on the way to Laguna.

She had to pass the Nightshade to get to Jacob's and decided to stop in. She'd left the gorilla there the night of the party. Becca wouldn't forgive her if she lost it. Her first boyfriend had won it at the Orange County Fair and given it to her. It had sentimental value.

There was a parking spot on the Coast Highway in front of the courtyard that housed the gallery, a rare occurrence. Rosie maneuvered her SUV into it and turned off the engine. She jogged to the Nightshade's front door, and stopped. It was closed. That's right. Peter had told her he'd be out of town for a few days.

She returned to the curb with slower steps. It struck her again that it was strange for Peter to close the shop for so many days in a row. But he did have customers all around the country. He sold pieces online and shipped them. She guessed the days of relying solely on the income from a brick and mortar store were over.

Lupe opened the door when she rang the tower's bell. Fury leaped around Rosie like she was his long-lost mother. He was so enthusiastic even Lupe smiled—a rare occurrence. "He loves you," she said.

Rosie kneeled, and Fury rolled over. She scratched his stomach. "He's really settling in, isn't he?"

"Most of the time. When Mr. Jacob is in a bad mood, he's in a bad mood too."

"Dogs are intuitive." Rosie stood and brushed dog hair off her pants. "Have you seen the furniture yet?"

"Yes. I got here while the delivery men were putting it together."

Rosie moved toward the stairs. "How does it look?"

Lupe followed her. "It's beautiful. Very sturdy. I think Mr. Jacob would like a table and chairs for his office from the same company."

"Did he say that?" Rosie said.

"No. I just think so."

It was such a strange comment, Rosie was going to ask her to explain herself, but they reached the upper landing, and Lupe disappeared into the closest bedroom. The furniture looked like the showroom pieces had, a rare thing. If anything, it was nicer than Rosie remembered, the color warmer. However, as Jacob had guessed, it wasn't where she wanted it. "Do you have a minute?" she asked Lupe.

"Sure."

The two women lifted and pushed the furniture into position, then went to the next bedroom. They rearranged all the guest rooms but Cecily's. "Is she still here?" Rosie said, looking at the closed door.

"She left with Mr. Jacob. They had an appointment in LA, then he was going to take her to the airport."

Rosie opened the door to Cecily's room. The bed was unmade. There were towels on the bathroom floor, but the room looked warm and inviting. She wanted to make the others as attractive. "I haven't had a chance to clean in here yet," Lupe said.

Rosie waved away her concern. "Just looking for inspiration." Lupe ignored her, strode to the bed and began stripping it. Rosie left her to it.

The next hour passed in a blur of new linens, lamps, and mirrors. Rosie was banging a picture hook into the wall above a dresser when Lupe came in. "I need to leave now. Can I show you how to set the alarm?"

Rosie set aside her hammer and followed Lupe downstairs. "You picking up your son from school?"

"Yes."

"He must be feeling better."

"This has been a good week."

"I'm glad. There's nothing worse than a sick child. When my oldest was three the doctors told me he had a heart murmur. I was a mess for at least a month."

Lupe's brow furrowed. "Is he okay?"

"He's fine. The murmur is still there, but nothing ever came of it. He'll never have to go to war if we ever reinstate the draft. That's the only impact it's had on him."

"Then it's a blessing." Lupe didn't sound as if she felt blessed. Her tone was somber.

"Your son won't have to go to war either." Rosie said, hoping to lighten the mood.

Lupe nodded. "Yes, a silver coating."

"Lining."

"Lining." Lupe struck her forehead with the heel of her palm. "I forget all the American expressions."

"I think you're doing great. If it wasn't for your lovely accent, I'd guess you were born here."

"Thank you, but I think you're being kind."

"No. Really. How long have you been in the States?"

"I came here from Nicaragua when I was pregnant with Luis. He's a citizen." She said the last words with pride.

"Did you come alone?"

"No." Lupe looked at her shoes, and Rosie worried she'd asked too much. A long second later, the woman met Rosie's eyes. "I came with my husband. He left us after Luis was diagnosed. He wasn't happy to have a… " She paused. "A defective child."

Heat flushed Rosie's cheeks. What kind of man leaves a woman in a foreign country with a sick kid? "You're better off without him." She blurted out the words without thinking.

Lupe shrugged. "In some ways."

She showed Rosie how to set the alarm and set off to her car. Rosie stood in the doorway and watched until she pulled away from the curb. She admired the woman. It must be difficult, starting over in a new country with an unwell child and no family to help. Maybe Rosie could recommend her services to some of her clients. If Lupe had time. She seemed pretty busy between Jacob and Lillian, but Rosie could ask. She wanted to show her support for the woman.

She shut the door and climbed the stairs. After another hour of pounding in nails and hanging pictures, she walked from room to room and surveyed her work. Three out of six bedrooms still had nothing but a single mirror on their walls.

Unlike the paint, furniture, and bedding, Rosie hadn't wanted the art in every room to be identical. No cheap prints for Jacob. He liked to collect, and these rooms were a good place to display the work of lesser known artists, maybe even some local ones.

The Coastal Gallery was close, about a fifteen-minute walk. After she cleaned up, she'd head over there and see if they had any smaller pieces, maybe something by the artist who'd painted the picture of the fortress Jacob had already purchased.

She gathered the paper and plastic wrappings that littered the floor and headed to the back stairway into the kitchen and through a side door to the outside trash cans. After dumping her load, she returned the way she'd come. At the top of the stairs her eye fell on the attic door.

She could take another look at the art Jacob already owned before going shopping. When she'd browsed through before, she'd been focused on Cecily's room and the larger spaces. She hadn't really been thinking about the guest rooms.

She banged on the door. "Okay spiders, run away." She gave them a minute to obey, opened the door, flipped on the overhead light and climbed the attic steps. The unpolished wood floor creaked as she stepped into the storage room. Orange-gold daylight streamed through the small window at its far end creating a pathway of light across its length.

The last time she'd been here the sun had been high in the sky and most of the space had been in shadow. Now she could see the entire room. It appeared to stretch all the way to the street, the length of the building. She decided to look out the front window, see if she was right.

Rosie made her way past the piles of Jacob's things and stepped onto the empty plank floor beyond. The wide sunbeam shone like a spotlight, and for a moment she was reminded of stepping onto that stage she'd so gracefully danced off years ago. She paused for a second then walked to the other end of the house, her steps clacking with purpose.

The window did look onto Cliff Drive. Through it, she could see over neighboring rooftops to the Coast Highway and almost as far south as the Coastal Gallery. *The Coastal Gallery.* That reminded her of why she'd come up here in the first place. It would be dark soon. She should get going.

After examining Jacob's stack of pictures again, she found one painting that would work in the small guest rooms. She pulled it from the pile, and as she did, she heard a rip. The hook had caught on the heavy paper backing of another piece.

She set aside the painting she was planning to use and lifted the one with the rip to assess the damage. Thank goodness only the backing had torn. Peter could fix it easily enough. She fingered the paper trying to guess the gauge and noticed there was what appeared to be another painting underneath it. Why would someone use a work of art rather than heavy cardboard to secure the frame?

Rosie hesitated, but only for a moment. She had to replace the paper, so she might as well give it a good tear and satisfy her curiosity. She grunted with understanding as soon as she saw what was beneath.

It was a portrait, a very amateurish portrait, of a woman. Who, Rosie was sure, wouldn't thank the painter if she saw it. Her skin tone had a blueish tinge that would have fit right in with some of the zombie paintings at the Nightshade. The scale was off, the neck too thin, the hands too large, yet there was something arresting about it.

Rosie carried it under the light. It was the eyes. They were a striking shade of green. They were Jacob's eyes. She remembered him saying his therapist told him to take up a hobby, and he'd tried painting but was terrible at it. This must have been one of his attempts. He'd probably used the canvas as backing because he wasn't happy with it. She folded the paper over the portrait again and returned it to the stack. She'd take it to Peter next time she went to the Nightshade.

Rosie left the attic and carried the painting she planned to use into its intended bedroom. After patting Fury goodbye and setting the alarm the way Lupe had shown her, she headed toward the Coastal Gallery on foot.

# 4.4.7

Rosie followed Cliff Drive through the North Laguna neighborhood and into Heisler Park. As she walked, the sky had faded from bright orange to blood red. Now it was the purple of old bruises.

Minutes after she entered the park the sun slipped beneath the horizon, and the last of the sunset worshipers headed for home. Soon the park was empty. Rosie wished she had Peach, or even Fury. She only had another quarter-mile to go on the cliff walk, however. Then she'd turn inland to the Coast Highway where there were people and lights. She picked up her pace.

A ground light popped on near her feet. Then another up ahead, and another. A side path was illuminated on her left. She knew it led up a short hill to a lookout bench. She'd sat there many times with Eric enjoying the sunset before walking into town for dinner. She didn't have much farther to go.

She passed the path, rounded a bend lush with shrubs, and headed toward an open area near the public restrooms where her children used to throw Frisbees. A dark shape lay in a puddle of light on the grass. As she drew closer, she saw it was a shoe. In a few more steps, she recognized it. A black Louboutin pump with a red sole. She stopped.

The image of a naked foot, black pump discarded, rubbing the back of a calf invaded her mind. Something heavy settled on her chest. No. There had to be hundreds of black Louboutin pumps in Southern California, all of them with a red sole. Like Twila's.

She bent and reached out a hand, but yanked it back before she touched the shoe. What if it was evidence?

Evidence of what? She was being melodramatic. A shoe. That's all this was. Someone must have taken them off to walk in the grass, dropped one but hadn't noticed. But even as that thought sprang into her mind, she doubted it. These were very expensive shoes. People were careful with expensive things.

She could call the police, but what would she say? She'd found a shoe? She pivoted, one hand on her head, and gazed back the way she'd come. She didn't know what she was looking for. A passerby she could talk to, the owner of the shoe, inspiration? What she saw made her heart thud harder.

Another shoe, black with a red sole.

This one hid halfway beneath the shrubbery she'd passed moments before, camouflaged by the leaves. From where she now stood, she could see it clearly. It looked like the mate of the one at her feet.

She walked, almost against her will, toward it and stopped again. Dropping a shoe out on the grass, she understood that. How could this shoe have ended up here, in this spot? Someone would have had to toss it under the bushes, unless...

Her gaze traveled up the slope behind the shrubbery to where the bench sat. Unless it fell from there, tumbled down the hill and dropped through the branches. It was the only thing that made sense.

She couldn't see the bench from her vantage point, couldn't see if anyone was sitting there. She would have to walk around the bushes and climb the path to satisfy her curiosity. Why did she care? Maybe a young couple had kicked off their shoes and ripped off their clothes on their way and were making passionate love on the bench at that moment.

There weren't any men's shoes on the path, on the grass, or in the bushes. No other articles of clothing. And people who could afford Louboutin pumps could afford a hotel room.

The arguments in her brain made sense—common sense. She

circled the bushes anyway. Most likely there was no one up there, the owner of the shoes long gone. Twila's bare foot, her empty shoe, paraded behind her eyes. Rosie stepped onto the path.

Two stars were out now. A small crescent moon seemed to bob in the sky as she walked. She felt like the heroine of a teen slasher flick. She could hear the audience screaming, "Don't go up there."

Twila was missing—or something. The police had questioned Eric. The shoes were a crazy coincidence, she was sure of it, but she had to look. For Eric's sake.

For Twila's sake. They'd been friends once. At least, Rosie had thought they were friends. They'd shared client stories and color wheels in those early days. Twila had worked for a big design firm. Rosie was just getting her feet wet, working on her own. Things hadn't gone south until Twila had asked Rosie to join her new firm, TW Designs, and Rosie had declined.

Twila hadn't seemed upset, but the comment she'd made haunted Rosie many times since. "We'll be rivals then," she'd said and laughed. It wasn't a nice laugh.

Rosie had joined in anyway, then said something silly like, of course they wouldn't be. Nothing would have to change, but it had. She wondered if Twila ever missed those days, envied Rosie's hands-on, personal career. Doubtful.

The path opened onto a small, paved area. In its center, facing the ocean, was the bench. No one was seated on it. She would see a head above its back if someone was there. If someone was lying down, however, she wouldn't be able to see them.

She made a wide circle, staying as far away from the bench as possible. Despite her anxiety, a smile cracked through the tense muscles of her face. She thought of Peach on the day they took her to rattlesnake avoidance training.

The trainers put a shock collar around her dog's neck and led her toward a rattlesnake they'd planted in the grass. The snake was alive, but it was muzzled. Eric had later joked that rattlesnake muzzler had to be one of the worst jobs on the planet.

The first time Peach saw the snake, she trotted forward, curious, tail wagging. As soon as she was within a foot of it, the trainer shocked her. It was awful to watch. Rosie's sweet dog yelped and spun around looking for whatever had pinched her tail. It had worked. The next time the trainer walked her toward a snake, she gave it a wide berth.

There was no snake on the bench, but it wasn't empty. Rosie saw a bare foot, a woman's foot, extending off the wood seat. She couldn't see the woman's face, but she recognized the foot. At least, she thought she did. She sucked in a shaky breath and walked closer, to be sure.

The form was still. She thought about trying to shake the woman awake. She wasn't dressed like the kind of woman who would pass out on a park bench alone at night, though. She wore an expensive black pants suit, just like the one Twila wore the night Rosie had seen her with Jacob at the Coastal Gallery.

Rosie sidestepped and faced the bench. There was nothing now between her and the form that lay there in a fetal position, head and arms curled so tightly their definition was lost. She paused, uncertain what to do. Contradicting thoughts screamed in her head. The woman is hurt, or ill. Help her.

There's no rise and fall of breath. She's dead.

The woman is sleeping something off.

She's dead.

The woman is Twila.

She's dead.

Rosie opened her mouth to call Twila's name, but shut it again. Because she saw something else, and knew there was no point. On the ground next to the bench was a book. It was Jacob's book. It was *Pillory*.

**MOLLY:** What? Twila Wilkes is dead. Rosie and the police must have considered that was a possibility, but did anyone expect her to be the next Pillory victim? I didn't when I first heard the story. And poor Rosie. Finding the body had to be the kind of experience nightmares are made of.

This new development raises a lot of questions in my mind, but before we get into that, let's hear what Patient Zero has to say.

# patient zero

Excerpt of Recorded patient
interview from the files of Dr. Lewis Carver:

As soon as I saw her, I knew she was trouble. My brother was besotted. Her skirts were too short, her lipstick and her hair too red, and her smile too phony. I tried to warn him, but he'd stopped listening to me by then. Teenage boys aren't known for their circumspection. Despite the reputation she had for breaking boys' hearts, he asked her to the Winter Formal.

Dad and the stepmom were thrilled. My brother had been a bit withdrawn since Mom's death, and they looked at this as a sign he was getting over it. I didn't agree. She actually reminded me of Mom.

Oh, she didn't look like her. Not at all. She was pretty in a trying-too-hard kind of way. People said Mom had been pretty once, but I never saw it. No. It was her personality that reminded me of Mom. She had a mean streak.

Once she got those ruby red claws into my brother, he didn't have a chance. He was like a rabbit caught by a hawk. He jumped and bowed and scurried whenever she snapped her fingers. It made me sick. I tried to stay out of the way, but the few times we did meet I could tell Mean Girl—MG, for short—didn't like me much either.

The night of the Winter Formal came, and I decided to tag along to keep an eye on things. I stayed in the shadows. Neither of them knew I was there. Not at first anyway.

I watched them dance, and show off for friends, and spike their punch—all the things you'd expect to see at a high school dance. I began to think I'd been overreacting. MG was behaving herself, and my brother was having fun.

I was thinking about fading away when the band struck up a song I especially liked, so I stayed a little longer. Good thing. Turned out my brother needed me. I was standing in the corner tapping my foot to the music, watching the couples wiggle by when I heard a hoot.

It came from a caveman brain-dead jock who was showing his appreciation the only way caveman brain-dead jocks know how. He was hooting because MG and Nat Gray were sucking face.

Nat was one of those big athletic guys that grow into fat slobs by the age of thirty. High school is their heyday. MG dated him on and off the year before until he dumped her for a brunette who played flute in the marching band. I'd never understood that one.

Anyway, there they were on the other side of the gym making out. I did my best to distract my brother. Tried to get him to leave, but he wasn't having any of it. He saw them, marched across the room, and got his lights punched out by Nat.

You'd think that would teach him—the black eye, the humiliation. It didn't. He couldn't get it through his thick head that MG and Nat were together. My brother might be mild mannered, but he's stubborn.

He did the Romeo thing. He moped outside MG's window at night, left flowers on her doorstep, stuck love sonnets into the crack of her locker. She didn't want anything to do with him. Kept telling him to get lost.

If she'd have left it at that, I probably wouldn't have stepped in. But, as I mentioned, she had a mean streak. She lured him, then mocked him. She gave the sonnets to the football team, and they were turned into locker room chants. She tripped him when he walked by her desk in class.

The final straw came on a cold winter afternoon after gym class. My brother had jumped into the shower to rinse off, and while he was soaping up Nat and the other boys on the team left the locker room. MG and others of her ilk sneaked in.

When my brother turned off the water, he found a crowd of jeering high school girls instead of a towel. He hid in the stall shivering until the bell went off, and the girls left. Then he ran, dripping, to his locker. But Nat had pried it open and left a juvenile note in place of his clothes.

My brother waited, naked, wet and cold, for a full twenty minutes until the next class began filing in and a compassionate kid lent him a pair of sweats. My brother ended up with walking pneumonia.

While he recovered, I pondered.

My brother had never been what you'd call a popular kid. He was quiet. He'd never drawn this kind of abuse, though. It was MG. She was the problem.

I'd started studying her habits when she and my brother began dating just in case something like this happened. I knew the whens and wheres of her life. It didn't take me long to come up with a plan.

MG took jazz dance classes at a private studio about a half mile from her house on Tuesday evenings. I'd watched her through the big picture window a half dozen times. She was terrible, but I digress.

The important thing was, she always took a short cut through an alley on her way home. She'd started doing it in the early fall when the sun didn't set until seven or eight and never stopped. It was a stupid thing to do in the winter when it was dark. Later, everyone agreed on that point.

One Tuesday night at 5:15, I took up my post behind a Dumpster. At 5:25 I heard her footsteps. When she passed my hiding place, I stepped out, raised a large rock over my head and slammed it into hers.

I hit her ten or eleven times just to be sure. It takes a lot more force to kill someone than you'd think. In movies the bad guy whacks some-body once, and they die. Not so in real life, I can attest to that.

I'd have liked to leave her alive so that when I stripped her, she'd feel cold and ashamed like my brother had, but I had to be satisfied with a symbolic gesture. When I left her, she was past feeling anything.

I took her clothes and the rock and started walking. Wednesday was trash day. Most people put their cans out the night before. I walked a mile or so from the alley and buried her clothes in a metal can under a bag of garbage, making sure no one saw me. Then I walked to the river and dumped the rock into the water.

I thought about the geeky kid's red wagon as I watched it disappear. Then I wiped my hands on my jeans, and headed home. It's not that hard to get rid of problems. You just have to be proactive, stop whining, and get it done.

**MOLLY:** And there you have it. The secret of success from the point of view of a murderer—be proactive, stop whining and get it done. His or her body count is now three that we know of, the mother, MG, and the Radio Flyer wagon.

Do you believe Patient Zero also killed Twila and the flight attendant? The MO in those murders was different than the ones recorded in the transcripts we've heard thus far. The bodies in the transcripts were intact—no missing heads and hands.

Of course, the transcripts must have something to do with the *Pillory* crimes or I wouldn't be reading them. But do you think we have more than one killer on our hands? Let's talk about it on the Facebook page.

Join me next time for more *Murders Under the Sun*.

**(cue music)**

**VO:** This episode is brought to you by The Fishbowl, your place for Pilates in the OC. *Murders Under the Sun* is edited by Jim Wilbourne, theme music is by Eclectic Blends, and I'm your host, Molly Shure.

# part six

# MURDER UNDER THE SUN
## SEASON FOUR; EPISODE FIVE

**MOLLY:** Welcome to episode five of *The Tower*. I'm Molly Shure, your host.

I received a lot of "duhs" and hand-to-forehead emojis this week. You all, without exception, believe there is only one killer—Patient Zero. And he, or she, murdered both Twila and the woman in the park. Which brings Patient Zero's body count up to four, minus the wagon. This week you'll find out if you're right.

Many of you took the question a step further and tried to guess who Patient Zero is. Some believed it was Twila Wilkes and were disappointed to move her into the victim category.

I get it. She was a good suspect primarily because we knew something was up with her, and she was—not to speak ill of the dead—unlikable. We also knew she spent time in Seattle because of her *Orange County Lifestyles* magazine spread. The backyard in the article was decorated with blown glass in the style of the Seattle Chihuly Garden and Glass Museum.

Now that Twila is out of the running, some have moved their suspicions to Eric, Rosie's husband. He also spent time in Seattle on business. He's been acting suspicious and if he was having affairs… Well, people have killed for less.

Others of you made a case for Peter of The Nightshade Gallery. He's certainly odd and has been making Seattle treks as well. Rosie also mentioned in one of the first episodes that he had a sibling, although she couldn't remember if it was a brother or a sister.

And, of course, some thought it was Jacob Rinehart, who we know was in all the right places at all the right times.

However, at this point in the story, Rosie doesn't know who the murderer is, therefore neither do we. Let's pickup where we left off last week, and see if we get any additional clues.

# 4.5.2

Despite the warmth of the blanket, Rosie couldn't stop shivering. It wasn't cold in the police station. She was in shock. The objective part of her brain registered that fact, and the fact that she wasn't in danger. Apparently, the emotional part of her brain hadn't caught up with the facts.

A policeman brought her a cup of coffee, hot and full of cream and sugar. She didn't usually take sugar, but the objective brain acknowledged she might need it, so she sipped. Investigator Sylla sat across from her patiently waiting for the answer to her question. "What made you walk up the path to the bench?"

Rosie took another sip of the coffee and focused on the comforting feeling of hot liquid traveling down her throat. She set the cup on the table and wrapped the blanket around herself again. "It was the shoes."

"The shoes?"

"Yes. I recognized them. At least, I thought I recognized them."

Sylla arched an eyebrow. "They're black pumps."

"Louboutin black pumps."

Confusion crossed the detective's face, and Rosie glanced at her footwear. She wore practical shoes. They had soft soles. They tied. They were shoes you could chase a criminal in. Detective Sylla wasn't a fashionista.

"They're very expensive, and they have a red sole. They stand out."
Rosie said.

Sylla made a note on her tablet. "Okay, then. You recognized the
shoes as, ah, Louboutin and you knew Twila Wilkes has a pair like
them."

Rosie nodded.

"Can I ask you something?"

Rosie stifled what could have become a hysterical giggle. That's what
the woman had been doing for the past half hour—asking her something. Why did she need permission now? Sylla didn't wait for it
anyway, the question came without a beat.

"Do you memorize all your friends' clothing choices? Or is it shoes
that interest you? Or just Twila Wilkes's shoes?"

Rosie felt her cheeks flush. How could she explain? She couldn't tell
the detective about the incident in Eric's office. Not only was it embarrassing, it would implicate Eric. Make it seem as if Rosie was concerned
about Eric and Twila's relationship. Which she was, but an affair was a
long way from murder. "I like shoes," she said. Her head began to ache.

Sylla didn't respond for a long moment. Rosie had the uncomfortable feeling that the answer didn't satisfy her. Gwen dealt with the
detective during what was dubbed the Real Estate Murders and
respected her. Rosie could understand why. The woman seemed to see
right through you. If Rosie had committed a crime, she wouldn't want
to be seated across the table from her.

Sylla let the shoe drop and returned to the original question. "So,
the bench?"

"After I saw the first shoe, I saw the other one under the bushes. I
thought it had to have fallen from above."

Sylla set her tablet on the table and leaned back in her chair. "You
saw Jacob Rinehart today?"

The shift in questioning took Rosie by surprise. Her heart rate, still
elevated from the shoe questions, sped up even more, and a new bout of
shivering wracked her body. Not because she minded answering questions about Jacob. It was a relief to change the subject, but in her
current state anything unexpected seemed to set off a physical chain
reaction. "No. I spoke with him, but I didn't see him."

"You said you walked from his home into the park at about 5:30."

"I did. I'd been working there alone."

"You have a key?"

Rosie shook her head. "His housekeeper let me in."

"Her name?"

Rosie told her.

"What time did you talk to Rinehart?"

"I don't know. Around 11:30 this morning, I think."

"When you were done working, at 5:30, you locked up, and instead of getting in your car, decided to walk through the park to..." she leaned forward and scrolled on her tablet. " ...The Coastal Gallery?"

Rosie nodded.

"Did Rinehart know Twila Wilkes?"

Another abrupt change in direction. It didn't throw Rosie as badly this time. She was getting used to Sylla's erratic style of questioning. "As far as I know they'd met a few times."

The door to the conference room opened, and a uniformed officer stuck his head in. "Eric Ring is here. He's asking for his wife."

The door closed, and Sylla returned her gaze to Rosie. "You look like you need a stiff drink and a hot bath."

She was human after all. Rosie hadn't been sure, but now saw a hint of something in the detective's unreadable eyes that could be compassion. "That sounds wonderful," Rosie said.

Sylla stood. "If you think of anything else, you know where to find me."

Rosie followed her into the station lobby where Eric waited. He opened his arms when he saw her, and she walked into them. After assuring himself that she was all right, he led her to the car. They didn't speak on the ride home.

Instead of a bath, Rosie settled on the couch with a blanket and watched Eric build a fire in the fireplace. Peach curled up on the floor next to her sensing Rosie's need for comfort. Eric's shoulders were tense, his movements jerky. He spoke in single words, no sentences. Maybe he was absorbing the shock that was leaking out of Rosie.

For her, the event had become like something she'd read about, something that had happened to someone else. Her climb to the bench was a movie she'd once seen. The emotions that had gone through her weren't hers but ones she was told about.

When she saw the copy of *Pillory,* she knew Twila was dead. It was all very logical. She knew the reason she couldn't see a head or hands wasn't because of the tight fetal position of the body. It was because they weren't there. And that was when her amygdala took over.

She'd run. As fast and as far from the awful object on the bench as she could, calling 911 as she went. She ran down the path, onto the cliff walk, across the grass, and to the street. Then she'd huddled in the light of a street lamp and waited for the police.

She would've called Eric, but the dispatcher kept her on the phone until the first black and white arrived. It hadn't taken long. Laguna Beach didn't have many murders and those they did have were usually domestic. By the time she got into Sylla's car to go to the station, Cliff Drive was lit up like Hollywood Boulevard.

Once the fire was blazing, Eric disappeared into the kitchen. A few minutes later he re-emerged with a drink in each hand. He set one on the coffee table next to her, then sank into a chair and stared at the flames.

Rosie reached for the glass. It was whiskey, neat. "They're going to try to blame Jacob."

"Why would he kill her?"

"I don't know. I just think that's what the detective thinks."

Eric's blue gaze shifted to her. "That makes no sense. Not after the conversation we had at the Halloween party."

Rosie waited for him to elaborate. He did. "He told me about the mob that gathered outside his house in Seattle every day, about the hate mail, about the media's invasion of his privacy. He's a victim, not a murderer. Like me. Like Bob. We may be alive, but we're casualties of someone else's crime."

"Who then?"

"Somebody who has a vendetta against him?"

"Why Twila?"

"Wrong place, wrong time? I don't know. Why the flight attendant?"

Silence fell again. Rosie's brain throbbed with unanswered questions. She studied Eric's face, as if she might find the answers there.

He was pale in the flickering firelight, a black and white version of himself. It struck her, she wasn't sure she knew this version. She'd married a full-color man, a man with changing shades and hues that had delighted and intrigued her. It was as if he'd been bleached, been through the wash too many times.

Evil did that to a person. She felt like a faded version of herself tonight. She took a long pull from her drink and closed her eyes.

## 4.5.3

Honey arrived as Eric left for work. Rosie had fallen asleep on the couch the night before. He'd covered her with a second blanket and gone to bed. She was there still, afraid to get up, afraid of what the day would hold.

Honey pushed Rosie's feet out of the way and sat at the end of the couch, her face a mask of concern. "I just heard. Are you okay?"

"I'm fine. Want coffee?"

Honey shook her head. "Have you talked to Jacob yet?"

"No. I'm sure the police were at his door last night."

"You think they suspect him?"

Rosie shrugged one shoulder. "They must. It doesn't look good. He moves to Laguna and there's another *Pillory* murder right here in SoCal."

"But why would he leave copies of his books like calling cards for the cops? That doesn't make sense. Murderers want to cover their tracks, at least they do on TV."

Rosie reached for the coffee Eric had left for her on the coffee table. It was lukewarm. She wanted a fresh cup, but she was too apathetic to get it. "I don't know what to think."

"Are you afraid to go there? Back to work?"

"Part of me is, but not because I think he's dangerous. He's a nice man. He's gentle. It seems like tragedy follows him around, you know?"

Honey nodded. Rosie assumed it was less in agreement and more in encouragement, so she continued. "We've become friends, not close friends, but it's more than a professional relationship. We're a lot alike—introverted, a little unsure of ourselves, more likely to run than fight. I can't see him committing such a... "

A vision of the body on the bench flitted across the screen of her mind, and she shuddered. "...horrible act."

Neither woman said anything for a long moment. Honey broke the silence. "We never really know people though, do we?" Then she patted Rosie's leg. "How about breakfast?"

Rosie was about to say no. She hadn't thought she was hungry, but her stomach rumbled when she heard the word breakfast. She followed Honey into the kitchen and sat at the counter. They'd been friends so long, Honey knew her kitchen almost as well as Rosie knew it herself. She soon had an omelet sizzling on the stove.

Honey dished up eggs, toast, and made a fresh pot of coffee. They took their breakfast into the dining room. As Rosie dug into the omelet's cheesy warmth, she realized she hadn't eaten anything since lunch the day before. She ate all the eggs, mopped up melted cheese with her last bite of toast then pushed the empty plate away, feeling stronger. "I should call Jacob."

Honey agreed. "You have to find out what's going on."

Rosie found her cell phone in her purse in the front hall and dialed. It rang so many times she was about to hang up when a female voice answered. "Hello?"

She looked at her phone screen to be sure she'd hit the right number. She had. "Hi, is Jacob there?"

"Is this Rosie?" Rosie recognized Lupe's voice by the way she said her name with a slight lift on the second syllable.

"Lupe? What are you doing with Jacob's phone?" Rosie realized she sounded rude. "I mean, it's not your usual day to be at the house."

"Mr. Jacob asked me to come over and feed Fury and take him for a walk. He was supposed to go to LA early this morning."

"He didn't?"

"No. He's in the apartment with a detective." Lupe's voice grew strained. "I heard on the news they found another dead woman."

Rosie had been thinking about going to Laguna. She wanted to talk to Jacob, to find out if he'd had time to make plans. If he'd thought about selling the tower last week because one local news van was out front, he'd be certain to do it now. It was more than that, however.

She'd been pulled into this drama in a way she'd never dreamed. If it wasn't so horrible she'd laugh. Eric had been afraid of bad press. He'd acted like Rinehart had a communicable disease. It had never entered either of their wildest imaginations she'd be the one to find the second *Pillory* victim.

"Yes," Rosie said in a soft voice.

"I don't know what to do."

"There's nothing you can do. Just feed Fury and take him for a walk."

"I can't."

"You can't?"

"There are people out front. Newspaper people. TV people."

Bad news travels fast as Rosie's father always said. Of course, they'd be there, swarming over the sidewalks, blocking traffic. "You could leave by the side door and go out through the trash area."

"I tried. They're there too, right outside the gate. I'm supposed to go to another job in a half hour. What if they are still here? What if they are still here when I have to get Luis?" Lupe's voice tightened like she was struggling to hold in tears.

Rosie spoke in soothing tones. "They're not there to talk to you. They want Jacob. Just put your head down and don't say anything."

"But..." And this time she did sob.

Rosie didn't enjoy being the center of attention, didn't like crowds, but Lupe's reaction to this situation seemed extreme even to her. She moved toward the living room, toward her jacket and purse. "Lupe, I'm going to come over."

"No, you don't—"

"I know you're upset. I can hear it in your voice."

"I am, but what can you do?"

Rosie glanced into a mirror. She needed to change, to clean up before she went anywhere. "Nothing probably. Moral support."

"You don't mind?" Lupe sounded calmer.

"No. I want to see Jacob anyway. I'll get there as soon as I can." Rosie said goodbye, and they hung up.

Honey leaned against the couch, arms folded over her chest. "You're going to Laguna?"

"I have to."

"And why on God's green earth is that?"

"Lupe needs me. Maybe Jacob needs me."

"Who is Lupe?"

"Jacob's housekeeper. She's terrified. The press is outside, and she's worried she won't be able to get out to her other jobs."

"That wouldn't be Lupe Perez would it?"

"I'm not sure what her last name is."

"Pretty woman, walks and talks like the Queen of England with a Spanish accent?"

"That's her."

"She certainly gets around."

"What do you mean?"

"She works for Marybeth, the woman I did the cooking party for last month."

"How do you know?"

"She was there, helping. I think she works for Estelle too."

"Bob's Estelle? Estelle Thompson?"

Honey nodded. Rosie couldn't imagine how Estelle could afford a housekeeper with all the problems Pacific Financial had been through. She and Eric had made major cutbacks and assumed Bob and Estelle had done the same. "Wonder how she pays for that."

"Maybe she doesn't work for Estelle anymore, but I'm pretty sure she did at one point. They definitely know each other."

Impatience tickled the back of Rosie's neck. "Well, regardless of who she knows or doesn't know, she needs someone to help her now."

"I don't see why it has to be you."

"Why not me?"

Honey widened her eyes and spoke slowly, as if she were addressing a deaf octogenarian with dementia, "Because you found the body."

Rosie blinked.

"If those reporters have even an inkling it was you that found Twila, they're going to be on you like ticks on a hound. Besides, what are you going to do for Lupe? Throw a bag over her head and steer her through the crowd? She's going to have to face them if she goes in or out of that place for the next month."

Rosie began rinsing dishes and throwing them into the dishwasher. Honey was right, what could she do? But the question didn't stop the growing sense of responsibility that had dropped into her shoulders. If she hadn't decided to walk through the park the night before, if she hadn't recognized the shoe, if she hadn't gone to investigate, Twila might have lain there all night. Some other poor soul would have found her.

But it wasn't some other poor soul. It was her. She'd found the body and now, as absurd as it was, she felt... Responsible wasn't exactly the right word. The killer was responsible. She felt involved, connected, a part of a small community who'd been impacted personally by the crime. They might be an unwilling tribe of mismatched people, but they were a tribe.

She slammed the dishwasher door and pivoted. "I know it doesn't make sense, but I have to go. I want to help. And I want to see Jacob. I'm worried about him."

Honey uncrossed her arms and left the living room. She returned a moment later with a sweater. "I'll go with you."

"I don't—"

"I'm going." Her lips formed a stubborn line Rosie recognized. It was useless to try and change her mind when she looked like that.

## 4.5.4

When Rosie turned onto Cliff Drive, she was glad to have Honey's solid presence in the car beside her. She'd be even happier to have her alongside as they pushed through the mass of reporters crowding the tower.

They parked halfway up the block and approached on foot. Rosie tugged the baseball cap she'd borrowed from Eric a little lower and adjusted her sunglasses. Two reporters, a good-looking man in a windbreaker with his station logo on the breast pocket, and a woman, blond and predictably pretty, watched them. Their expressions reminded Rosie of Peach's when a ball was in play.

As soon as it became apparent that Rosie and Honey were headed to the tower, the pair left the group, microphones extended, and ran toward them. "Are you friends with Jacob Rinehart?"

"Can you tell us anything about his state of mind in light of the recent discovery of another body?"

"I'll bet he's not as cheerful about it as you all are," Honey said under her breath.

Rosie grabbed Honey's arm and dragged her forward dodging a barrage of questions as the rest of the group realized where they were headed. She'd sent a text to Jacob's phone before they parked, and hoped either he or Lupe would be waiting by the door to let them in.

The reporters legally couldn't follow them onto the property and yelled their questions across the grass. Rosie raised her hand to knock, but the door opened before she got the chance. She and Honey ducked inside, and it slammed behind them.

The quiet in the dim hallway was a balm after the commotion outside. She stood, back against the door for a long moment to slow her hammering heart. The hush that enveloped her was comforting and disturbing at the same time. It could've been the contrast between what was on either side of the door, but she felt something was missing.

"Wow," Honey said.

Despite everything, Rosie smiled. She'd forgotten Honey had never been inside the tower. Rosie allowed herself to relive the awe she'd felt the first time she crossed the threshold. It was an impressive sight, the long, long hallway culminating in radiant blue like a near death experience—the bright light at the end of the tunnel.

"Thank you for coming." Lupe's voice was almost a whisper, as if she was afraid the reporters could hear her through the thick wood door.

"Are the police still here?" Rosie said.

She shook her head. "They just left. He's in the apartment."

Rosie and Honey followed her in that direction, Honey's head swiveling right and left as they passed open doorways. "I'm surprised they didn't take him into the station," Rosie said.

"I think they didn't want to make him walk outside." Lupe wrapped her arms around herself as if the thought left her cold. Rosie wondered again why the woman felt so threatened by the news cameras. Maybe it was something to do with her past, the reason she'd left Nicaragua.

As they entered the apartment Rosie realized what she'd felt was missing in the hallway, Fury. Where were the frantic barks and scrabbling paws that usually greeted her? "Where's Fury?" she said when she saw Jacob.

"Hello to you too," Jacob said.

"Sorry, hi. But where is Fury?"

"He's been crated. He had an accident."

"I didn't walk him," Lupe said, her gaze on a wet looking spot near the couch.

"Good thing we don't have the new rugs yet." Jacob's tone was droll. Rosie had expected him to be upset, shaky, emotional, the way he'd been the day they'd discovered the local news van out front, but he wasn't. He was composed. As cool as an ocean breeze.

Honey jammed an elbow into her ribs. "Jacob, this is Honey. Honey, Jacob," Rosie said.

"The master chef. I know Honey from the Halloween party."

"That's right, you were there," Honey said. "I didn't recognize you."

"That was the goal. Pity others didn't have the same trouble."

Rosie couldn't focus on small talk. "Lupe said the police were here this morning."

Raised eyebrows and a sigh were his sole response.

"What did they say?"

"What do you think? They wanted to know where I was during the estimated time of death."

*And where were you?* Rosie wanted to ask, but she didn't. He answered her anyway. "I was here, with Cecily all night. Then in the morning, we left for LA. I didn't get home until late. The detective was able to talk to Cecily on the phone, and she corroborated, so I guess I'm in the clear. Although why they think I'd do this to myself, I don't understand."

"Book sales," Honey said. Rosie's cheeks flushed. Sometimes she wished Honey wasn't so direct. If it was in her head, it generally came out of her mouth.

"I sold enough after the first murder to keep me flush. Going for a second would just be greedy," he said. Then to Rosie's shock he grinned at Honey.

"What are you going to do? Are you going to leave town until things settle?" Rosie said. She wondered if he'd return to the idea of selling the property.

"I'd like to, but Detective Sylla prefers I remain." He turned his palms to the ceiling. "She needn't worry. With the hounds of hell at the door, I'm not going anywhere."

The tower may have been built to keep others out, but it had become a prison.

"I had deliveries scheduled for later in the week. I can put them on hold," Rosie said, thinking out loud.

Jacob shook his head. "No need. I think the best thing to do is go on with life as usual."

"That won't be easy," Rosie said.

"No, but it's necessary."

"You're right," Honey said. "Show the world you've nothing to hide, and they'll stop hunting."

"Exactly."

Honey wandered to the central bank of windows. "What an incredible view."

Jacob followed. "Isn't it? Look to the right..." He began to show her points of interest, and Rosie walked into the hall to find Lupe. She'd told Rosie on the phone she had an appointment in a half hour. That was at least forty-five minutes ago.

Lupe didn't appear to be anywhere on the main level, so Rosie climbed the central stairs. When she reached the top, she called her name.

"Here." Lupe's muted voice came from the master bedroom.

Rosie found her sitting in a chair near a dog crate, Fury on her lap. When the dog saw Rosie, he yelped and squirmed until Lupe was forced to drop him. He ran to Rosie with even more frantic joy than usual.

"You need to leave, don't you?" Rosie said after greeting him.

"Yes." Lupe looked nauseated.

Rosie took off Eric's cap and put it on Lupe's head. "Do you have sunglasses?" Lupe nodded. "Hats and sunglasses help. I'll take Fury for a walk and go with you."

The two women walked downstairs, Fury trotting in front of them. Rosie expected Lupe to offer an explanation, tell her why the media presence outside upset her so much, but she didn't.

When they entered the apartment, Fury hung back. He lay just outside the doorway and waited for them. His reluctance to go in seemed strange. Maybe he didn't want to face the scene of his crime. Peach gave Rosie the cold shoulder after being left home alone for a long period or being sent to the groomer. Dogs were emotional creatures.

"Will you be here Saturday?" Jacob asked Lupe as she walked toward the hallway.

She turned nervous eyes his way. "If the reporters are gone."

"They won't be." Jacob's voice was flat. "I've been through this before. They won't go until they get what they want, until I talk to them. Unless, of course, someone else is killed, or the police make an arrest. They're distracted by fresh blood."

"Are you going to talk to them?" She said.

"Nope. That's Cecily's job, but she can't come for at least a week, so we're out of luck." The smile he'd been wearing disappeared. "I'll need you before that, though. Rosie's going to need you."

"I don't—" Rosie started to say.

Jacob held up a hand. "I'm not going to let those vultures run my life. So, I repeat, will you come Saturday, Lupe?" Jacob's face was hard.

Lupe played with the strap of her purse, folding and remolding the frayed leather for a long moment. She appeared to be weighing the question. "Yes," she finally said.

A slow angry burn filled Rosie's gut. Why was Jacob being so insensitive? Couldn't he see how upset Lupe was? She turned to him. "I'm going to walk her to her car and get Fury out for a bit. I'll be back."

## 4.5.5

Sunglasses on and Fury leashed, Rosie opened the front door. She felt naked without the baseball cap, but Lupe seemed to need it more than she did. *They're not here to talk to you.* She exited the house. Lupe followed.

When the first flashbulb went off, she felt the woman cower against her back. The ember of anger in Rosie's gut that had been lit by Jacob's insensitive attitude, flared. It was so unfair. She didn't know what Lupe had gone through in her life, but whatever it was she didn't deserve this.

Maybe Lupe's visa had expired. Maybe she was no longer legal. Could that be the cause of her anxiety? That hadn't occurred to Rosie before, but even so, her earlier words held true: no one in this throng cared. They were after blood, but it wasn't hers.

Rosie stepped over the property line and began shoving her way through the media wall like a linebacker. She ignored the physical contact, the lights, the questions being hurled at her and kept her eye on the finish line—Lupe's car.

By the time they reached it, the rumble of voices had faded to white noise. Lupe slid inside and closed the door. Rosie stood guard until she pulled away, then marched up Cliff Drive toward town. Adrenaline flooded her veins. She needed to walk it off. Fury must have felt the same. He pulled at the leash as if he was trying to put as much distance between himself and the tower as possible.

Rosie was breathing hard by the time she reached Heisler Park. She stopped. The pounding of emotion that had propelled her was now a dull throb. Memories of the last time she'd been in the park threatened to start a new attack.

The sheer horror over the discovery of a dead body hadn't faded, not yet, but a new emotion had joined it—grief. She was grieving over Twila's death.

Rosie hadn't liked Twila. She had admired her in a distorted, agonized way, but she hadn't liked her. Why grieve?

Rosie pivoted and stood with her hands on her hips. She couldn't go forward into the park. She wasn't ready to face that scene, and she dreaded going back.

Her return trip was slower, her footsteps more hesitant. A thought inserted itself into her consciousness. She'd had Twila on a pedestal. That was the cause of the grief. Rosie tried to argue with the idea but couldn't. It was true. She'd seen Twila ascend the winner's platform over and over. Watched her receive trophies Rosie had never won but had worked hard for. That Twila stood in that coveted position had altered Rosie's view of life.

It had given her ambition. The spirit of competition had spurred her on to bigger things than she might have accomplished without it. Rosie had spent so many years lamenting Twila's luck, and her own lack of it, it had become a part of her. She wasn't sure how to function without it.

Twila was broken now. A cracked trophy. No longer a force to be reckoned with.

Rosie elevated some people and made villains of others. It was wrong. She knew it, but it didn't always stop her from doing it. Eric had brought it to her attention their first year of marriage.

She'd met Eric at a college basketball game. He was sitting behind her with a group of guys she knew through her roommate. By the time the game was over, he'd dropped to the seat next to her and gotten her phone number.

He was working on his MBA, and she'd thought he was brilliant.

He was handsome. No one would argue with her about that, but it was his brain she'd bragged about. Especially to Liz.

Once Liz got over Derek Johnson, her high school jock sweetheart, she only dated intellectuals, guys in med school, law school, and engineers. One of her boyfriends was a rocket scientist—literally. Eric's degrees were in mathematics and business, not science, but Rosie had been sure he could compete with anybody Liz dated and told her so. The first Christmas after Rosie and Eric married, her challenge was tested.

They'd gone to stay with her family for the holidays. Liz brought home the boyfriend *du jour*, a journalist who wrote for a national magazine. After the dinner table was cleared, the family gathered for games. It was a tradition. Eric held his own and even won a few rounds of Rummikub, a numbers game that combined luck and skill. Then the Scrabble board came out. He crashed and burned. Liz's boyfriend dominated.

As irrational as it was, Rosie got mad at Eric. She couldn't tell him why, because then she'd have to admit how small minded she was, so she didn't talk at all. He'd asked what was wrong repeatedly, and she pleaded headache.

On the way home, he finally got the truth out of her. They still laughed about it. It was immature to put people into categories: good, bad, smart, stupid, caring, hard-hearted, and expect them to stay there. Yet she often did. Eric said for someone whose business was color she was awfully black and white. Ironic, but true.

Before Rosie reached the house, she lifted Fury into her arms to protect him. He'd almost been trampled on the way out. He immediately became a snarling, snapping shield. If reporters got too close, he became her protector. Relief washed over her when she reached the front yard and broke free of the crowd. She'd only have to do this once more today.

The relief was short lived. As she put a hand on the doorknob, one voice rose above the others. It called her by name. "Rosie Ring. You're Rosie Ring, aren't you?"

She turned, looking for the source of the voice. A tall man in black-rimmed glasses, stood on the property edge. "You must have been very upset when you found the body. Can you give us your impressions? What was your relationship with Twila Wilkes? Isn't it a strange coincidence that you were the one to find her?"

Rosie's veins filled with ice water. She fled into the house. How had they known? Sylla had promised she'd try to keep Rosie's identity from the public. Her fingers trembled as she unleashed Fury. The dog scampered up the stairs. She walked to the apartment in long, panicked strides.

"How do they know?" she said as soon as she entered.

Honey and Jacob's faces pivoted to her in unison. They wore almost identical expressions of confusion and surprise. "Who knows what?" Jacob said.

"Those, those idiots outside know I found Twila. How would they know that?"

Nobody said anything for a long moment, then Honey and Jacob spoke at once. "Someone on the force must have leaked it," Honey said.

"They're a scourge," Jacob said.

"Cops talk. Booker hears all kinds of things." Honey turned to Jacob. "My husband is a firefighter."

"But Sylla—" Rosie started to say.

"You can't trust them. They do whatever they think they need to do. The investigation is the only thing that matters," Jacob said.

"How does giving the press my name help the investigation?" Rosie was baffled. Before either came up with an answer, her phone rang.

She fished it out of her purse. It was Eric. Had her name made it onto the news already? "I'm okay. I'm at Jacob's. The press is all over the place, but I'm okay," she said.

"Rosie." Eric's voice was soft.

"I couldn't believe it. Sylla said—"

"Rosie." He spoke with more volume.

"She would keep my name out of it. And she did. For a whole twenty-four—"

"Rosie." Eric shouted this time. "Listen to me."

Rosie shut her mouth with a jarring clack. She hadn't heard this level of panic in his voice since Seb's crimes were revealed in the press.

"I'm in Santa Ana at the station. They brought me in for questioning. I need you to find a lawyer."

He was still speaking, but she couldn't hear the words. They were drowned out by a roaring in her ears. Questioning? Eric? Why? She tried to voice the thoughts, but her mouth had gone dry. She swallowed. "What are you talking about?"

"They brought me in for questioning."

"What for?"

"The blood on my saw was Twila's."

Jacob and Honey stared at Rosie with furrowed brows. "What happened?" Honey asked when she ended the call.

"They've got Eric at the station." No one said anything for a beat, and Rosie went on. "I don't know much. He couldn't talk. He said they've been questioning him, and he wants me to find him a lawyer."

"Questioning him about Twila Wilkes death?" Jacob said.

Rosie nodded.

"That's crazy," Honey said. "What possible motive could Eric have? He hardly knew Twila."

"Motive is secondary. First, they need evidence. Do they have any evidence?" Jacob said.

"A saw. Eric took a saw into the office to cut some bookshelves, and he left it there. The police bagged it and showed it to him the other night, when they questioned everybody from Pacific Financial. I guess they found Twila's blood on it."

Jacob stood. "I'll make some calls. Cecily had a lawyer lined up in case the police got more interested in me when the flight attendant died. Maybe he can recommend someone here."

Jacob was acting like the kind, concerned man she'd always known him to be. He'd been so tough on Lupe; she wondered if she'd misread him. It was probably the stress, which was understandable. People didn't fit into nice, neat boxes, she reminded herself. Tears stung her eyes, and her throat tightened. "Thank you."

He took his cell from the coffee table and walked toward the hallway. He placed a hand on her shoulder as he went past. "I'll be in my office."

Honey patted the couch next to her. Rosie sat, and Honey put an arm around her shoulders. "Nothing will come of this, Rosie. You can't prove something that didn't happen. Jacob will get you a good lawyer, and that lawyer will prove Eric had nothing to do with it."

Rosie dropped her face into her hands. "I don't know. I don't know what to think."

They sat that way, Honey rubbing circles onto Rosie's back until Jacob returned. "I got a name. She's supposed to be the best."

Rosie looked up, and Jacob handed her a slip of paper. The name Rachel Widmark and a phone number were written on it. "I hope you don't mind, I asked Cecily to call and make an appointment. I figured you had enough to worry about."

She took the paper. "Thank you. I'd better go. I have to pick him up."

"Wait a minute," Jacob said and jogged from the room. When he returned, Fury trotted behind him. "A few vans have left. Maybe you should wait…"

"Why don't we look online? See what the media knows before you go out there," Honey said.

Jacob sat on a chair adjacent to the couch and opened his laptop. A moment later, they were looking at a video of the street in front of his house.

"There's breaking news in Laguna Beach." It was the man with the black-rimmed glasses. The one who knew who Rosie was. "The woman who found the murdered interior designer—the second crime in what is being called the *Pillory* murders—is here, inside this house." The camera panned on the fortress. "Jacob Rinehart's home."

The reporter explained who Jacob was and that his book had been found on the bodies of both victims. "No one knows what to make of the fact that Jacob Rinehart's interior designer, Rosamond Ring, was the one to find the body of another local interior designer, Twila Wilkes.

All we know is it's a strange coincidence." The man signed off with his station call letters and the promise of a full report at six.

Rosie crossed her arms over her gut and groaned. It sounded so damning when it was put that way.

Jacob shut the laptop, and Honey stared into space. "There's one thing I don't understand."

"Only one?" Rosie said.

Honey continued as if Rosie hadn't spoken. "Twila and Eric knew each other, but he didn't know the flight attendant. And that murder didn't happen around here. It happened in Seattle. Why are they interested in Eric?"

"I'm sure they're looking for links. Does Eric ever fly Western Airlines, or go to Seattle for work?" Jacob said.

"Yes, to both." Rosie felt nauseated.

"Well, there you go."

"There you go nothing," Honey said. "Just because Eric does those things doesn't mean he knew that flight attendant."

"She was on one of those cheating sites," Jacob said.

"What are you implying?" Honey's voice rose.

Jacob put up both hands. "I'm not implying anything. I'm just saying those are the kinds of things the police are going to investigate. If Eric ever—"

"He's not that kind of guy. He and Rosie have been married for twenty-five years."

Rosie listened to Honey defend Eric, and her heart sank. She'd been concerned herself that Eric may have played around. A year ago, she'd never have believed that of him, but things had changed. He was often distant. He was rarely ever home. The phone conversation she'd overheard played in her mind, *I don't want her to be hurt*. Then he'd lied to her about it, said he wasn't talking to Twila.

"He wouldn't be the first guy who cheated on his wife after twenty-five years of marriage. In fact, there are stats that say after the seven-year itch phase, the next most dangerous time is when the kids go off to college."

"How would you know? You're not even married." Rosie heard the defensiveness in Honey's voice.

"*Pillory*. Everybody in that book is cheating on somebody. I did a lot of research."

Honey stood in one abrupt motion. "Rosie, we need to go."

Jacob stood with her. "I'm not trying to upset you, either of you. I'm also not saying this is what I think. I'm trying to prepare you for the kinds of things you could hear when you walk out that door."

He pointed toward the front of the house. "This is what people will say. It's what you'll hear on the news, on social media. Hell, you'll hear it in the grocery store. I've been through it."

Rosie examined Jacob's face. His forehead was creased with concern. His eyes, deep green wells of sympathy. He was trying to help.

"Maybe, but Rosie has to go pick up her husband. She doesn't need to be thinking about all this now."

"I'm just saying, it's good to be prepared before you walk out that door."

Honey set her jaw in a stubborn line. "No comment. Isn't that what you're supposed to say?"

"Right, and have you ever seen how guilty they can make someone look by provoking them? Even if they say nothing, if they look angry or aggressive, the world thinks they're guilty."

"Well, I am angry." Honey's eyes flared.

"That's my point." He put a hand on her arm and drew her onto the couch, resuming his position in the chair. "We need to think this through, for Rosie's sake. For Eric's. Don't go running out there half-cocked."

Honey heaved a sigh. "Alright then. What do you suggest?"

"I'll go out."

"You?"

"Yeah. They want to talk to me. They always want to talk to me."

"What are you going to say?"

"I don't know." He shrugged. "I'll tell them Rosie is a wonderful woman, that neither of us knew Twila well, that I believe it was a coincidence that Rosie found the body. The point is, I'll distract them while you two go out through the side gate."

Rosie sat up straighter. "You'd do that for me?" She knew how much Jacob hated to engage with reporters, and that his publisher didn't want him to.

He reached across Honey and took one of Rosie's hands. "I've been where you are. I know what it's like. Cecily stood up for me, but you don't have anyone."

Tears threatened to overwhelm Rosie for about the tenth time that day.

**MOLLY:** The police are looking hard at Eric. Finding Twila's blood on his saw isn't a great development, at least as far as he and Rosie are concerned.

Let's hear from Patient Zero. Maybe we'll learn something that could shift the suspicion yet again.

# patient zero



My brother was questioned in the death of MG, but nothing came of it. The case went cold in a few months—chalked up to stranger-danger. She became a cautionary tale. Mothers used the story to teach their kids about the dangers of dark alleys, and that was that.

The next fifteen years were pretty copacetic. I began to think more about my own life, what I wanted to be and do. I had an awakening of sorts when my brother went to college. Living and sacrificing for him was fine, but it was time to focus on myself.

I never expected roses and chocolate. I mean, he didn't know what I'd done for him. He didn't know about Mom or MG. So, I wasn't bitter, not exactly, but I'd grown a little tired of everything always being about him.

We grew up and, in some ways, grew apart. I had a life. He had a life. Everything was good, until the flight attendant. Marianne Kennedy, *née* Pulaski. It took me a while to figure out who she was. She looked so different.

Marianne was one of the few people I knew for whom the years had been an advantage. She'd been a skinny, pimply teenager. I only noticed her then because she'd followed MG around like a pilot fish follows a shark, looking for leftovers.

I'd visited an art event that day, and stopped into a nearby pub for a drink. I was sitting at the bar minding my own business when she sidled up and asked for a chardonnay. Our eyes met, and her face lit up. She was sure she recognized me.

I told her she was wrong. I said I had one of those faces, you know, the kind everybody recognizes. Which is true, by the way.

She wouldn't leave it alone. She returned to the table she'd been sitting at. There was a group there that looked like other airline people. Every time she passed my seat to order another drink or go to the restroom, she made a comment.

She reminded me of MG. Attractive in a trying-too-hard kind of way, loud, and flirty. I wasn't surprised when I read in the paper later that she'd been cheating on her husband, the poor slob. It justified my actions. I like to think I'm a pretty good judge of character, and in this case it was true.

After a while her friends left, and she pulled up to the bar. She was drunk by then. Sloppy drunk. You know? The kind of drunk that likes to hearken back to the good ol' days.

She started talking about MG in a loud teary voice, telling everyone at the bar the tragic story. I acted as if I was hearing it for the first time. She eyed me over the rim of her glass, and said she never believed it was stranger-danger. She'd always thought it was someone from school.

This made me nervous. I read things into the droop of her gaze and the narrowing of her lips that may or may not have been there. Now, I think I should've paid my bill and left, but hindsight is twenty-twenty.

I'd had a bit too much to drink by then too. I don't imbibe frequently. It tends to make me question things, fall down paranoid rabbit holes. Which I did that night. I became sure she knew. She knew I'd killed MG, and not only that, but she was threatening me.

I'm Mr. Proactive, right? Maybe too proactive. Anyway, while she went to the girls' room, I managed to palm the knife the bartender was using to cut limes. Kind of crazy, I know. But hey, as I said, I was concerned. Turned out to be a good thing, but I'm jumping ahead of myself.

She got back, and I leaned over and whispered why didn't we go somewhere more private. Believe it or not, I can be charming when I want to be. I turned it on. Full beam. I told her the bartender knew my girlfriend, so we couldn't leave together, or I'd be in a world of hurt. Which of course wasn't true, but she swallowed it. Cheaters always figure other people are cheaters too.

I said I'd leave first, then she should wait ten minutes and follow. We planned to meet in a park a couple of blocks away. I had more time to plan with my mother and MG but desperate times and all that.

I hurried to the park. My plan was to hide behind a stand of bushes, but a junkie stumbled past before I reached them. I almost tossed it up at that point. Thought I'd walk away, hope for the best, you know?

I chewed a fingernail and watched him disappear around a bend. Had he noticed me? That was what was going through my head. He was in a bad way. After a long, tense minute, I decided it was game on. Even if he had seen me, he wasn't in any state to make connections.

I hid. She came along, and the rest is history, as they say. It was after I hit her with the rock that I had my brainstorm. I thought: What is the best way to cover a crime? The answer: With a bigger one. One that would overshadow the first and knock it right out of people's minds.

I happened to have a copy of *Pillory* in my backpack, which was what gave me my big idea. I took off my shirt and jacket and wrapped my shirt around my waist like an apron. The key is to wait a minute or two for the heart to stop pumping. That sucker can keep going long after the lights go out. Despite my patience, it was messy business. The knife was sharp enough, though. I managed to cut off her head and hands without getting too much blood on myself.

I wrapped her head and hands in my shirt and shoved them into my backpack, then set her up on a bench with the novel. I used the book to cover the face that wasn't there. I thought that was a clever touch at the time. Did not expect the extent of the media hype, though. Not at all.

Couldn't believe it when I heard the flight attendant was using one of those swingers' websites. Talk about coincidences. The whole thing blew up when that came out.

Anyway, I put my jacket on, walked a mile and hailed a taxi. I dropped her head and hands off the boardwalk at the waterfront. Another problem washed away.

Really, it couldn't have gone better. The press went crazy, and I did a good deed without meaning to. Jacob Rinehart sold a million books. Which proves the point, sometimes the best offense is diversion.

**MOLLY:** So, what did we learn? Those who believed there was only one killer were correct. The *Pillory* killing was not this dude's first murder. We also learned that he didn't kill Marianne Kennedy because he was having an affair with her. In fact, her death had nothing to do with the fact that she was in a swingers' club. It was because he was nervous that she might put two and two together and nail him for the murder of MG years earlier.

The question of the week, then, is this: Do you believe the police are on the right track about Eric? Is the blood on the saw damning or merely circumstantial? Hop into the Facebook group and let me know what you think.

Join me next time for more *Murders Under the Sun*.

**(cue music)**

**VO:** If you enjoyed this episode, please leave us a five-star review on your favorite podcast service-it really helps. *Murders Under the Sun* is edited by Jim Wilbourne, theme music is by Eclectic Blends, and I'm your host, Molly Shure.

# part seven

# MURDERS UNDER THE SUN
## SEASON FOUR; EPISODE SIX

**MOLLY:** Welcome back to *The Tower*, Episode Six. I'm Molly Shure, your host.

For listeners who haven't yet joined our podcast Facebook group, I need to fill you in on what went on there this week. If you've been following the series, you know that last week I asked if people thought the police were off base with their suspicions of Eric Ring. Well, the opinions in the group were pretty volatile. The pendulum swung from "He couldn't be the killer without Rosie knowing about it," to "His saw had her blood on it. He's guilty as sin."

I thought I'd put in my two cents today. First, yes, it's difficult to imagine Rosie being married to a cold-blooded murderer for all those years yet have no idea. But stranger things have happened.

Judith Mawson, wife of Gary Ridgway, the notorious Green River Killer, had no clue she was married to a man who'd killed so many people that he'd lost count of the number. He was charming—to her. She thought she had the perfect husband.

Paula Radar didn't know her husband Dennis was the BTK killer. According to her daughter, she would never have knowingly exposed her children to such a dangerous individual. Linda Yates thought her husband Robert was having an affair, not killing sex workers.

Julie Baumeister believed her husband Herb's story about the remains their son found on their property. He'd said it was a medical school skeleton owned by his father, an anesthesiologist. In actuality, authorities believe he may have been the most prolific serial killer ever in the state of Indiana.

The point is, throughout history many family members have been completely in the dark about the nefarious deeds of their loved ones. Just because Rosie doesn't believe Eric could kill doesn't mean he didn't. At least, not as far as the police are concerned.

Having said all that, my guess is Rosie would know if his childhood was as difficult as Patient Zero's apparently was. She hasn't discussed his past in the interviews to this point. It's possible she didn't know about it. It's possible it never seemed relevant to her so she didn't bring it up. It's also possible Eric isn't our villain.

Let's dive in and see what we learn today.

# 4.6.2

Why were chairs in governmental facilities always so hard? Tax dollars are funny money. You'd think spending a little extra on something comfortable wouldn't be that difficult. Rosie slumped lower in the uncomfortable chair.

She'd been waiting for forty-five minutes. That was another thing about governmental institutions, they loved to make you wait. You had to get three days off work and bring a sleeping bag to renew your drivers license at the DMV.

Her anxiety over Eric's situation had morphed into irritation and was moving toward outrage. Why was her family under scrutiny? A reporter showed up outside Becca's classroom that morning. Somehow the woman had discovered Rosie worked for Jacob, and Becca was Rosie's daughter.

Thankfully, she didn't know Rosie was also the one to find the body. What would happen when that got around? Rosie wanted to call the kids before they saw it on TV, but here she was stuck in the lobby of the sheriff's station.

Another thought hit her with a jolt of adrenaline. The kids couldn't hear about the police's interest in Eric. If this made it into the press, the Skandalis crimes would certainly be resurrected. That wound was finally healing. She couldn't bear the idea of having it ripped open again.

They'd all suffered enough. Especially because they'd had nothing to do with Seb's crimes. Just as they had nothing to do with the deaths of the flight attendant or Twila.

*The saw.*

Okay, there was blood on the saw. That bothered her, but they had to have more than that. Didn't they? Even if it was her blood, it didn't mean Eric killed her.

The saw was convenient that was all. It was at Twila's house. She was probably killed at her house. She wasn't killed in the park. There hadn't been enough blood.

Rosie shuddered.

It was cold in the waiting room. With all the tax money the state of California took out of their paychecks every month, you'd think there'd be enough to heat public buildings. And buy comfortable chairs. She squirmed in her seat. When would they be done with Eric?

Why were they keeping him so long? He didn't do anything. Surely, that was obvious.

Jacob's words, *after the seven-year itch phase of a marriage, the next most dangerous time is when the kids go off to college,* rang through her mind. Anecdotally, she knew it to be true. A third of the couples they used to socialize with when the kids were in grade school and high school were divorced today. But not Eric and her.

They were good together.

A naked foot massaging a lovely calf appeared behind her eyes. She massaged her forehead. She didn't believe it. He wouldn't.

She stood. The chair was unbearable. She crossed to a window and looked out at the parking lot.

Even if he did have an affair with Twila, he wouldn't murder her. A vision of a blood-soaked Eric in his grilling apron, saw in hand, made her laugh out loud. The sound startled her into silence. She returned to the chair and sat.

A door opened and Eric entered the lobby. Finally. He looked terrible. His hair stood in tufts. His shirt was untucked and rumpled. Everything about him was rumpled. "Thanks, Rosie," he said when he saw her.

"Stay available, yes?" Rosie hadn't noticed Detective Sylla standing behind him until she spoke.

Eric nodded, but didn't look at her. His eyes remained on Rosie. "Let's go."

They didn't speak until they cleared the parking lot. "How long were you in there?" Rosie asked.

"Forever."

"What on earth did they ask you? What could possibly take all that time?"

"My life story. I think that detective knows more about me now than you do."

Rosie had to focus on her driving as she merged onto the 5 freeway. It gave her a chance to think. Eric's answers were vague. She wanted details. "Did she talk about Twila?"

"Of course. Twila is the woman of the hour." He barked a laugh. "That's one way to get attention, get yourself murdered. If she's looking down on us now, or up, she's probably thrilled."

Rosie shot a glance at him, shocked by his words. "That's harsh."

He dropped his head onto the headrest. "I'm sorry. Twila wasn't my favorite person, but she didn't deserve this. Can't say it surprises me though."

"What do you mean?"

He didn't answer her for a long moment, then he said, "I'm going to tell you something I didn't tell the police."

Rosie's pulse jumped. Was the information she was about to receive going to change her life? If Eric had an affair with Twila, and she knew about it, nothing would ever be the same in their marriage. Suspicion was one thing. She could talk herself out of that. But knowing, that was something else altogether.

"Twila was blackmailing me."

Eric's words filled the emptiness in the car like something solid. They had mass, weight. Blackmail. Not an affair. Blackmail. Rosie didn't know whether to laugh or cry.

The relief lasted a brief instant, however. Because blackmail couldn't happen without an indiscretion. Could the indiscretion be what she feared?

"Over what?" Rosie's voice shook with the words.

"Seb may be dead, but his mess never dies."

Seb. Not Twila. Not an affair. Rosie inhaled and exhaled slow and deep.

Eric told her the whole sordid story between Santa Ana and Laguna Niguel. Twila found evidence that Skandalis had used Pacific Financial to launder funds from his trafficking business. He'd padded clients' investments, created fake clients, and hid funds in plain sight. She'd used the information to get the design job at Pacific Financial and more.

"The reason the credit cards were maxed wasn't identity theft." Eric's head was in his hand now. "I had to borrow to pay her."

"Why didn't you tell me?"

"I didn't want you to know. It was humiliating."

Rosie pulled into their driveway and turned off the engine. She pivoted in her seat so she could face him. "None of those things were your doing, Eric. Seb started the problem. Twila perpetuated it. You're not to blame."

"Maybe, but if it got out... Pacific is on such shaky ground. It would sink us. Bob and I agreed, we'd give her the job, and we'd each make a financial settlement with her."

"Why would she stop? Isn't that the thing with blackmailers? You can never get rid of them."

"Not in this case. The business is only worth so much, and Bob and I, our crime was stupidity. Last I checked, not prosecutable. Once we paid her, we were fairly certain we'd be done. We could start over. Put the disaster of the past behind us."

The darkness began to close around them as they sat there in the car. It was easier to talk about some things without facing each other.

"We need to tell the police," Rosie said.

"About the blackmail?" Eric's voice was incredulous.

"Yes. Don't you see? If Twila was blackmailing you, she was probably blackmailing other people. It's a motive."

"Right. It's a motive. The police already view me as a person of interest. Why would I hand them a motive?"

"Because..." She couldn't end the sentence. Of course, he was right.

"I'm not going to tell the police anything else until I talk to a lawyer. I need advice."

"What about Bob?"

"What *about* Bob?"

"What if he tells the police about the blackmail? It will make you look even more guilty if you keep quiet."

"He's not going to say anything."

"How do you know?"

"This isn't the first time Twila has blackmailed him."

Rosie stared at Eric in the dying light. "You're kidding?"

He laughed. "No. Not kidding. First time was three years ago. He and Estelle were meeting with interior designers for a home improvement project. They were going to use someone else. A guy from Newport, but when they called Twila to give her the bad news she mentioned they might want to reconsider. She happened to know their daughter, Sam, had plagiarized a college essay. Bought it from one of those Internet sites. Said she'd turn her in."

"What?" Rosie was stunned. "How could she know that?"

"Good question. How did she know about the money laundering?" Eric put a hand on the door handle.

"I wonder how many other people she's blackmailed over the years?"

He opened the door, and the car flooded with light. "Plenty, I'm sure."

Rosie sat in the dark for several minutes after Eric left trying to digest the information she'd just heard. Twila blackmailed her way into jobs. She wasn't sure if she should feel good, or outraged, or both.

It was as if the woman died a second death. Not only had Rosie's rival been taken out of the game, she'd never fought fair. Rosie would never know if she'd lost clients to Twila because she was better at her job, or because she'd coerced them.

Rosie stepped out of the car into the night. She remembered the year when she'd learned the truth about Santa Claus. She'd been six. Liz had broken the news, and it had changed Christmas forever. She had a similar, forlorn feeling now. What she'd longed for, pined for, tortured herself over, had never been real.

## 4.6.3

"It all makes sense now," Honey said.

"What makes sense?" Rosie and Honey sat in Honey's office at the back of Sweeter. Eric hadn't wanted her to talk to anyone about the blackmail, but Rosie couldn't keep it to herself. She had to talk it out with someone.

"Twila and her big deal clients. She just wasn't that good. I could never figure out how she got them."

"She was talented. She could have gotten clients without blackmail."

"She wasn't good enough to get them all."

"She did have that sixth sense. You know, how she read people," Rosie said.

Honey shook her head. "You mean like she just happened to know someone was about to have a baby boy, not a girl, and suggest blue in the nursery? Or how she knew that sports memorabilia was a marital issue? Come on, Rosie. Don't be naive."

"If she wasn't psychic, how did she get the information?" It was driving Rosie nuts. She'd thought about it all night, picked at every thread, but all she'd done was create more knots.

Honey's eyes widened. "Good question."

"It doesn't really matter, though. This crime is like the Seattle crime.

Unless the police find a connection between the flight attendant and Twila, we have to assume the victims were random."

"Twila liked married men. The flight attendant liked married men. Maybe it was someone who'd been involved with them both? Maybe the ladies threatened to expose the relationship?"

"I think that's what the police believe about Eric. That he's that guy."

Honey's mouth formed the stubborn line Rosie knew so well. "That's stupid."

"I agree, but what else could it be?"

"A copycat?"

"You think someone local wanted to get rid of Twila and misdirect the police?"

Honey shrugged. "It's not a bad plan."

"I'm pretty sure they have ways of knowing if the crimes were committed by the same person," Rosie said.

"They do on *CSI*. They solve every crime there, but that's not real life."

"If your theory is correct, it would have to be someone who knew Jacob had moved to Laguna."

Honey sat up straighter in her chair. "Right. Planting the body in Heisler Park less than a mile from his house. It's so obvious." She put a hand on Rosie's leg. "Okay, this is crazy, but I have an idea."

Rosie waited.

"What if we made a list of all Twila's big money clients of the past three years—"

"Then compared it to the list of people who knew Jacob had moved to town," Rosie interrupted her.

The front door bell jangled and Rosie jumped. They'd been so intent, she'd forgotten where they were.

Honey wrinkled her nose. "Yes. And I'll be quick."

Rosie reached for a yellow legal pad on Honey's desk and a pencil. She drew a line and divided the page into two columns. One headed, "T's CLIENTS," the other, "KNEW J IN LAGUNA."

She began filling in the names she knew off the top of her head: Bob and Estelle, Marybeth, and a few others went into the left column. Peter, Lillian, and Sid were on the right.

She chewed on the pencil eraser. Bob and Estelle may have known about Jacob. Eric probably told them when she got the tower gig. She drew an arrow from their name to the other side of the page.

She stared at the ceiling and tried to remember the names of the people who were mentioned in the *Orange County Lifestyles* article. Even if she could remember them, she didn't know anything about them. How could she find out?

Peter.

She stood, ripped the top sheet off Honey's pad, and headed for the door. Peter knew everybody. He'd done a lot of work with Twila, and he was nosy.

Honey and a cute elderly lady were examining one of the new pressure cookers that had made a comeback recently. As Honey explained the advantages of the pot to the woman, her eyes shot to Rosie. "It's much safer than the one you used to have."

Rosie pretended she was holding a phone to her ear and mouthed, "Call you soon."

Fifteen minutes later she pulled into the parking lot behind Nightshade. She jogged from the car to the door and threw it open. Peter looked up, surprise on his face. He was seated at the long table he used for a desk, catalogs and fliers littered its top. "Rosie."

"Hey." She pulled out a chair and sat across from him. "I need your help."

"At your disposal."

"I need a list of all the big money clients Twila has worked with in the past two or three years."

"Oh, is that all?" His voice was heavy with sarcasm. "What makes you think I'd have that information?"

Rosie waved a hand at him. "Will you help me?"

He leaned in his chair. "Can I ask why you want to know?"

"Nope."

"In that case, of course."

Rosie pulled the legal sheet out of her purse and spread it out on the table, ironing out the folds with the side of her hand. "This is what I have so far."

Peter adjusted his glasses and peered at the paper. "I assume J. Is Jacob?" He pointed to the column headed "Knew J. in Laguna."

Rosie gave a curt nod.

"Why are these connected?"

"I thought you weren't going to ask questions."

"I didn't say that. I just established that you weren't going to answer me if I asked why you needed this information."

"Same thing."

"It's not. If you want me to help you fill out this interesting little grid, I'm going to need some of the facts."

Rosie sighed. "Alright. Bare bones facts, but—" She pointed a finger into his face. "You can't divulge one word of this to anyone. It's crucial."

"I'm insulted."

"Right. So the police hauled Eric in for questioning yesterday."

Peter's forehead turned into a field of deep furrows as Rosie filled him in on the events of the past twenty-four hours. The one thing she didn't tell him was that Twila had been blackmailing Eric. Instead, she'd said one of Pacific's clients admitted they'd been blackmailed by her.

"So you decided to do a little investigation on your own," he said when she was done.

"We can't tell the police about the blackmail. Eric promised his client."

Peter stared at the paper for a long moment, then picked up a pen.

Twenty minutes later Rosie's list had grown by twelve names on the Twila side of the page. On the Jacob side, Peter pointed out that the move was leaked by the local news and there were too many people to make the distinction meaningful.

"I don't see what good this list is going to do you. How can you know who was being blackmailed and who wasn't?" he said.

"I can't." Discouragement dampened Rosie's earlier excitement. "I forgot about the press."

"You want my opinion?"

"Do I have a choice?"

"Eric needs to come clean with the police about the blackmail. He doesn't have to say who it was or what it was about, but he needs to let them know the kind of person she was."

"The kind of person who had a lot of enemies."

"Exactly. They are probably focused on trying to find a link between the flight attendant and Twila. When, as Honey so brilliantly pointed out, there might not be one."

"The flight attendant was in a swingers' club. Most likely, she had dirt on a lot of people. Maybe she was a blackmailer too," Rosie said.

Peter turned both palms to the ceiling. "The plot thickens."

Rosie refolded the paper and put it into her purse. "Thanks. You've been a big help."

"Tell Eric what I said, will you?"

"I will. He's not going to do anything until he talks to a lawyer though."

Rosie headed toward the door but stopped short. Leaning against the wall near the door was a painting that made her catch her breath. "I thought you said you'd never carry this."

"It's terrible, isn't it?"

It was terrible. The one she'd seen on the flier was disturbing, but it hadn't done the real thing justice. The painting depicted the woman with the blue-gray face she'd seen before. Up close and life-sized, the eyes — stitched closed with thick, black metallic looking thread—seemed to plead for release. It sent a frisson of horror up her back.

"Why?" Was all she could manage to say.

"Special order. A gallery owner in Seattle said he had a customer who wanted to pick it up here. Didn't want it delivered to his home."

"Who would want something like this?"

Peter shrugged. "There's no accounting for taste."

"But this is a nightmare."

"I should turn her around. She's been looking at me, or not looking at me, all day."

Rosie picked up the portrait, stared into the woman's unseeing eyes for a moment, then turned it to the wall and walked out the door. It struck her as she did that Peter had spent a lot of time in Seattle over the past few months. Could he have known the flight attendant?

He also worked with Twila, and was vocal about the fact that he didn't like her. Could he have been one of her blackmail victims? She knew so little about his personal life.

A stab of disloyalty hit her. He was her friend. Peter might be many things, but a murderer wasn't one of them. Of course, she'd had no idea Twila was a blackmailer, but that was different. Completely different.

## 4.6.4

Rosie calmed a joyous Peach, grabbed a glass of water from the kitchen and carried it into the sunroom. Her laptop sat on the wicker glass-top table between the chairs. She opened it, took the yellow sheet from her purse, and began her research.

If she could find a common thread between Twila's clients, perhaps she could figure out how she was able to dig up dirt on them. On her way home, she'd called Gwen Bishop, read her all the names, and asked her to search the property databases for addresses. Rosie wanted to compare the locations of the homes. One nosy neighbor might be able to provide information on a dozen others.

While she was waiting to hear from Gwen, she thought she'd try professions. If each were in a similar career, there could be a secretary, or co-worker, or colleague who was hungry for a payoff.

After a quick search on LinkedIn, she found Twila's clients were everything from doctors, to lawyers, to accountants. No connection there.

She closed the LinkedIn window, and her phone rang. It was Gwen. The addresses of Twila's clients were all over the map from San Clemente to Newport. From the beach to the mountains. So, that was no help either.

The light from the windows began to fade and so did Rosie's enthusiasm. Her body was stiff from sitting for so long. She rose, stretched, and padded to the kitchen to refill her glass. Peach trotted next to her. She stared out the kitchen window onto her backyard as she downed water.

A breeze had kicked up, and the red swing swayed. One Easter morning she'd taken a picture of all three of her children piled onto that swing in their pajamas, baskets in hand. They'd gotten up early and searched for eggs in the yard before church.

Becca's canary yellow PJs, Ryan's Spiderman ones, and Conner's dark blue sweats had created a stunning collage of color against the bright red paint of the swing. She'd had more comments on that picture on Facebook than on almost any other she'd ever posted.

Facebook.

Why hadn't she thought of that?

She set her glass on the counter with a thump and ran to the sunroom. She logged into her Facebook account then searched for the first name on the list she and Peter had made. It was a private page, she couldn't see much. She chewed a fingernail and thought. Why not? She hit the friend request button.

Rosie had lived in Laguna Niguel for years, had a personal page and a professional page. She was Facebook respectable, and chances are they had some friend in common. Why wouldn't they accept her request? She moved on to the next name on the list.

Within forty-five minutes, she'd found five public pages, and been accepted to two private ones. She combed the pages one by one. She didn't know what she was looking for. Something. Anything.

She scrolled through photos of one of the homes that had been featured in *Orange County Living*. After ten or twelve professional shots of the house, the pictures became more personal—the family on vacation in a mountain community, out to dinner with friends, everyone bundled up for a boat parade.

Rosie was about to move on to the next Facebook page, when she saw a picture that featured a woman she recognized from a previous page, another woman on the list. This shot showed a long table, filled with women, all toasting the camera with glasses of wine.

She stared at it for a long moment. There was nothing very

surprising about the fact that some of Twila's clients knew each other. Many of her own clients were friends. Referrals were a primary source of business for many people in service industries.

She moved to the next photo in the album and the next. There were three that appeared to be of the same event. In one, a group of women stood near long, elegant windows. In another, two women leaned on a kitchen counter with guilty expressions and mouths stuffed with food.

Her eyes roamed this last picture, hoping to find a clue. She stiffened. She saw something she hadn't noticed before. There was a woman in the background. Her head and shoulders were cut off, but Rosie could see she wasn't dressed like others at the party. She wore black pants, and a stark white blouse. She was hired help.

Rosie backtracked. The caterer or maid wasn't in the photo by the windows, but there was a face in the first picture—the one at the table— she hadn't noticed before. It was a pretty face with olive skin surrounded by a halo of dark hair. It was Lupe's face.

Rosie set her laptop on the side table and stood. She walked to the windows and gazed at her yard. She'd found inspiration there earlier, maybe she would again.

She began to review everything she knew about Lupe. She was an immigrant from Nicaragua. She'd come with her husband who'd deserted her when he'd found out his young son had diabetes.

Lupe was a hard-working, likable woman. Rosie respected her. She seemed like a good person. Trustworthy. Rosie couldn't imagine her feeding Twila dirt.

Unless Twila had something on her.

The fear that had overwhelmed Lupe when she'd had to face the reporters who surrounded Jacob's house was extreme. At the time Rosie had thought perhaps Lupe was no longer legal, and she feared deportation. If her son was ill and wouldn't receive the same medical treatment in Nicaragua that he was receiving in the US, it gave her an additional reason to be afraid. Rosie would do almost anything for her children. She was sure Lupe would as well.

This was all supposition, however. That fact that Lupe worked for one of Twila's clients didn't prove anything.

Rosie returned to the yellow sheet of paper and began checking off the names she knew Lupe had worked for. She'd worked for Estelle and Bob, and Marybeth. She currently worked for Lillian. That niggled at Rosie. Lillian had thrown Rosie over for Twila, despite Rosie's connection to Jacob Rinehart. Sid hoped to be San Clemente's next mayor. A man running for a political position would be particularly vulnerable to blackmail.

Lupe also worked for the woman whose home was featured in *Orange County Lifestyles*. Four out of twelve was a high number, but it wasn't conclusive. Lupe probably had clients who weren't Twila's. She worked for Jacob.

Rosie had an uncomfortable thought. Was it possible Twila hadn't had time to blackmail Jacob before she died? Rosie had started working for him before Lupe had come on board. The first day she'd met with Jacob at the tower, he'd made a joke about not having servants when he showed her the servant stairs. The next week, Lupe was there. How did Jacob come to hire her?

She strode to the hall, found her purse where she'd left it on the bench by the front door and fished out her cell. Jacob answered after four rings. "I have a funny question."

"Good," he said. "I need some humor in my life."

"How did you hear about Lupe?"

There was a long silence.

"Jacob?"

"I'm trying to remember. It wasn't Craigslist, or one of those things. Someone referred her to me."

Rosie heard a sharp intake of breath through the phone.

"I know," he said. "It was Twila Wilkes. Weird, huh? It was that night I met her at the art gallery. I guess she was trying to ingratiate herself with me, get my business, but I didn't catch on. I did take Lupe's name and number from her though. Why?"

"Just trying to connect some dots."

"Okay." He waited a beat, but when Rosie didn't elaborate, he said, "How's Eric?"

"Shook up. The police questioned him for about three hours. It was grueling."

"Sorry to hear it. I know what that's like."

"I bet you do."

They spoke a moment more about the delivery scheduled for the next week, and Rosie disconnected. She added Jacob's name to the list of clients Lupe and Twila shared.

It seemed too coincidental to be coincidental. She had one more thing to check, and if the evidence kept rolling in, she'd confront Lupe. She wanted to show all this to Honey. Honey may know if Lupe worked for any of the other women on the list.

Twila frequently had her clients hire Honey for an in-home cooking class and dinner to show off her work. Since Honey didn't bring along staff, the homeowner often helped or hired someone to help.

Rosie grabbed the yellow sheet and headed to Honey's house. If she could add the name of even one more of Twila's clients to Lupe's list, Rosie would confront her. Detective Sylla needed to know who Twila Wilkes really was.

4.6.5

Monday morning, Rosie waited until Eric left for work before heading to Laguna. She'd had to keep her suspicions about Lupe to herself all weekend. He'd come home so depressed Friday night; it had been difficult. She didn't want him to be disappointed if it turned out to be a dead end, however. Hopefully the three o'clock appointment with the lawyer Cecily had found for him would be encouraging.

Yesterday after talking to Honey, she'd wanted to call Lupe right away. If Lupe would tell the police about Twila's little habit of blackmailing her clients, the police would have a whole new line of inquiry to explore. She'd resisted the urge. It would be better to talk to Lupe face to face.

Rosie parked around the corner from the tower. Most of the media were gone, moved on to muddier pastures. There was only one van and a handful of reporters and photographers still hanging around out front. She tipped her face to the ground, hunched her shoulders and strode forward with purpose, ignoring the questions hurled at her.

Lupe opened the door only seconds after Rosie knocked. Fury raced down the hallway and threw himself at her. She squatted to pet him. "Has the furniture arrived?" she asked.

"No, not yet." Lupe, unlike Fury, was subdued.

Rosie didn't have to be there for the delivery, but it made a good excuse. She wanted to get Lupe alone, and have it out with her. "Where's Jacob?"

Lupe pointed to a door a third of the way down the hallway. "In his office."

Rosie knocked and waited until she heard Jacob's voice. She pushed open the door, and stuck her head in. "Hi. Don't want to bother you. Just wanted you to know I was here."

Jacob was seated in an old leather easy chair, his feet on a matching ottoman. Sunlight streamed through the south facing window and warmed the worn oriental carpet beneath him. A vintage mahogany desk the size of a small pond took up a corner of the room. Bookcases stuffed with paperbacks, hardcover novels, and resource books lined two walls.

Rosie wouldn't do much to this room. Distraction free was the goal. This was Jacob's space, not a place to entertain.

He gazed at the air over her head, his green eyes glowing with creative heat. "Wonderful."

"Working on the new book?"

He nodded. "Can you look over the delivery and sign for it if everything is in good shape?"

"Of course."

"I'm in a zone."

"Right." His eyes returned to his laptop before Rosie closed the door.

She followed the sound of a vacuum into the apartment. Most of its furniture had been cleared and the old rug rolled and propped in a corner. Lupe was vacuuming the empty space, readying it for the new couch, chairs, carpet, and coffee table.

Fury lay on the kitchen tile. He must have gotten over his vacuum phobia. When Lupe saw Rosie, she turned off the machine. "Can I get you something? Coffee?"

"You're busy. Can I get you a cup? I'd like to talk."

Lupe's eyes widened and a line creased her forehead. "I'll be done in a minute."

Rosie went to the kitchen, dumped the dregs of coffee from the carafe and made a fresh pot. She took two mugs from the cupboard, and cream from the refrigerator.

Lupe switched off the vacuum as the coffee maker sputtered out its last drops. Rosie filled the mugs and took them to the table. Lupe sat on the far end, closest to the exit, and took one of them.

"How's everything going at Lillian's?" Rosie said. She didn't actually care but thought the question might set Lupe at ease. She might think Rosie wanted to reclaim that job now that Twila was dead. It seemed to work. Lupe's shoulders relaxed.

"Up in the air. Mrs. Rawlinson isn't happy that..." Lupe stopped. How would you put it? Isn't happy that Twila died, and she had nobody to decorate her living and dining rooms for her Christmas party? That sounded harsh but was most likely the truth.

"It'll be difficult for her to find someone else now who'll work under her time constraints."

Lupe scratched her nose. Rosie thought she did it to hide a smile. "Yes. I don't know what she's going to do."

Rosie was happy to pass on that client. Let some other designer deal with her. "Certainly a First World problem. I won't lose sleep over it." Rosie stirred her coffee. She needed to get to the point before the delivery men arrived, and she lost the opportunity. "Twila left a lot of people hanging," she said. "For others her death was a relief."

Lupe's shoulders tensed, but she didn't respond.

"You know my husband was questioned by the police about her murder," Rosie continued. "He doesn't know anything about it, but he does know something that gives a large number of people motives."

Lupe stared into her coffee mug as if something fascinating was happening inside it.

"I think you know what it is," Rosie said.

Lupe's head jerked up. She looked like a horse that was about to bolt, eyes so big the whites showed, nostrils flared. Rosie put a hand on hers to keep her.

"I don't want to get you in trouble, Lupe. No matter what you've done. I believe you were one of her victims, but I need you to level with me."

Lupe snatched her hand away. "I don't know what you're talking about."

Rosie reached into her purse which hung on her chair and took the yellow sheet out. She spread it on the table and spun it so it faced Lupe. Lupe stared at the writing. Understanding crawled across her face like a spider.

"I didn't think I was doing a bad thing. Not in the beginning." Her voice was a harsh whisper.

"What happened?" Rosie kept her voice soft, matching Lupe's.

"I was cleaning for Twila, and she asked me how things were. They weren't good. Luis's healthcare is expensive. Even with insurance there are things." Lupe met Rosie's gaze, a pleading look in her own. "Twila said there was a way I could make more money. She would help me get jobs with rich people, lots of jobs, if I would do a favor for her. I thought she was being kind."

"Twila wasn't a kind person," Rosie said.

Lupe massaged the hand Rosie had held with the other. "No. She wasn't."

"What was the favor?"

"All she wanted me to do was to talk to people, listen when they talked to each other, find out things about them."

"Bad things?"

"Not at first. At first, it was only where they went on vacations, what kind of music they liked, if they had parties, big families, those kinds of things. She would use the information to make herself look good, to get them to hire her. It seemed like a game."

A dishonest game, Rosie thought but didn't say. But was it dishonest? In this social media day and age didn't everybody follow people online to learn more about them? Didn't every good service provider do their due diligence when approaching a prospective client?

Lupe massaged her hand more aggressively, like she was trying to rub something away. "It wasn't a game though. Soon those things weren't enough. She wanted me to find out more. To look at their files, at their email if I could get onto their computers, listen to private conversations. When I said no, she said I'd never be able to find a job in Orange County again."

"Then she found out my visa had expired. She said she would go to the police, tell them that I was illegal. She said they'd send me back to Nicaragua."

"I don't think that would've happened. Luis is a citizen."

"I couldn't take a chance. Luis's doctors are here."

Rosie placed a hand on Lupe's to still them. "Lupe, you have to go to the police now. They need to know. It might have something to do with Twila's murder."

"I can't."

"Talk to my husband's lawyer. Maybe you can make a deal with the authorities. I can tell you they'd rather catch a murderer than send a hard-working woman out of the country."

A mix of emotions collided in Lupe's face. There was fear and dread, but there was something else as well. It looked like hope. "Many of the people were good to me. I felt so bad."

"Of course," Rosie said, "but they all have a motive for killing Twila." As soon as she said the words she realized they were a mistake.

Lupe's face clouded. "I don't want to hurt them again."

"If they're innocent, nothing will come of it. The police are investigating a murder, not whatever missteps these people are guilty of."

*Then why didn't Eric want to tell them Twila was blackmailing him?* Rosie knew the answer. He was afraid it would not only make him look guilty, but that the information would be made public. All the other victims would feel the same way. Not all the other victims had a bloody saw with their fingerprints on it, however.

The saw tightened Rosie's resolve. She had to get Lupe to cooperate, even if she had to resort to the same threat Twila had used. She hoped it wouldn't come to that. "Just talk to Eric's attorney. Anything you say to a lawyer is confidential. They can't tell anyone without your permission."

"If I could afford a lawyer, I wouldn't have done the things I did." There was bitterness in Lupe's voice.

"I'll pay for the lawyer," Rosie said without thinking. She wasn't sure if she and Eric could afford his legal fees, never mind Lupe's, but it had to be done.

The doorbell rang, and Fury careened by her, barking. "It's the delivery men." Lupe pushed away from the table and hurried after him. Rosie wasn't going to let this go. She couldn't.

The next hour was spent inspecting furniture, rugs, and lamps and directing their placement. When the men cleared the last of the cardboard and plastic from the room, Rosie stood back to take in the effect.

She loved this part of her job—watching her imaginings come to life. She wasn't disappointed. The room had been transformed. In place of the earlier dull tones, was now a contrast of muted and vibrant colors that, like the beach, was restful and exciting at the same time.

The painting of the tower, like royalty, connected the room and held sway over it from its prominent position. When the rest of the artwork, vases, and throw pillows were in place, it would be perfect. Although she appreciated the moment, she couldn't enjoy it the way she usually did. Eric's problems covered the beauty before her like haze on a sunny day.

She turned to Lupe, who was running a dust rag over the coffee table. "Eric is meeting with his lawyer at three."

"I have to pick up Luis at three."

"You could bring him to the lawyer's office. He can sit in the waiting room and do homework or something."

Lupe straightened and looked out the window. "We could be there by four."

Relief washed over Rosie. "I'll call and let them know."

"Let who know what?" Jacob said from the hall, then, "Wow. Oh, wow." Rosie didn't have to answer. The room drove everything else from his mind.

4.6.6

Time inched forward. Rachel Widmark seemed to be asking the same questions over and over again. Rosie was ready to scream. Eric had already given the lawyer the dates he was in Seattle during the past six months. He'd told her repeatedly he'd never set eyes on the flight attendant until he saw her face in the paper.

"The problem—" Rachel took a sip from one of those fifty-dollar water bottles that keep liquids freezing cold or boiling hot for days "—is you were in Seattle during Marianne Kennedy's estimated time of death." She rifled through a file. "The medical examiner said she died between 9:00 PM and 2:00 AM on Thursday, June 12th. You have no alibi."

Eric lifted his hands, beseeching. "I went to my hotel room right after dinner. What can I do about that? That's what happened. I never met the woman."

"I believe you. I'm just trying to make you understand what's going through the mind of the investigators. You, unfortunately, were her type."

Eric snorted. Rosie reddened. It was hard to sit here and listen to assertions that her husband was anyone else's type, especially a woman whose type happened to be married men. "What about the blackmail?" Rosie said.

"That only makes him look guiltier. If I were investigating these crimes, I might assume that Eric had a fling with Marianne Kennedy, and she decided to blackmail him too."

"Twila wasn't blackmailing only Eric. She was blackmailing a lot of people, which gives them all motives."

"Hearsay, until your friend shows up."

Rosie looked at the time on her phone again. It was 4:20, ten minutes since the last time she checked. Lupe was late, and every minute that ticked by cost her seven more dollars. "Maybe I should call her."

"That's a good idea," Rachel said. Eric and Rachel watched Rosie stand. Feeling self-conscious, she took her phone and left the office.

The waiting room was empty except for the young male receptionist who'd shown them into Rachel's office earlier. He smiled at her, teeth white against a dark complexion. Rosie shot him an obligatory smile in return and headed out of the office into the corridor.

She punched Lupe's number into her phone and counted the rings —five and it went to voice mail, like the last time she'd called. Rosie left a brief message and hung up. Maybe Lupe was driving and couldn't answer. Maybe she was lost.

Rosie's gaze fell on a restroom placard a few doors up the corridor. She went in. When she was done, she took a long drink from the water fountain next to it. She looked at the time, 4:32. She called Lupe again. Five rings. Voicemail. She didn't bother leaving a message this time.

She wandered to Widmark's outer office door and pushed it open. She wasn't ready to return to the meeting. She wanted to give Lupe a few more minutes and try again. Against the far wall, there was a couch, blue and expensive looking, and a coffee table covered with magazines and the day's paper.

Rosie sat on the couch and picked up the *Los Angeles Times*. She began leafing through the national news section, not really reading, just wasting time until she could make another call. Three pages in, a picture made her suck in her breath.

It was Twila.

***Second Victim Likes Married Men Too***

Rosie scanned the article. It focused on the rumors about Twila Wilkes's affinity for married men, speculated that perhaps she'd frequented the same site Marianne Kennedy had, and recounted several other cases where murderers had found their victims online.

Rosie wasn't sure whether to feel relieved or concerned. She knew Eric had never, would never, stoop so low. At least, she thought she knew that. If someone would have asked her three months ago if her husband would ever cheat on her, she would've denied it emphatically. Although she would still deny it today, it might not be as emphatically.

She leaned forward to set the paper down, but stopped. There was another photograph in the article, part way down the page. It was the flight attendant, but not the smiling, photoshopped shot Rosie had seen on the internet. This picture was raw. Marianne Kennedy looked like the camera had taken her by surprise. She wasn't smiling. Her hair wasn't perfectly combed.

Rosie stared at the photo for a long moment. It reminded her of something, of someone else. An unpleasant sensation settled on her like the aftermath of a nightmare. The feeling was vague and unfocused. She knew it had a source, but she didn't know what the source was.

She took her thumb and covered Kennedy's mouth. Maybe the eyes were someone else's eyes. Who did she look like? Maybe it wasn't the eyes. Maybe it was the mouth. Rosie covered the upper half of the face, and she knew. When she'd last seen this face, the eyes had been stitched closed with metallic thread.

Rosie dropped the paper as if it was on fire. What did this mean? Who would paint such an awful thing? The killer? Or just some twisted artist who wanted to make a statement about the case?

She looked at the office door, then at her phone. It was 4:40 now. Lupe wasn't coming and suddenly Rosie wanted to find her, make sure she was all right. The memory of the painting in Peter's gallery filled her with unease.

The office door opened. Eric and Rachel emerged. "I'll have to make another appointment to meet with Ms. Perez," Widmark said. "I'm out of time today."

"I'm concerned. She's a responsible person. This isn't like her," Rosie said.

"Have her call my office when you get in touch with her." Rachel dropped a hand on Eric's shoulder. "Try not to worry. It's uncomfortable, I get it. But based on what you told me, the police don't have enough to build a case."

Eric nodded. "Not yet, anyway."

"Maybe not ever."

"Maybe."

What did he mean by that? Was there damning evidence out there Rosie didn't know about? Eric opened the door for her and followed her into the corridor. "She seems to know her stuff," he said after the door closed behind them.

"Did she make you feel better?" He didn't seem as relieved as Rosie had hoped. Then again, neither was she.

"Better than what? I'm being investigated for the murder of a women who bled me dry, and today I got to drop a grand on a lawyer. No. I don't feel better, but I feel like I'm in capable hands if this thing escalates."

They didn't speak in the elevator, or on the walk through the parking lot, or the drive home. By the time they pulled up in front of their house, Rosie's uneasiness had grown. She wasn't sure what gave her the most anxiety, the photo in the paper, Lupe's absence, or Eric's attitude, but she felt like she'd had a triple shot of espresso. Eric exited the car, and Rosie slid into the driver's seat. "I'm going to drive over to Lupe's," she said through the window.

His eyebrows shot up.

"She lives in San Juan Capistrano. I won't be long."

"Want me to go with you?"

"No. I'm okay." She wanted to be alone, to think. Besides, Eric's presence might spook Lupe.

He shrugged and headed inside.

Rosie wasn't sure what she'd say to Lupe when she found her, but she knew she wouldn't be able to sleep without making contact. It was the painting. It had the same air of the evil she'd felt when she found Twila's body. That night had been heavy with it. It had surrounded her like a bad odor. She was catching whiffs of it again.

She found Lupe's apartment after making a few laps around the side streets of San Juan Capistrano. It wasn't far from the Mission, one of Rosie's favorite places to visit, despite what had happened there. Seven months ago, Abby Travers had watched as a young girl was dumped on the grounds there and left to die.

The tragedy Seb had set into motion was a terrible thing, and the reverberations continued. Rosie decided she wouldn't let it tarnish her feelings about the Mission.

If she lived as close as Lupe did, she'd volunteer to tend the gardens, or at least spend more time in them. She hoped she would anyway. She'd become so focused on her business, on Eric, on their marriage, things that used to give her pleasure had lost some of their luster.

Enjoyment, relaxation, peace; Seb Skandalis had stolen so much from so many. She'd visit the Mission as soon as Eric was cleared. *If he was cleared.* She shoved that thought away and replaced it with one of her sitting in the sun on a Mission bench reading a novel.

She'd do that soon, but not today. Today she needed to find Lupe.

She parked in front of Lupe's apartment, climbed the metal staircase on the outside of the worn, stucco building, and located apartment 2B. Rosie knocked. She waited a long minute, then tried the bell. She knocked again. No one came. There was no sound coming through the dingy white door, no light peeking out between the slates of the blind on the window. Nobody home.

**MOLLY:** You can feel Rosie's anxiety. We now know why Twila was killed, or we can guess. She must have been blackmailing Patient Zero. Has Lupe become his next victim because of her involvement in Twila's schemes? If I were Rosie I wouldn't be able to rest until I found her. I hate to break away from Rosie's narrative here, but we have another patient excerpt to read before our time is up.

# patient zero



In looking back on the first *Pillory* killing, I realize I'd finally found myself. Before that I'd always acted to help my brother. Some might say gassing Mom was for both of us. Honestly, it was an act of selflessness.

I was more worried about him than myself. I'm tougher. I could've stood the abuse. It was destroying him.

The flight attendant was a danger to me, not to him. This was pivotal. Her murder was the first thing I did solely for myself, and the results were staggering. I became famous. Me, the quiet one. The sibling in the background.

It was a funny kind of fame, because of course no one knew who I was. That didn't seem to matter though. It felt great to be the one in the spotlight for a change. Everybody was talking about it, coming up with their theories. Which were all bogus, by the way. No one had it right. Not CNN, not ABC, not FOX, no one. It's a rush talking about it even now, even though the cat's out of the bag.

Anyway, I had a lot of energy to channel, so I painted her—the flight attendant. I'd been dabbling for several years. Had a few pieces sold on consignment here and there. I wished I'd have saved her head so

I could've used that for a model, but I had to settle for a picture I found on a news site.

I called the portrait *Invidia*. That's Latin for envy. At least, that's the closest word we have for it in English. I figured you didn't go around sleeping with other women's husbands unless you had a thing about wanting what someone else already had.

I'd read somewhere that in Dante's *Divine Comedy*, in the *Purgatorio* section, the envious were punished by having their eyes sewn shut. In life they wanted whatever they saw whether it belonged to them or not. In death they were deprived of sight. Deep, right?

*Invidia* is also associated with witches, and their ability to curse with the evil-eye. That's the threat Marianne Kennedy held. She looked too closely at me, at the death of MG. She needed to be blinded, so I did it. Metaphorically anyway.

I took the painting to a gallery in Seattle that had sold stuff for me in the past. I was worried it might be too deep, too dark, but I shouldn't have been. Snapped up. Sold in a week. So I did another, slightly different angle and color palette. The gallery took it on consignment right away.

I thought I had a pretty good thing going there. Maybe I'd do other portraits, like Lust and Greed and Sloth, the sins. But I got sidetracked. My brother got in trouble again, and this time it was going to bite me in the ass too. I had to take a break from painting to take care of business.

**MOLLY:** So Patient Zero was the painter of the awful portrait of Marianne Kennedy. This clue seems to point away from Eric. Rosie, an artist of sorts herself, would know if her husband painted. But if the murderer isn't Eric, who is it?

That isn't the question of the week, however. This week, let's talk about the ability narcissistic and sociopathic people have to justify their heinous acts. It's staggering isn't it?

Do you know people like this? Now, I assume the vast majority of you don't know any murderers. However, we have probably all had boyfriends or girlfriends or relatives who've justified less horrific, but still reprehensible, deeds. This is your week to vent, people. Tell me your worst stories in the Facebook group.

Join me next time for more *Murders Under the Sun*.

**(cue music)**

**VO:** This episode is sponsored by Oasis Air, your wings to paradise. *Murders Under the Sun* is edited by Jim Wilbourne, theme music is by Eclectic Blends, and I'm your host, Molly Shure.

# part eight

# MURDERS UNDER THE SUN
## SEASON FOUR; EPISODE SEVEN

**MOLLY:** Welcome back to *The Tower*. I'm Molly Shure, your host.

Before we get into the last episode of the season, I just have to say some of your stories in the Facebook group almost gave me a coronary. It's unreal how many self-absorbed, selfish and completely clueless people there are in the world.

I expected the ex-husband/ex-wife stories. What I didn't expect was how many of you had terrible bosses. Seriously, people, I think you can take employers like that to court.

All the talk about employers reminded me to fill you in on the most recent tidbit we learned about Ariana Blackstone, our third missing CSU-Fullerton student. It's not much, so don't get excited.

Since we were having such a hard time getting hold of a relative, we decided to talk to the owners of The Raven's Perch. Remember, Ariana had been a waitress there back in the day.

The owner believes Ariana's grandmother must have had some kind of windfall in the months after her granddaughter's disappearance. The poor woman was suffering from dementia, so the facts are hazy. But Ariana's boss remembers Ariana always talking about how she was saving up to put her grandmother into a home. So, when her final paycheck came in, he decided to send it to the grandmother—very honest of him. Especially because he had to track her down to do it.

Turns out, she'd moved only weeks before to a very nice memory care home. He wondered at the time where she'd gotten the funds. It is pretty curious.

That's all we have to report at the moment, but we'll continue digging and let you know what we find next season.

Now, let's get back into Rosie's narrative. When we left off last week, she couldn't find Lupe and was really getting concerned.

# 4.7.2

Rosie drove aimlessly. Worry gripped and left her restless. The palm branches whipping in the rising wind mirrored her mood. Where was Lupe? Had Luis had an episode? Had fear overwhelmed her, and she'd run? Left Orange County?

Rosie rejected that idea. The reason Lupe was so afraid of being deported was because of Luis's health issues. He had good doctors here, doctors who knew his history, doctors who were helping him. Why would Lupe run from that?

The road Rosie had been on dead ended into the Coast Highway, and she turned right. Ten minutes later she found herself in front of the Nightshade Gallery. She pulled into the lot behind the building and parked.

The painting of the flight attendant had scared her, upset her, but more than that she couldn't shake the feeling it was significant. If she knew who the artist was, or who ordered the painting, maybe she'd understand.

Peter was wrapping a piece in butcher paper when she arrived. "Twice in one week. What did I do to deserve this?"

Rosie walked to the coffee pot and poured herself a cup. She took it to the table. "Who painted that painting?"

"Are you still thinking about that?"

"Yeah. I know who the model was."

Peter glanced up from his work, surprise on his face. "Really?"

"Yes. Can I borrow your laptop?"

Peter pushed his computer toward her. Rosie logged into the online version of the *Los Angeles Times* and looked for the article she'd read in print. She found it, scrolled until she came to the picture of Marianne Kennedy and turned the screen toward Peter.

He raised his glasses and examined it. He nodded slowly. "I see a resemblance."

Rosie put her finger over the eyes. "Look at it now."

He shrugged. "Okay, a strong resemblance."

"Who is the artist?" Rosie asked again and felt a fleeting stab of fear. She had wondered if Peter was involved with Twila's death, hadn't she? Logic dictated that whoever had painted the piece was likely the flight attendant's killer. And the flight attendant's killer might also be Twila's.

But Peter seemed as curious to find the artist as she was. His brow furrowed in concentration as he typed into his laptop. "Jarod Reynolds. He's from Seattle."

"Does he have a website?"

More typing. "No. Not even an Instagram account." Peter looked at her. "That's unusual. How does an artist grow a business without an online presence these days?"

"What shows up when you search his name?"

"A real estate agent in LA and three Jarod Reynolds in other states, none of them Washington."

"Washington?"

"The painting came from Meyer's Gallery in Seattle," Peter said. "We collaborate quite a bit. There aren't many galleries that carry exclusively dark art. I could call David. Find out what he knows, but what do I say? Why do I care?"

"You have a client who might be interested in another painting?"

Peter's eyebrows rose and fell and his mouth twitched. Rosie could tell he found showing interest in artwork he considered inferior distasteful, but he picked up his phone.

"David, Peter here. The special order you sent me, I had a customer asking about the artist. Do you have more work by him?"

Peter listened for a long moment. "Interesting. He must be an odd bird." A laugh. "Okay. Let me know. No, no hurry."

He hung up and gazed at Rosie. "David doesn't know much about him. He walked in off the street, a brochure of his work in hand. David took one painting on consignment and it sold, quickly. So, he took another. But he has no way to get in contact with Reynolds. Has to wait for Reynolds to contact him."

"What was the first painting of?"

Peter's lips thinned into a disapproving line. "A dead woman with her eyes sewn shut."

Rosie set her coffee mug down, realizing she'd been cradling it. "That's creepy. It's creepy, isn't it?"

"Yes. Creepy, but I've seen worse."

"Creepier than only painting people with their eyes sewn shut?"

Peter tipped his head to one side. "You'd rather he depicted multiple forms of torture?"

Which was worse? She didn't know. Didn't want to know. She changed the subject. "Who ordered the painting to be delivered here?"

"I didn't sell it. Just held it for a day or two." Peter apologized as he dug through an inbox of paperwork. He pulled a slip from under the pile. He handed it to Rosie. The name printed at the top of the page was J. Richmond.

Rosie's pulse jumped. "Richmond. Reynolds. The names are so similar."

"A man picked it up and signed for it. I hadn't noticed the name was like the artist's."

"Did you see him?"

"Yes. Briefly."

"What did he look like?"

Peter stared at the wall as if trying to conjure a face there. "I was on the phone. Not paying close attention. He wore a baseball cap. Had a beard. Pretty nondescript."

"I wonder if this is worth taking to the police."

"They have resources we don't. They might be able to find Jarod Reynolds. But even if they do, nothing illegal has transpired."

"But it's—"

Peter cut her off. "Creepy, yes I know. Last time I checked it wasn't against the law to be creepy."

"If J. Richmond is really J. Reynolds, why would he buy his own painting?"

"Maybe he found someone who would pay more than he would have made on consignment. Maybe he decided he couldn't part with it. Who knows?"

"Don't you find it strange that Marianne Kennedy is killed in Seattle, and the painting ends up in a gallery in the same town? Then Twila dies in Laguna Beach, and the piece is brought here?"

Peter shrugged. "It is a coincidence, but Reynolds may be following the crimes because they inspire his art. Painting the dead doesn't make him a killer any more than writing a murder mystery makes an author a murderer."

Rosie pulled a hand through her hair. Another dead end, no pun intended. Ever since Eric had come under suspicion, she'd run into one wall after another. Now it felt as if those walls were closing in. Peter was right, there was probably nothing here. Just a strange man who liked to paint dead women from high profile crimes.

Lupe had answers. Where the hell was she?

"Thanks," Rosie said.

"Didn't really do anything."

"You did. You humored me." Rosie patted Peter's shoulder on her way out the door.

She navigated her car out of the parking lot. The night promised to be a blustery one. Eric was waiting for her at home. She should pick something up for dinner, go home, put a fire in the fireplace and watch a movie. She wasn't accomplishing anything besides wasting gas. However, instead of turning left toward Laguna Niguel, she made a right.

She'd drive by Jacob's house and see if Lupe was there. It was a meaningless gesture. Lupe never worked after 3:00, but Rosie was out of ideas.

Five minutes later she sat in her car, engine idling, in front of the tower staring at Lupe's Honda. She jockeyed into the small space behind it.

The news vans were gone. The street deserted. As she approached the house, she noted the front door was a few inches ajar. Jacob never left the door open.

Rosie's palms pricked with tension. She placed them on the wood, and pushed. "Hello. Jacob?"

Her voice echoed through the dark house. The setting sun illuminated the far end of the hall, made it a red, glowing fire. She stepped inside, closed the door behind herself, and headed toward the light. Her footsteps rang in the silent house.

"Lupe?" She called. No answer.

She reached the apartment. It was as empty as the hallway. The ocean, deep purple in the dying day, made a striking backdrop. The room was beautiful, but it did nothing to relax her. The infusion of violet felt arrogant, challenging.

Rosie fled to the kitchen. There were dirty dishes on the counters and in the sink. Lupe never left dirty dishes behind. The door to the servant staircase was wide open. Someone had exited the apartment in a hurry.

She walked to the doorway and gazed up the steps. No one there. Not that she expected to see anyone, but the quiet house felt like a presence. The sensation was so powerful, she glanced over her shoulder to see if she was being watched.

If Lupe was upstairs, injured or unconscious, it could explain why she hadn't made it to the lawyer, why the front door had been left open, and dishes in the sink. "Lupe." She called the woman's name again.

When Rosie reached the upper landing, she stopped and listened. A faint whimper reached her ears. She followed the sound into Jacob's bedroom.

She stepped over a pile of dirty linens. The bed was stripped. The bedspread and sheets puddled on the floor. The whimper came again, louder now.

Rosie rounded the king-sized bed and saw Fury huddled in his crate in the corner. His tail thumped on its floor when he saw her. "Fury, baby, what are you doing in there?"

He crept forward. His whimper became a whine. Rosie unlatched the door. The small dog crept out and into her arms. He was shivering. "What's the matter, baby?" She hugged him to herself. "Where's Lupe? Where's Jacob?"

Rosie stood, and hugging Fury to her chest she left the bedroom. She walked through the upper hall, going from room to room. Lupe wasn't there.

Maybe she'd gotten a call about Luis? An emergency? Maybe she'd run out leaving the door open. That didn't explain her car. It was still out front.

Maybe Lupe had been in no state to drive, and Jacob had taken her wherever she'd needed to go. A calm came over Rosie at that thought. That must be what had happened. Luis had an episode. Lupe got a call. Jacob had insisted on taking her to the doctor's office, or the hospital.

Fury stopped shivering, and was now squirming to get loose. He must have to go out. Who knows how long he'd been in that crate?

Rosie set the dog down, and he trotted through the door to the back staircase. She decided to take him home with her and return him tomorrow. An emergency must have come up for Jacob to leave the dog crated like that. She'd text Jacob and let him know, so he wouldn't worry.

She followed the dog through the doorway, but Fury hadn't run to the side door as she'd expected. He'd stopped at the attic door.

"Come on." Rosie started down the stairs, but he didn't follow. Instead Fury pawed at the attic door. The anxiety she'd felt when she'd entered the empty house tripped up her spine again.

"Fury, come." He didn't. "Fury." He ran to the top of the stairs, gave a sharp bark, then returned to the attic door.

He wanted her to follow him. Could Lupe be in the attic? The scenario she'd constructed, Lupe and Jacob off to the hospital together, didn't seem as solid suddenly.

Why would Lupe go upstairs? What reason would she have? And if she did, why wouldn't she come out on her own? Despite her internal argument, or maybe because of it, Rosie turned and climbed the stairs.

Lupe wouldn't be there. Fury must smell a mouse, or maybe a cat had wandered in. She'd check just to placate the dog. Besides, the attic was the one place she hadn't searched.

She stopped with her hand on the door. Fury turned in a tight circle at her feet. "Okay. But you're coming with me," she said, and pushed the door open. Fury scurried up before she could flip on the light. She hurried after him.

## 4.7.3

The scrabble of claws on wood faded as Fury moved toward the front of the house. Rosie knew before she got there he wouldn't be in the pool of electric light at the top of the stairs. He'd run across the dark expanse of the attic to the sole window that looked onto the street.

She could hear his whines and snuffles from the top of the stairs and see his small shape silhouetted in the dim glow. He was sniffing the windowsill with rapt attention.

Rosie took one cautious step, then another, then strode after him. As she drew closer, she saw a dark rectangle leaning against the wall near him. "Fury, come here boy." Her voice sounded calmer than she felt.

When she reached the dog, she squatted on her haunches to lift him, and her eyes came level with the windowsill. She drew back. A maroon stain, so dark it was almost black, dripped down the wall. Blood? Had someone fallen and hit their head on the sill? Had that been the emergency that had taken Lupe and Jacob out of the house so quickly they'd forgotten to lock the front door? Forgotten about Fury?

Her gaze traveled from the stain to the rectangle. It was the back of a painting. She stood, holding Fury under one arm, flipped it over, and took a sharp breath.

The gray light emanating through the window made the face in the painting even more pallid and deathlike. The eyes were darker slits. The black stitches thicker. Rosie dropped it and resisted the urge to wipe her hand on her pants. J. Reynolds's work stared at her sightlessly.

Why was this here? In Jacob's house?

J. Reynolds. She looked at the scrawl of signature at the bottom of the painting and something niggled at her memory. She set the dog down and strode across the long room to the stack of art leaning against the wall.

She leafed through until she came to the painting with the torn backing. She brought it under the overhead bulb and pulled aside the paper. Yes. She was right. The same signature, J. Reynolds, graced the bottom right corner. When she'd glanced at it before, she'd assumed it had read J. Rinehart.

The painting itself was more amateurish than the one of the flight attendant, but there were similarities in style, in brush stroke. Examining it with a more careful eye, she recognized what had bothered her when she'd first seen it. Although the eyes were open—their green depths the most arresting part of the work—they were unfocused. The woman's complexion too pale. Her mouth too slack. She looked dead.

Rosie set the painting down. Fury nuzzled her leg. She picked him up and hugged him to her chest and felt her own heart beat against his side. What did this mean? Was J. Reynolds a friend or relative of Jacob's? Was it Jacob's pen name?

*My shrink said it would be good for me to have a hobby, but I was terrible.* She remembered his words. Why would Jacob buy his own painting from the gallery in LA and have it sent to Nightshade? And who had picked it up for him? Peter would have recognized Jacob even with a disguise, wouldn't he? Had Peter ever met Jacob without his Invisible Man costume?

All she had were questions, no answers. The only thing she knew was that Jacob wasn't the man she'd thought he was. He was much more complicated. Possibly dangerous.

Leave.

The word reverberated through her skull.

Take Fury and leave.

Rosie hurried from the attic, closing the door behind her. She didn't want Jacob to know what she'd seen. When she reached the kitchen, she crossed to the south facing wall where Fury's leash hung from a hook and fastened it to his collar. As she pivoted to retrieve her purse from the long table, movement outside the window caught her eye. A flash of white on the beach below flickered on then off like a firefly, brilliant in the growing darkness. The white like the white of Lupe's blouses.

Lupe. The painting had driven her purpose for being here from her mind. Rosie let Fury go and walked to the telescope Cecily had given Jacob. She carried it to the window and trained it on the cove. She didn't know what she expected to see. Not Lupe. There was no reason for the woman to be on the beach when a storm was brewing. But she felt compelled to look.

It took her a few moments, focusing and tilting, to find the white flash again. It was a blouse, and above the blouse was a head of dark hair. Lupe. It had to be.

Rosie stepped away from the telescope to the window and peered out without its help. Was there a second shape? A second person with her?

She moved to the telescope again. It didn't take her as long to find what she was looking for this time. There were two people on the beach, huddled against the wind, walking toward the rocky outcropping at the end of the cove.

Could the second be Jacob? They were too far away for Rosie to be able to see faces. She'd never have noticed them at all if it wasn't for the white blouse waving like a flag.

Rosie turned from the window, grabbed Fury's leash, and raced through the gloom to the front door. There was only one way to know if it was Lupe on the beach. She had to go there.

The air was thick with moisture. Her face was wet and cold before she'd gone half a block. The foolishness of her act hit her like that spray, light at first but building in intensity until she couldn't ignore it.

If it was Jacob on the beach with Lupe, they weren't taking an evening constitutional. Lupe wouldn't have willingly stayed past Luis's pickup time, wouldn't have missed the appointment with Eric's lawyer.

If Jacob was the murderer, and he'd discovered Lupe's role as an informant, she'd be a threat to him. The smear of black blood on the wall in the attic flashed across Rosie's mind. What if he'd found Lupe looking at the painting?

Rosie began to walk faster, then broke into a trot. The rocks were dangerous at high tide. He'd mentioned that on more than one occasion. People had been swept off them when the surf was big, been sucked into the crevices between them and drowned. Could that be Jacob's plan for Lupe?

The distance from the tower to the beach access ramp was two blocks, but it seemed like miles. Anxiety haunted her every step. What was Jacob planning?

Another voice, a voice she'd always associated with reason, chided her. She was being dramatic. Hysterical. Jacob was a nice man. A kind man. A gentle man. He wouldn't hurt Lupe. He rescued dogs, for goodness sake.

Then, an image of Fury refusing to enter the apartment when Jacob was in one of his moods stuck in her mind. There were times Fury seemed afraid of his owner. He was a man of contradictions.

When Rosie reached the top of the beach ramp, she stopped. If he was dangerous, if he was intent on harming Lupe, what was she going to do about it? Try to talk him down? She had no plan, just instinct.

She pulled her phone from her purse. Should she call the police? And say what? Say that Jacob, at least she thought it was Jacob, was on the beach with a woman she thought was Lupe and could they come check it out?

By the time they came, if they came, it would be too late if her fears were real. Eric. She'd call Eric. He'd believe her, and he could call Sylla, make her understand.

Eric sounded irritated when he answered. "Where are you? I thought you were coming right home? I got a chicken—"

"Eric, listen to me." Her voice sounded desperate even to her own ears. He stopped speaking. "I can't talk long, but I'm on my way to the beach at Crescent Bay. I saw two people from Jacob's window—"

"What are you doing at—"

"Please, just listen. I'll explain later. I think the people I saw are Jacob and Lupe, and I think he's going to hurt her."

"Hurt her?"

"Yes. I found a painting... It's too complicated to explain now, but I found something in Jacob's house. It's bad. He may be the one who killed Twila and the flight attendant. I think he knows about Lupe too."

"Don't do anything stupid." Eric's voice dropped an octave. "I'll get there as soon as I can."

"I can't wait."

"Rosie, you have to. You could get yourself killed."

"Lupe needs help."

"Let the police help her."

"They won't come because I saw people walking on the beach."

"Tell them you saw someone fall off the rocks. You think they're drowning. They'll come."

"Can you? I need to get down there."

"Rosie—"

"Please." She hung up. He'd call. She had to help Lupe.

# 4.7.4

Her feet sank into wet sand with each step. The mist had become a drizzle and saturated the air, the ground, Rosie's jeans and thin sweater. The faster she tried to move, the heavier and more awkward she felt. She envied Fury who trotted beside her seeming to float on the surface of the world with light, sure feet.

The rocks loomed charcoal against a deep purple sky. A crescent moon hung over the water. She no longer saw the couple she'd seen from the window. Had they climbed to the next cove? The surf was high. Waves crashed over the outcropping, and she was sure the tide pools nestled in the rocks were under feet of water. It wouldn't be an easy crossing.

Cold splashed her right leg. The tide had taken over much of the beach. She navigated to a thin dry strip closer to the cliff. The sand was loose here and slowed her progress even more. She swore under her breath. What was she doing? She didn't even know if the people she was chasing were Jacob and Lupe. Lupe wasn't the only woman on the planet who wore white blouses.

The voice of reason spoke more loudly now. *Turn back. This is pointless.* But she ignored it, and plodded on. The drizzle became rain that spat in her face and blurred her vision. She wiped her eyes with her sleeve.

Then she saw them. They stood on the rocks now, two silhouettes, moving together and apart like shadow puppets. One man. One woman. One taller. One smaller. One the aggressor. One the defender. It was them, Jacob and Lupe. There was something in the way they moved, something familiar in the gestures.

"Hey." She screamed without thinking.

There was no sign they'd heard her. No stopping, no head turning. She began to run. The figures came together, forming one monstrous shape with too many arms and legs. A spider on the rock.

Rosie stumbled. The sand grabbed at her feet as if it was trying to stop her progress. The spider moved toward the ocean in steps as staggering as her own. Jacob was going to throw Lupe off the rocks into the washing machine of the crevasse. She was sure of it.

The rocks were slick with water and algae. Rosie slipped as she attempted to climb. She caught herself with her hands. Pain. Abandoned mussel shells cut into her palms like knives.

On her feet again, she scrabbled to the top of the first outcropping. She could see them clearly now. Jacob, face twisted into a portrait of rage, struggled with Lupe. His arms were around her, pulling her almost limp form forward. Blood cascaded along the left side of her face.

"Jacob." Rosie yelled over the roar of the waves. He heard her this time and stopped. His head pivoted. She saw the glint of moonlight in his eyes.

"Jacob, stop. It's over."

"What's over, Rosie?" His voice was deep with menace, so different than his usual soft tones.

"I know it was you. I know you killed Twila. Killed Marianne Kennedy."

"You don't know anything."

"I saw the painting, Jacob. I know you painted it."

He turned his face to the sky and laughed. "Jacob doesn't paint."

Fury growled. A shiver of fear traveled up Rosie's spine. "Don't hurt Lupe. Luis needs her." She changed tack.

"Poor Luis." His words dripped with sarcasm. "At least he's had a mother who cared for him for some of his pathetic life. It's more than I've had, and look at me." One arm released its hold on Lupe, and he flung it out from his side. "I turned out okay. And, Jacob, Jacob did even better."

Lupe sagged against him. The movement must have jarred her awake. Her head jolted upright, and her eyes opened.

Jacob was crazed. He made no sense, but Rosie needed to keep him talking. Draw him toward shore, toward safety.

"I'm sorry your childhood was difficult, but why punish Lupe for that? She's a good mother."

"I'm not punishing her. I don't have anything against Lupe, except that she's a sneak." He yanked her into him when he said the word "sneak." Her hands flew to his arm and gripped it. Her eyes widened.

Rosie took a step toward them. "She didn't want to. Twila threatened her."

"Right. And she did what she had to do to protect her son. I'm doing what I have to do to protect my brother and myself."

"Your brother?"

White water splashed around the man on the rocks, covering him in a shower of foam. He raised his voice to be heard over the noise. "Jacob isn't a strong man."

Confusion wrapped around her head like a storm cloud. Who was this man? An identical twin? A twin she never knew existed? "Who are you?"

His right arm wrapped around Lupe again. He took a large step backward. "I don't have time for this."

"Wait, Jacob." Fury tugged at his leash, struggling to get to Lupe.

"Jarod. I'm Jarod, Rosie." He sounded offended.

"Jarod." The name felt foreign on her tongue. "The police are on their way. What's the point of this?"

He hesitated, as if considering her logic. "It's my job take care of Jacob."

She pressed on. "If you want to protect Jacob, you'll tell the police what you've done. They're going to blame him for the murders if you don't."

A sad smile spread across his face. "They'd lock him up. That would kill him."

Rosie turned her palms to the heavens, pleading with him. "Exactly. That's what I'm saying."

"If I confess, they'll lock him up."

"Only if he's an accomplice, but you could tell them you acted on your own. That Jacob never knew."

Jarod shook his head and stepped toward the edge of the rock. A wave the size of a nightmare appeared behind him.

Before Rosie could react, three things happened in quick succession: Lupe pulled a knee up and kicked back. Fury slipped his collar, leaped forward, and attached himself to Jarod's shin. Jarod released Lupe and fell to his knees.

"Lupe." Rosie reached for her as she scrambled toward Rosie. They clung together. A second later the wall of water struck.

The world became a whirl of deep blue and cold and stinging salt. The ocean slapped and pulled and yanked. Rosie and Lupe fell onto the rocks, but Rosie felt herself been torn away. She fought for a hold, anchored a foot against something hard and clung.

When the water receded, she lay on her side bleeding, Lupe in her arms, and the sound of sirens faint but persistent in her ears. "Get to the beach." Her voice was a rasp.

Lupe nodded, released her, and began to crawl toward the sand. Rosie climbed to her knees to follow, but a high-pitched cry stopped her. Fury. Where was Fury?

She pulled herself to the edge of the rock split and peered into the churning water between the outcroppings. The small, black dog paddled desperately in the wash. Jarod was about five feet away.

He swam toward the dog with long strokes. When he reached him, he gripped his small body with both hands. Would he hurt him? She didn't know what this man who looked like Jacob would do.

Rosie lay on her belly and extended her arms. "Here. Give him to me."

Jarod lifted the squirming bundle in the air fighting against the power of the water. Wet fur grazed her fingers but was torn away. Rosie pushed herself farther out and waited for current to bring them close again. An eternity later, she gripped Fury by the scruff of his neck and lifted him onto the rocks. He lay next to her, panting and whimpering for a moment, then ran toward the shore after Lupe.

Jarod tossed in the foam below. Everything in her screamed to leave him. He was a murderer. Let the ocean steal his life the way he'd stolen life from others. Or let the authorities save him. They must be close.

"Help me." His voice rose above the crash of water. She peered over the side. His eyes were wide with fear, his resemblance to Jacob so strong. A pang of empathy struck her. She reached out a hand without thinking.

He bobbed in the water, pushed this way and that by the strength of the tide. He tried to grab her proffered hand, but couldn't reach her. Rosie scooted farther out until her hips were the only things anchoring her to the rocks. She stuck out both arms. This time he gripped her wrists.

"Climb as I pull," she said, but when she looked in his eyes, she realized her mistake. Jarod wasn't Jacob.

He smiled and yanked.

**MOLLY:** I'm sorry. I've got to interject. What. The. Heck. Who is this guy? Could Jarod be an identical twin? Or someone who had a lot of plastic surgery to make himself look like Jacob? Or is there a darker answer? Is he some kind of doppelganger? A Mr. Hyde to Jacob's Dr. Jekyll?

Obviously, you're about to find out. We're in the final episode of the season. But I wanted to get your wheels spinning. Now, I'll shut up and get back to Rosie.

# 4.7.5

There was no up, no down, no air. Rosie was blinded by blue just as she'd been blinded by the spotlight many years ago. Which way should she swim? Small mistakes in judgment had dire consequences. Small mistakes in judgment meant the difference between safety and pain, air and no air. She wanted to propel herself into the dark, to hide, but she swam toward the light.

Airless, panic-filled seconds passed before her head popped to the surface of the water. Rosie took in mouthfuls of wet air. She gagged and choked as a wave splashed into her gaping mouth. She blinked the foam from her eyes and tried to get her bearings. The walls of the crevasse rose above her like the walls of the tower, massive and unassailable.

*Drowning was a horrible way to die.* No. She couldn't think about that. She'd heard the sirens. Help was near. She would hold on.

"Rosie."

She paddled in a circle, panic giving her energy. Where was he?

"Rosie."

He was three arm-lengths away, closer to the open ocean than she was.

"Help me, please." He reached a hand toward her. She stared at it.

"We can help each other. Pull me closer."

Rosie kicked toward the cliffs, away from him.

"Rosie, what's wrong with you? Grab my hand."

A flood of water tossed him toward her, and his head submerged. She fought to keep hers above the tide. He was farther out than she was. If the police didn't hurry, he would drown. That thought came without emotion. She didn't care if he drowned.

A moment later, he popped to the surface like a cork, sputtering and coughing. "Rosie, please." His eyes were black and unreadable in the dying light.

She made no move toward him. "The police are coming. They can help you."

He held up a hand again. "I'm so tired."

So was she, but she wasn't about to admit that. Another wave pelted them, pushing him closer, pulling him back, tugging her from her corner, closer to the open ocean. Closer to him. Fear, cold and stinging, pricked her skin. She couldn't think with the constant noise and motion of the waves. *Hang on. Hang on.* She began to shiver.

"Rosie." Jarod's voice was shrill. He was a yard from the opening of the crevasse. The waves were brutal tonight. Riptides coursed through these waters. Even if help came, they might not be able to rescue him if he washed out into the sea.

He wasn't her problem.

She needed to focus on the rock walls around her, use her energy to stay within their protection. "You're on your own." She could hear the bitterness in her voice despite the slamming of water on stone.

He was on the edge of hysteria. "Why you won't you grab my hand?" He reached out, his face pleading.

She didn't answer him. She wouldn't waste her breath, her precious, precious breath. She breast-stroked toward the wall of the outcropping, fighting the tide. If she got there maybe she could find something to hold on to. But when she reached it, there was nothing.

She corkscrewed her legs, attempting to stay afloat, but Jarod flailed in the water. Earlier he'd swum long, strong strokes to rescue Fury. Why was he flapping like an angry bird now?

Water cascaded over his head, his pleading eyes disappeared. Should she go to him? It might be a trick. Like the last time. It had to be.

He emerged, eyes wide and terrified, sucking at the air. "Rosie." It was all he said, and he was under again.

She was so exhausted she could hardly keep herself afloat, how would she manage him? He surfaced. Farther out this time, at the ocean's edge. Rosie treaded water, struggling to maintain her position. If she followed him, they'd both die, but leaving him seemed inhuman.

"Damn it." She pushed off the rocks, planning to swim toward the last place she'd seen him. It was a suicide mission.

He rose to the surface, but before she reached him a shape blocked the night sky above her. She craned her neck to look. It was a man. Relief shivered through her weary limbs. "They're here, Jarod. We made it," she said, but he didn't hear her. He'd gone under again.

Strong arms lifted her onto the rocks and wrapped her in a foil blanket. Those strong arms handed her off to a woman in uniform. Rosie stumbled as her feet hit the sand. The woman put an arm around her and led her toward the red lights blinking on the cliffs above.

Two police officers hurried past, moving away from the scene. "Did you get him? Did you get Jarod?" she called after them. They didn't hear her. At least, they didn't answer.

The same men passed her again, when she reached the beach access ramp. She didn't repeat her question. They carried a stretcher between them. They'd gotten Jarod then. Alive, or dead? She'd have to wait for the answer.

An ambulance pulled away as she reached the street. Its siren shattered the night. Lupe. Rosie had forgotten her. Bands of worry tightened around her chest. *Please, God, let her be okay.*

The uniformed woman helped Rosie into the back of a second ambulance and onto a gurney. A paramedic inside dried Fury with a towel, manipulating his limbs and speaking soothing words. The man's muscles bulged under his uniform, but he held the small dog gently. "This your dog?" he said.

She shook her head. "I know his owner."

The woman began to examine Rosie. "We'll get you over to South Coast as soon as we get the other guy in here."

Through the open doors, Rosie saw the two policemen she'd crossed paths with on her trek from the beach. They carried a stretcher. The muscled paramedic handed Fury to Rosie and jumped through the open door with athletic agility. Together the men hoisted the stretcher inside. The woman left Rosie and started work on her new patient.

Jarod's eyes were closed, his lips blue, his face pale. He looked hypothermic, not dangerous, but Rosie pushed as far away from him as she could. Despite the blanket and the warmth in the small space, she shivered uncontrollably. Fear, shock, and cold were a deadly combination.

A policeman, dark hair plastered to his head from the rain, leaned through the open doors. "Were there two men in the water with you?" he asked Rosie.

"No. Just one."

"What did you say his name was?"

"Jarod. Jarod Reynolds."

"This man said he's Jacob Rinehart."

**MOLLY:** So, who is he? Jacob or Jarod? Make your guesses now, because the last patient interview reveals the answer.

# patient zero

EXCERPT OF RECORDED PATIENT INTERVIEW
FROM THE FILES OF DR. LEWIS CARVER:

Twila Wilkes, now she was a case. A real problem. I'd been watching her for a while. She had more money, bigger clients, closed bigger deals, than her talent qualified her for. I pride myself on my artistic eye, and I can tell you she wasn't that good. Rosie Ring is much better. But back to the point.

Twila.

I didn't know her well, but she made me nervous. I knew her type, the mean girl. Like MG, only Twila wasn't a girl anymore. I watched her from a distance and tried to keep mine. She approached my brother. I swear, he's a magnet for women like her.

Twila got her hands on an old letter from Jacob's publisher. It was written when his sales were sliding. It referenced that his three-book contract had been fulfilled by *Pillory.* Then said that as much as they appreciated their past association, his work didn't fit into their future catalog plans. *Blah, blah, blah.* He was being fired. Of course, that all changed after Marianne Kennedy's death.

The hypocrites backpedaled. Oops. They didn't mean it. Just

joking. Point was, he thought it was all over before the flight attendant's death.

Twila cornered him at that Halloween party. She told him she would take the letter to the police along with a fake ID she'd found. An ID with the name Jarod Reynolds and Jacob's picture. It didn't prove anything, but it would put him on their radar again.

All he had to do was get rid of Rosie and hire Twila to do the design work on the house, and it would all go away. She had other demands, as well. She wanted to pitch articles to national magazines, wanted referrals, and so on, but the first was the worst. Having to see her every week, living at her mercy; it wasn't going to happen.

Of course, Jacob was completely confused. You need to understand; my brother is fragile. I hadn't told him anything. Truth is, we don't really talk. Until recently, he didn't know I existed. He was aware of memory lapses. That's it.

I went to Twila's that night after Cecily went to bed. I was going to knock and tell her I wanted to talk, but I didn't have to. The sliding glass door to the backyard wasn't locked.

I didn't have much time to plan, but after my success with the flight attendant, I was more comfortable thinking on my feet. More confident. I killed Twila in the library with a candlestick. Just kidding. I killed her in her living room with a stone vase.

I found a handsaw on her kitchen counter next to her car keys of all places. Convenient, right? I used it to remove her head and hands, then put them in a garbage bag I found under the sink. I dumped her and the bag into the trunk of her car.

You're going to think I was crazy. *Ha.* You probably already think that. Look who I'm talking to. But, anyway, after all that, I went inside and poured myself a drink. Bold, huh?

I had things to think about. The first was, how had she found my ID? I kept it in an old suitcase of Dad's in the attic. How'd she found the letter from the publisher? Hell, how'd she gotten into the house without Jacob or me knowing about it?

I couldn't get past the login on her computer. I'm not much of a hacker. So, I poked around in her files and found some information that pointed to a particular person. It wasn't conclusive though. I figured I'd better watch the situation for a while. You know, to be sure.

I set Twila up in the park, minus her head and hands which I threw off the rocks in Diver's Cove. I left another copy of *Pillory* by the body, kind of my signature move. Plus, I knew it would get those reporters' shorts in a bunch and sell more books for Jacob. Which it did.

The cosmos stepped in once again. I guess I shouldn't have been surprised. Blackmailing is a dangerous profession. Twila must have had a lot of enemies. The police focused their attention on one of them, Eric Ring. I felt badly about that. He seemed like a decent guy, but he was also a convenient diversion. I needed a diversion. It bought me time to figure out who my other problem was.

I guessed it was Lupe. Lupe, or Rosie. Considering Rosie's feelings about Twila, I was leaning toward Lupe. I ended up blundering into the answer.

What happened was I got nervous about having that second painting of the flight attendant in a gallery. Thought somebody might recognize her and trace the thing back to me. I bought it using a fictitious name and had it sent to the Nightshade. Figured it wouldn't attract a lot of attention there. It fit in with his other stuff. Then I put on the fake beard I wear so people don't confuse me with Jacob and picked it up.

A few days later, I heard noise in the attic. That's where I'd stowed it. Sure enough, Lupe Perez, my sweet little housekeeper, is staring at the painting. She was the one. She was the informant. Why else would she be up there poking around? I'd liked her too.

What made it worse was that Twila was dead. Lupe didn't have to dig up dirt for her anymore. I thought she must have been digging for herself, so she could take over the blackmailing business. It was a real betrayal.

We got into a scuffle, and she hit her head on the windowsill. She wasn't unconscious, but she was pretty out of it. I had to think fast. I grabbed a board that was laying around and whacked her a couple of more times so I could think.

I knew I didn't want to leave her in a park like Twila and the flight attendant. She worked for Jacob. There was a direct connection there. I decided to make it look like an accident.

Right away I thought about the washing machine, the crevasse in the rocks on the beach below the house. People have drowned there in the past. A storm was coming. The waves were big. The conditions were perfect. The cops would assume she'd gone for a walk and been washed off the rocks.

I tied her up in case she came to and waited for dark. When the sun began to set, she started coming to. She was wobbly and confused, and obviously didn't remember what had happened. She believed me when I told her I was taking her to the hospital.

I leaned her against me and walked her outside. No one was on the street. I wasn't worried either way though. If we passed anyone, they'd think we were drunk, or taking a romantic stroll, or both. Lupe didn't get suspicious until we reached the beach ramp, but she wasn't in any condition to fight. It would have gone without a hitch, except Rosie showed up.

Why did I abandon Jacob in the water? That's a good question. I knew he couldn't swim. I'm not a bad swimmer, but he's always been afraid. You have to understand, I didn't think we were going to make it. If we were going to drown, I wanted to let him be himself before he died.

It didn't seem right to take away his final moments of life. He came into the world first. I didn't show up until he was four, and Mom started drinking. He was first in. He should be last out.

I'm glad we didn't drown. I know he doesn't agree. He hates being here. Hates the whole thing. Probably hates me. But I'm happy enough. I get to talk to people. Tell my story. It's not all about him for a change.

I appreciate him sharing the ball, though. I do. I was worried when Jacob found out about me, he'd try to shut me down. He hasn't. In fact, it's kind of the opposite. He's hiding out and letting me do most of the talking.

And, yeah, I think the whole integration thing is worth a try. I admit I'm a bit skeptical, Doc. Jacob and I are very different people, and he's not thrilled with me at the moment. But it's worth a try. He's my bro. I'd do anything for him.

**MOLLY:** Those of you who believed Jacob Rinehart was the murderer were partially right. Jacob has an unusual form of DID, Disassociative Identity Disorder. It's a controversial diagnosis. Many in the mental health field don't believe it exists. However, there are doctors who do and patients who claim to suffer from it.

Most of these patients have one thing in common, a very traumatic childhood. Doctors who accept the diagnosis believe that when a young child is regularly exposed to extreme abuse or other traumatic experiences, a protective mechanism takes over. A secondary personality emerges to handle the difficulty so that the primary personality is freed from it.

I am not a physician. I'm simply reporting the diagnosis of Dr. Lewis Carver, the psychiatrist who treated Jacob Rinehart. And this is the defense Mr. Rinehart's lawyer presented in the murder cases. It worked. Rather than getting life in prison, Jacob Rinehart was sent to a high security hospital. As tragic as this is, there is hope that he will be made well. Meanwhile, his books are selling like hotcakes.

Now, let's return to Rosie. We're picking up her story a month after the rescue at the beach.

4.7.6

ONE MONTH LATER

Cliff Drive looked the same as it always had. The tower too, except for the red and white "FOR SALE" sign staked in the grass out front. It felt different, though. The feeling was something like what Rosie experienced the Christmas she crossed the invisible line between belief in Santa and no belief. The tree was decorated, the lights were up, the presents wrapped, but the magic was gone. The mystery of the tower had been better than its reality.

Time stood still at the big house. So much had happened to her and in her, but here the days and weeks felt compressed, as if no time had passed at all. She had to remind herself of the very thankful Thanksgiving holiday she and Eric had just spent with their children to keep her perspective.

She sat in her car now enjoying the sun coming through the windshield as she waited for Gwen Bishop. She would be assisting her in staging the house for sale. Gwen was late, but Rosie didn't mind the wait.

She hadn't felt warm for a month. The chill of the ocean had seeped into her bones, and she couldn't seem to get enough sun to leach it out. She closed her eyes and dozed.

A tap on her window snapped her awake. She glanced out to see Gwen's face haloed by her auburn hair. "Wake up, sleepy," Gwen said.

Rosie exited the car. "I'm so tired."

"Not sleeping at night?"

"Not much."

"That happened to me too. I dragged myself around all day and stayed awake all night for months." Gwen was referring to the aftermath of her experience in that other house on Cliff Drive two years ago.

"I'm surprised you took this listing." Rosie gestured to the fortress with her chin.

Gwen walked up the path to the front door. "Gotta walk toward the fear if you're going to conquer it." She turned the key in the lock and threw open the door. "This house doesn't have a basement."

Rosie followed Gwen from room to familiar room. Her heart squeezed when they stepped into Jacob's office. *I'm in my zone,* he'd said, his green eyes blazing. It was hard to think of his creative spirit caged.

"Cecily said we can keep all the furniture. She's already been through Jacob's personal things and taken what he needs," Rosie said.

"What's happening? Have you heard?"

"Jacob's lawyer hired a doctor to help ferret out the truth. His personality fragmented when he was just a child, and Jarod, the alternate personality, is the only one who knows about the murders. Jacob has no memory of them. I'm sure they'll plead insanity."

"They're all insane." Gwen's voice held an edge of bitterness.

Rosie put a hand on her arm. "Jacob was different. He really didn't know, Gwen. I believe it. I spoke to Jarod. It was like talking to an entirely different person. I thought he was Jacob's evil twin."

Gwen's lips thinned. "I hope he doesn't end up back on the street."

"That won't happen. This case is too high profile. The media will follow it like hawks."

Neither said anything for a long moment, then Gwen said, "What do you think about the living room? There's nothing in it yet."

The two crossed the hall and got to work. An hour later, iPad full of notes, Rosie sipped coffee at Jacob's old wood table. "I think we can pull it together this weekend. There's not that much to do. Eric will help."

"How is Eric? This has been a real roller coaster for him too."

"You're not kidding. However, the good news is my assistance in Lupe's rescue was greatly exaggerated by the local papers. It seems to be helping Pacific Financial's reputation. New clients aren't busting the doors down, but the old ones have settled. And they're starting to get referrals again."

"Speaking of referrals, I want to recommend Lupe to other agents at the office, but I can't until she's legal."

Rosie had asked Gwen to help her get Lupe's name in front of new home buyers. She was fearful it would be difficult for her to find work after everything that had happened. If Jarod confessed and pleaded guilty to all the murders, there wouldn't be a trial. Her part in Twila's blackmailing scheme might never go public, but there was still ICE to deal with. Jacob had already paid for an immigration lawyer to help expedite her citizenship, but that would take time.

"She should have a new visa soon," Rosie said.

"Let me know when she does. I could use her at my place meanwhile. I have three kids. It's always a mess."

"Jacob has agreed to cover her medical bills and supplement her living expenses until she's on her feet. She's making good progress, but she still has headaches. He's trying to make amends."

"There's no amount of money—"

Rosie held up a hand. "I don't think she feels that way. I know you don't understand, but we still care for Jacob."

After making plans for the weekend, Rosie said goodbye and closed the tower door behind herself. The extreme fatigue she'd been fighting ever since that night on the beach overwhelmed her again. She wasn't terrorized as Gwen had been after her ordeal, but she wasn't sleeping either. Rosie was sad, and the sadness was exhausting.

Her career had benefited from the media attention just like Eric's. The world finally knew she was Jacob Rinehart's designer, not that the news came out the way she'd have liked it to. But her wish to make a splash had come to pass. Her calendar was packed with appointments for the next three months. Funny it didn't make her feel as happy as she'd thought it would when Twila was the one pulling in all the big clients.

On her way home, Rosie stopped by Nightshade. She still hadn't gotten that stupid stuffed gorilla from Peter, and Becca had noticed its absence when she'd been home for Thanksgiving.

The lights were on and the door was open for a change. Peter had closed up shop so many times in the past few months she'd started to worry about him.

"Rosie, my dear, you're just in time." A grin split his face.

"In time for what?"

"My private celebration." He disappeared into the rear of the gallery and returned a moment later with two bubbling champagne flutes. He handed her one, then held his up for a toast. "To freedom."

Rosie clinked. "To freedom." She sipped, then said, "From what?"

"You heard, I'm sure, about the accusations against Wes Fellman?"

It took Rosie a moment to place the name. Wes Fellman was the founder of Manifest, the self-actualization program that posed as a business coaching organization Peter had once been a part of.

"The plaintiff's lawyer presented me with an ultimatum several months ago; testify against Wes, or the spotlight would be turned on me next. I agreed, of course."

He waved his champagne glass. "Not that I had anything to hide. I'd never been inappropriate with anyone, but these things are difficult to prove, especially when emotions are high."

"Was Wes guilty?" Rosie asked.

"As sin." Peter set his glass on a table and crossed his arms over his chest. "He is also rich, powerful, and well-connected. Testifying was the right thing to do, I like to think I'd have done it even without the threat. It was terrifying, however. If he hadn't been convicted... " He shook his head as if denying the possibility.

"Was that why you were away so much the past two months?"

"Yes, back and forth to Seattle for depositions, statements, etc..."

"Sounds like a nightmare. I wish you would have told me. I could have kept the shop open for you some of the days," Rosie said.

"You had your own nightmare to deal with."

Rosie finished her glass of champagne and promised to have Peter over for dinner soon. It was time for him and Eric to bond, she decided.

Before she reached the door, Peter called her name. "Forget something?" He tossed her the gorilla.

## 4.7.7

As Rosie pulled onto her block, she saw Honey's van in the driveway next door. She decided to stop before going into her own house. No sense getting Peach all excited, then leaving again right away.

Honey's front door was open. The scents of baking and fresh ground coffee wafted out. "Hey." She entered and closed the door.

"Hey, yourself," Honey called from the kitchen.

Rosie made her way around a stack of library books, three unopened Amazon delivery boxes, and two pairs of shoes. "Aren't you worried that he's going to get out?"

"Look," Honey pointed. At her feet sat Fury, a cube of pumpkin bread balanced on his nose, eyes riveted on Honey's face. Rosie caught her breath and waited. After a long moment, Honey said, "Okay." Fury tossed the bread into the air and snapped it up before it hit the ground.

Rosie clapped, and Fury wiggled over to her for pets and love. "You're doing so good with him. How did you teach him that?"

"Persistence. We tried to teach Bruiser, but he didn't have enough nose to balance anything on." Bruiser had been a boxer.

"Cecily told Jacob you took Fury. He's so glad. He was worried about him."

"It was time to get another dog. You can't mourn forever, and this little guy is so smart."

"He is, isn't he." Rosie lifted him from the floor and hugged him. "If it wasn't for him, I wouldn't have thought to look on the beach for Lupe and Jacob. He's the one who led me into the attic. And he was the only one who knew who Jarod was."

"What do you mean?"

"At the time I couldn't figure it out. Sometimes he loved Jacob more than anyone else in the world. Other times, he seemed afraid of him. Fury knew the difference, and he didn't like Jarod. He attacked him on the rocks that night."

Honey took Fury from Rosie's arms. "Don't be getting a big head." She kissed the offending head and set him down. "How about coffee and a piece of bread."

"Coffee sounds good, but I'll hold off on the bread. Getting close to dinner."

"See, that's the difference between you and me. I see home baked pumpkin bread, and I don't look at the clock. I eat it."

"I could have a small piece." Rosie felt chastised.

"No. No, you're better than me. I went to the doctor today, and I have to learn to be more like you."

"More like me?"

"Yes. My cholesterol is high, and she said I'm pre-pre-diabetic or something."

"You mean insulin resistant?"

"Right. That's what she said, insulin resistant. She wants me on a low carb, low animal fat diet." Honey thudded a mug of coffee on the counter in front of Rosie. Rosie raised it to her lips. She'd been trying to get Honey to cook and eat healthier for years, but Honey had only laughed and said she didn't know how to cook without cheese and butter.

"She wants me to start exercising." Honey said the last word like it was a curse.

"Booker will like that," Rosie said.

Honey's gaze traveled to the ceiling. "He does. He's already got hikes planned for the weekends he's home. He's taking me shopping for shoes on Friday, and I don't mean heels."

"Well, that's good." Rosie made her voice hearty.

"I don't know how to cook without—"

"I know butter and cheese. You're such a great cook, you'll come up with amazing, healthy meals. I know you will. Last time Becca was home she made a vegan shepherd's pie that was delicious."

"Please don't tell me it had tofu in it."

"Okay, I won't tell you." Honey buried her face in her hands and moaned. "We gotta keep you healthy. Fury needs you," Rosie said.

"That's what Booker says."

"Everything alright with him? Did getting Fury change his mood? I know you thought he might be missing Bruiser."

"Bruiser had nothing to do with it." Honey rubbed at an invisible spot on her counter. Rosie waited for her to continue. "It was his brother."

"The one who got in trouble with the church fund?"

"That's the only brother he's got."

"Something else happen?"

"I guess he wasn't exonerated like Booker told me he was. Turns out Booker went into our savings and lent Joe the money he'd stolen. The church said if he paid them back, they wouldn't press charges."

That sounded like something Booker would do. With him, family always came first. "Did Joe get into more trouble?"

"Either that or he doesn't want to pay us back. He's missing. The good news is, Booker has come to grips with it. He was worried about Carla and the kids, but they're okay. Her parents are well off, and she has a good job. He was looking for Joe. Was calling his buddies on the police force back in Kentucky, trying to track him down."

"Why didn't he tell you about it?"

"He knows I don't like Joe. Didn't want to make it worse. But seems like now he's come over to my way of thinking. Said if his brother is going to be such an idiot, so be it."

"At least you know what was wrong," Rosie said.

"Yeah. It's not good news, but it's a relief he's not fooling around or got cancer or something."

"Booker? Never happen. He's too loyal and too healthy."

"I know that. I really do. But things bother you even when you know you're being crazy."

Rosie circled the counter and gave Honey a hug. "That's never happened to me," she said. They promised to walk the dogs together the next day, then Rosie headed home.

The phone rang as she opened her front door. It was Eric. "What are you doing next weekend?" he said without saying hello.

"Hang on. I have to dump my stuff." Rosie put her purse and the gorilla on a chair, walked into the sunroom and sat on the floor. Peach plopped into her lap. "I haven't thought that far ahead," she said.

"Good. Block out five days. We're going away."

"Where?"

"I got a rental in Cambria. We're going to eat good food, go wine tasting, hike in the hills and—"

She cut him off. "Sleep?"

"We'll definitely be spending time in bed."

Rosie smiled. Ever since Eric had been cleared of suspicion in Twila's death, it was as if a black cloud had been lifted from their home. He'd been cheerful, helpful, attentive, a regular Boy Scout.

When things were bad, when he wasn't communicating, when she thought he might be having an affair, she'd called Liz. After she poured out her fears and worries, Liz admitted she'd never liked Eric because he was too perfect. "I hate to tell you this," she'd said. "But I've always been envious of your marriage. You were the talented one. You were so artistic. You made everything beautiful, and then you had this amazing family. It didn't seem fair. So I decided Eric was too good to be true. I decided not to trust him."

"But hearing you say the words I'd been thinking, it's obvious I was wrong. He's a good guy. I'm glad he's yours."

It took Eric becoming less-than-perfect to turn Liz around. Rosie didn't plan to tell her about his current behavior. She might go back to hating him.

"Cambria sounds wonderful," she said. "But can you get away? I thought you guys were short-handed."

"I told Bob he's going to have to get his pudgy butt in the office and put in the extra hours. I was there all those weekends slamming book-shelves together when he was begging off because of his back. It's his turn to cover for me."

"It's good timing. I'm out of Red Ravish."

"Can't have that."

"That's right."

"Love you, Rose."

"Love you too."

They hung up, and Rosie leaned onto the chair behind her. When Eric met her at the hospital that night, he'd wrapped his arms around her and wept. She hadn't seen him weep since Conner was born. "I'm sorry," he'd said when he could.

"What for?"

"For getting my eyes on the wrong thing, Rose. All I could see was what I didn't have. What was wrong. I couldn't see what I did have. I was so stupid. I could've lost you." Then he teared up some more, and she patted him some more.

Ever since, he told her he loved her when he left for work, hung up the phone, and went to bed at night. He'd even popped his head out of the bathroom door the other morning to tell her he loved her before he got in the shower. She wondered how long it would last.

Eric was right about getting his eyes on the wrong thing, but he hadn't been the only one. Her eyes had been on Twila's success, or what she'd perceived to be Twila's success. She'd felt like a failure because she didn't have the clients, the income, the prestige that Twila had. She'd been too blinded by the spotlights to see the truth.

Rosie pulled an orange pillow off the chair behind her, wrapped her arms around it and rested her chin on it. Gold light diffused the sun room. The furniture, Peach's coat, the art on the walls glowed with it. This was where she was content.

Yes, she was happy her career was picking up steam. She was even more happy Eric's morose mood had lifted, and they were a team again. She was thankful for friends like Honey and Peter and thankful for her blossoming friendship with Lupe. But if there was one thing she'd learned over the past two months, it was that if you weren't at peace with yourself, nothing else mattered.

Jacob had split into two entirely different individuals trying to fix the tragedies of his life. Thank God that didn't happen to most people, but how many were truly integrated? Truly accepting of all their personality quirks? Never wished they were someone else, or had another's gifts and talents instead of their own?

If she lost contentment with this, this core of her being, Rosie Ring in all her shifting colors, she now knew nothing else would satisfy. She stuck the pillow behind her head and closed her eyes. Peach's snoring warmth traveled through her jeans, her muscles, and into her bones. And Rosie fell asleep.

**MOLLY:** I love that last line. It's so peaceful. Finally, Rosie can rest.

We can't, however. Abby and I are gearing up for Season Five of the podcast. In it, we'll be hearing from Honey, Rosie's friend. If you haven't guessed from their conversations at the end of this episode, a mystery has already reared its ugly head in her life. Apparently, Joe, Booker's brother, has gotten himself into some kind of trouble.

You will learn all about that trouble next season, my friends. *The Keep* will take us to some of the most remote spots in Southern Orange County. We'll spend time in a monastery out on rural, twisty Trabuco Road and a prepper compound in Blackstar Canyon—considered the most haunted hiking trail in SoCal. We'll also learn more about Honey's business, both in the shop and her gourmet cooking classes.

Meanwhile, if you haven't read the story that started this entire crime wave you can get a copy at the link below.

Join me next season for more *Murders Under the Sun*.

**(cue music)**

Local author, Greta Boris, has graciously offered free digital copies of *The Dark Room* to our listening audience.

Get your free digital copy of *The Dark Room* at
https://bookhip.com/ZQMTCLP

If you enjoyed this book, please do one or more of the following:

- Leave a review on your favorite book review site
- Tell a friend about the *An Almost True Crime Story* series
- Ask your local library to put Greta Boris's work on the shelf
- Recommend Fawkes Press books to your local bookstore

VISIT US ONLINE
www.FawkesPress.com
www.GretaBoris.com

# also by greta boris

*An Almost True Crime Story:*

The Cliff House

The Garden

The Hiding Place

The Tower

The Keep

The Manor

The Cabin

*The Mortician Mysteries:*

To Dye For

Mortuary School

Hair Today, Gone Tomorrow

Bald-Headed Lies

A Permanent Solution

Buzz Cut

Splitting Hairs